BILL
MYERS

he presence

Book Two

ZONDERVAN™

GRAND RAPIDS, MICHIGAN 49530 USA

ZONDERVAN™

The Presence
Copyright © 2005 by Bill Myers

This title is also available as a Zondervan audio product.
Visit www.zondervan.com/audiopages for more information.

Requests for information should be addressed to:

Zondervan, *Grand Rapids, Michigan 49530*

Library of Congress Cataloging-in-Publication Data

Myers, Bill, 1953–
    The presence / Bill Myers.
        p. cm.—(Soul tracker series; bk. 2)
     ISBN-10: 0-310-24236-3 (softcover)
     ISBN-13: 978-0-310-24236-9 (softcover)
     I. Title.
    PS3563.Y36P74 2005
    813'.54—dc22

                                                   2005006083

Published in association with the literary agency of Alive Communications, Inc., 7680 Goddard Street, Suite 200, Colorado Springs, CO 80920.

"How Great Thou Art," words and music copyright 1953 by S. K. Hine. Assigned to Manna Music, Inc., 35255 Brooten Road, Pacific City, OR 97135. Renewed 1981 by Manna Music, Inc. All rights reserved. Used by permission. (ASCAP)

Interior design by Michelle Espinoza

Printed in the United States of America

---

05 06 07 08 09 10 11 /❖ DCI/ 10 9 8 7 6 5 4 3 2 1

For Mackenzie . . .
Who makes my heart smile

author's note

This is Book 2 in the Soul Tracker series. If you haven't read the first, don't worry—I've included enough background information so you won't be lost. Of course, reading this one ahead of the other might ruin a couple surprises in the first (like who manages to survive and who doesn't), but that's about the only problem I can see. And, hopefully, when you're finished, you'll be intrigued enough to go back and read the first.

With this second book there are a few more characters, so I'll list them for your reference. Don't be concerned about them now, but if you get sidetracked and come back to the book later, the list should help jump-start your memory. From the first book we have . . .

David Kauffman—Lost his daughter (Emily) as well as a good friend (Gita). Has been asked to disprove the claim that we can contact the dead.

Luke Kauffman—David's teenage son.

Preacher Man—Street evangelist and friend of David's.

Nubee—Mentally and physically impaired brother of Gita.

Starr—Young teen living on the streets.

Norman E. Orbolitz—Media tycoon who will do anything to control his fate, even through death.

And the new folks on the block are . . .

Rachel McPherson—A television medium growing in popularity.

Savannah—Ex-model trying to contact her dead
husband.

Albert Sinclair—Friend of Savannah's. A software
entrepreneur.

Reverend Wyatt—Savannah's spiritual advisor.

There you have it. Thanks for beginning or continuing
this series. It's certainly been an interesting journey for me
and has caused me to do some thinking along the way. I
hope it will do the same for you.

Blessings,

Bill

www.Billmyers.com

"The LORD does not look at the things man looks at. Man looks at the outward appearance, but the LORD looks at the heart."

1 Samuel 16:7

the presence

the presence

part one

one

Some presence has joined us. Yes, something has definitely decided to visit us from beyond."

David Kauffman tried not to smirk at the melodrama. Honestly, the medium sounded like she was out of a bad 1950s movie. The only thing missing were some cheesy special effects. Then, sure enough, right on cue, the table candles flickered as if someone had opened a window. But of course no window had been opened. Nor door. Nor anything else in the lodge's spacious dining room of pine paneling and hardwood floors. Just the fan or whatever it was the medium had obviously switched on by hidden remote.

Still, it had its desired effect. None of the participants moved; they waited in breathless anticipation. This is what they'd been preparing for. What they'd traveled so many miles to experience.

A chill crept across David's shoulders. Apparently the medium hadn't turned on a fan but an air conditioner. He could literally feel the temperature of the room dropping. A neat trick that made an instant believer of the woman to his right.

"Is it ... him?" Her voice was thick and husky, cured from years of tobacco smoke. Savannah (she used no last name) was an ex-supermodel edging out of her prime—with thick blonde hair, complete with fashionable dark streaks, an indigo butterfly tattooed on her left shoulder, silver and turquoise jewelry, pink capris, and a silk camisole sheer enough to show off her lacy black bra. Nearby was the water bottle she took frequent drags from. In further efforts to kick her nicotine habit, she perpetually clicked and rattled sugarless candy inside her mouth.

"Ashton . . . baby?" She gave a sniff and gripped David's hand tighter, her fingers damp and cold. "Is that you?"

There was no answer—except for the slapping candles against the air and the rattling of sugarless lemon drops.

Directly across from her sat a young man—Albert Sinclair. He'd barely met David before mentioning he'd sold his first software company at twenty-six, for 2.5 mil, and was working on his second. He sported a shaved head with fuzzy stubble, mandatory goatee, and casual khakis. In an effort to hide his nerdiness, he wore a black T-shirt just tight enough to indicate he'd been working out. He nearly succeeded.

"Man," he sniffed, "it's getting cold in here."

David fought off another shiver. The kid was right. It had dropped a good ten degrees.

"It often happens when one contacts those on the other side."

David shook his head. He'd written better lines than that in junior high. He turned to the medium, Rachel McPherson. She was in her midthirties and had that handsome sophistication that sometimes follows pretty girls when they grow up. Smart, personable, sensitive—the perfect combination for a con artist who bilks the grieving by "contacting" their dearly departed. Now if she could just do something about that corny dialogue. He had studied her bio on the flight up from LA. She had two books out, a syndicated TV show with a growing audience, and a PSI rating by the National Psychic Board of Level Three—a classification held by only a dozen or so in the country. A classification that to David meant she was simply good at not getting caught.

Ever since they'd started the séance some fifteen minutes earlier, he'd been silently evaluating her performance. Her eyes were closed in concentration, her head tilted to the side as if listening, allowing her shimmering copper hair to brush against some very bare and lovely shoulders. It's true, he'd been taken by her beauty the moment they'd met—which explained his immediate shifting to a cooler, more professional approach, a curtness that bordered on rudeness. He didn't enjoy it, not in the least, but it seemed to be necessary if he was to do his job.

She had offered her hand at the lodge's front door when he and his son had been dropped off by the chopper less than an hour earlier. "Good morning, Mr. Kauffman. We were beginning to wonder if you would make it." It was a good-natured barb, softened by kind eyes and the slightest flirt to her smile.

He nodded, glancing at the hand-carved beaver near the entrance, the beamed cathedral ceiling, the stuffed bobcat crouching on the table—anywhere but to her green, low-swooping, cowl-neck sweater. It was a clumsy defense, one he knew she saw through, but it was the best he could come up with on such short notice. He kept his answer simple and to the point: "Then let's not waste any more time, shall we."

"Don't you want to see your room? Get unpacked and settled?"

He shook his head. "The sooner we get on with this, the better."

That was it. No pleasantries. No apologies for missing the first day. Just his attempt at trying to be direct and pro-fessional.

The woman's smile remained, but it grew a few degrees cooler. Just as well. He may have been taken in by her looks and winning personality—but he would not be taken in by her scam.

Initially, David had declined the request to fly up to Washington state and take part in the séances. He was an author, for crying out loud—not some psychic ghost buster. But Savannah, widow of the famous rock and roller, Ashton

Hawkins, had been very persistent . . . the twenty-five thousand dollars she'd offered hadn't hurt, either. All she asked was that he attend the gathering with a couple close friends and the acclaimed psychic, Rachel McPherson. Savannah insisted that they had made several contacts with her dead husband over the past few months. And it was during those contacts that his spirit claimed again and again that David had seen him in hell. More importantly, he insisted that David could actually help him escape from it.

Far-fetched to say the least. And David would have written Savannah off as a nutcase—except for the gold pendant. The swirling gold pendant he had seen around the neck of an individual suffering and burning when he had visited the Lake of Fire. The very pendant Savannah had later sent him as proof that he had actually seen her dead husband during those awful minutes he'd spent in hell.

Even then, David had declined. Although a relatively new believer, he'd read the Bible's warnings against contacting the dead. Besides, according to his research, most were merely hoaxes and con jobs. A good friend of his, Dr. Gita Patekar, had made a career exposing just such frauds . . . until she gave up her life to save him in a very different type of supernatural encounter, one that was anything but fake.

Unfortunately, it was this last argument that the widow turned on him and successfully used in one of her later phone calls. "If you're so sure it's not true, then you'd be doing me a favor by coming up here and proving it."

"I really don't—"

"You wouldn't believe the money I'm pouring down the drain on these people."

"I can appreciate—"

"Not to mention my emotional instability."

"I'm sure it's very diffi—"

"I'm a wreck, David—I can call you David, right?"

"Certainly, but—"

"I got this cool place all rented up in the Cascades. So deep in the mountains you have to charter a helicopter. You can bring the family. You got family?"

"I have a son."

"Perfect. Bring him up. Three days is all I'm asking. Make a vacation out of it."

"I'm afraid you don't—"

"Just think it over, please? 'Cause for me it's a real life or death thing. Not to mention for Ashton."

"But—"

"Just think it over."

It took a few more calls to finally wear him down, though it was the offer to bring his son that had clinched it. Who knew, maybe a little father/son bonding in the wilderness would help heal their ever-widening rift.

The chandelier above their heads, the one made of intertwined deer antlers, started to rattle. All eyes shot up to it.

"Just a little tremor," Reverend Wyatt assured them. He was the last of the party—an elderly denominational pastor in his seventies. Savannah had brought him along as her "spiritual advisor." He was not at all the type David figured for someone of her lifestyle. Then again, by the way he constantly scrutinized and corrected her, maybe she felt he was exactly what she needed. Although he was a definite stuffed shirt, David felt the closest to him. Probably because they shared equal skepticism about the proceedings.

The shaking grew harder, accompanied by a low rumble.

"We are located upon some unstable geological plates," the Reverend calmly explained. "The same ones that created all that activity with Mount St. Helens and are currently creating the steam vents you may have witnessed while flying over Mount Baker."

David threw a look to his son. He was alert but showed little concern. And why not? After all, Luke was California born and bred. A little tremor now and then was only natural.

What was not natural was the icy blast of wind that suddenly exploded from the center of the table. It burst out in all directions, striking their faces, blowing their hair, their clothes. David squinted into the wind, searching the table for a vent, for some sort of opening. He saw none. He looked up at the ceiling, around the chandelier. Nothing.

"Rachel?" Savannah cried.

"We're okay," the medium shouted. "Everything's all right."

But things were not all right. The concern in the woman's voice made that clear. So did the shaking of her hands. The gold Tiffany bracelet on her right wrist, the one Savannah had ogled earlier, banged loudly on the table.

There was also the matter of the computer geek's chair. It started to move.

"What—what's happening?" Albert cried.

David dropped his head to look at the legs of the chair just as it began rising from the floor ... with the kid in it!

Albert screamed, immediately trying to climb off, but the wind pressed against him with such force that he could barely move. "Make it stop!" he shouted as he continued rising. Soon his ankles were level with the top of the table. "Put me down! Put me down!"

"Jump!" Rachel yelled.

"I can't!" He struggled, but it was no use. "I can't move!"

Savannah shrieked and David spun around to see her chair also rising. Eyes bulging in terror, she continued screaming, "Rachel! Rachel!" She tried moving, but like Albert she was pressed into the chair, her hair flying in all directions.

"Noooo!" Rachel cried.

David turned to see her screaming directly into the wind.

"They are innocent! I am the one who disturbed you! I am the one you—"

Her chair also began to rise, her eyes growing as big as Savannah's. If this was a hoax, it was more elaborate than anything David had ever seen or read about. And Rachel McPherson was a far better actress than he'd imagined.

With sudden concern, he turned to his son . . . just as the table between them exploded! The air filled with wood. "Luke!"

If the boy answered, David didn't hear—not over the roar of the wind and the crashing debris. He leaped from his chair and tried lunging into the swirling vortex of wood and splinters. Pieces stung his cheeks, cut his forehead. He threw his arm across his face, squinting into the wind as he stepped forward, but the power and force drove him back.

And then he heard him. "DAD!"

He caught a glimpse of his boy beside the Reverend, peering through the wind.

Another scream. He whirled around to see Savannah's chair blow apart, throwing her ten, twelve feet across the room. Then Albert's chair disintegrated, flinging the young man in the opposite direction—just as Rachel's chair exploded, tossing her hard into the far wall.

"DAD!"

He spun back to Luke. The boy had left the Reverend's side and was stepping into the swirl of wind and wood.

"NO, LUKE, STAY—"

But his son did not listen. He fought through the whirlwind toward his father. David lunged forward, doing likewise. Each struggled toward the other, barely staying on their feet, until they finally arrived and David wrapped his arms around his son to protect him. Only then did he notice the wind decreasing, the roar lessening. Swirling bits of wood began to clatter to the ground around them. Soon there were only sputtering gusts, then uneven wisps. Then, nothing at all.

"Savannah!"

He turned to see Reverend Wyatt stumbling through the clutter toward the supermodel. She lay crumpled on the floor. There was no blood, and though she was stunned, she was struggling to sit up.

A groan brought David's attention to Albert on the other side of the room. Like Savannah, he had no blood on him, though he was definitely bruised and battered as he fought to get back to his feet.

Only Rachel McPherson did not rise. Instead, she sat curled in a ball against the far wall. She gripped her knees tightly, her eyes wild and unblinking. And she shivered. So fiercely her entire body shook.

flashes of light?" Norman E. Orbolitz shouted. He turned to his division head, Dr. Lisa Stanton. She was in her late thirties, a nervous, rail-thin researcher whose wardrobe showed she had no concept of her gender and whose shoes squeaked annoyingly every second or third step. It was difficult moving his head with the heavy goggles on, not to mention the bulky cable that attached his goggles to the control console. "Twenty-one million dollars and you give me flashes of light!"

"Sir, that's at our lowest setting. We wanted your system to have a moment to adjust. Remember what happened when we exposed—"

"Forget my system, girl. We're on a deadline! Now crank this baby up and let's see what she's got."

Through his goggles he watched the glowing image of the woman as she turned to her two assistants behind the console. "Increase the power, Charles. On my count."

"Yes, Doctor."

She turned back to Orbolitz. "We're at Level Two. I'll call off each level as—"

"Just do it! Quit wastin' my time and do it!" Orbolitz had every right to be angry. He'd been assured the goggles would be up and running by now. In fact, their completion determined the start-up date of the entire project. A project that had cut sizably into the assets of his multibillion-dollar communication empire. But a project that would be worth every penny ... if it worked.

"Bring us to Level Three, Charles."

The hum from the headgear increased as Orbolitz continued staring through the goggles. In some ways they reminded him of the night vision gear used by the military, though they required far more power. And instead of green and white images that registered the body's heat, these images registered something much more substantial.

There was another fleeting smudge of light, off to his left—four, five feet wide, traveling less than a yard before disappearing. Then another, over by the console. Orbolitz sighed impatiently.

"Level Four, please, Charles."

More lights, wider now, growing brighter, more distracting. "Lisa, this is not what we—"

"Implement the filters, please, and take us to Level Six."

The room grew several shades darker and the darting lights all but disappeared. Now he could clearly see the glow coming from the doctor and her colleagues. This was the focus of their studies. The light smudges were only a distraction, unwanted interference to what they were really after.

Orbolitz smiled. "Now we're cookin'."

"And Seven, please."

The glow from the doctor grew brighter, radiating two or three inches from her body, except for the glow around her head, which was slightly larger, reminding Orbolitz of the halos in old religious paintings. He knew that the holistic crowd would mistake the glow as some type of aura photography—a technique developed in the 1890s and made popular in the 1970s by Kirlian Photography. But the team had quickly debunked that myth. Instead, what they discovered and what he now witnessed came from hard, scientific research—most of it from his Life After Life division, a department devoted to the study of death—more precisely, how to control one's life *after* death. At seventy-eight, controlling his afterlife was just about all Norman E. Orbolitz cared about these days. Forget increasing his empire, forget any philanthropic outreaches—what good would they do him once he was gone? Instead, he invested his sizable wealth into making sure he could maintain control even after he'd left.

"Level Eight, please."

The glows shimmered, growing brighter. He could see colors now—oranges and reds, swirling and folding into one another—all encased in a thin, much darker, violet-blue shell.

Orbolitz grinned. "Oh, yeah."

They'd first noticed the glow when visiting the virtual reality lab down on the third floor. By entering the chamber, participants could experience the first few minutes of death recorded from the dying brains of over thirteen hundred volunteers. This data was then processed and assembled into a virtual reality program that allowed the participants to experience heaven, hell, and everything in between. It was a fascinating study, but soon opened the doors to much more important research . . . research that focused upon the glow.

They found it to be the strongest on the other side of the tunnel, in what they called the Garden. Here people, animals, even plants seemed to radiate it. And by isolating the information and studying it, the Life After Life team had been able to develop special and complex opticals to capture glimmers of it in our world. Glimmers that were amplified several thousand times, allowing the wearer of the goggles to see what Orbolitz now saw.

"We're at Level Nine, sir."

The faint flashes of light reappeared. He frowned. "I'm gettin' them light things again."

"Double the filtering, please."

"Doubling now."

The room dimmed again. The interfering lights disappeared, and the doctor's glow increased. He turned to her assistants. The first had a glow similar to the doctor's, though tinged with a bit more red. And the second? Orbolitz squinted. His shell was much thicker, the purples and violets starting to encroach upon the warmer colors underneath. Orbolitz mused. He'd have to ask for the background on the kid—his psychological profile. Because, as their research continued, Life After Life had discovered a clear pattern between a person's interior life and their glow. More importantly, the pattern between the person's glow and their final destination after death ... which, of course, was the whole purpose of the little quarter-billion-dollar event they were about to stage.

"Mr. Orbolitz?"

He turned back to Stanton. By now her glow was so vivid it was nearly impossible to see her physical body.

"We're at maximum power now."

He nodded, examining each of the three glowing figures. "It's still not like the implants."

"No, sir, you'll never see what our subjects will see, but it should definitely give you the idea. And, as we increase the power, as they experience more and more of the Presence, you'll be able to see and evaluate their various reactions."

Again he nodded. If it was the best they could do, it was the best they could do. "Well, then," he sighed, "let's get our heinies down to the screening room and see what we got."

david in trouble. We go see David." Once again Nubee Patekar grabbed his pillow, rolled his wheelchair backwards to the foot of his bed, and dropped the pillow into the suitcase.

"Nubee . . ." Once again Starr patiently reached into the suitcase and removed it. "David's up in Washington state with Luke."

"We go see David—we go see God."

Starr raked her fingers through her greasy blonde hair. The two of them had been stuck in this rut ever since she'd entered his room at the nursing home twenty minutes ago.

"We go see God. You'll like God." He started for the pillow again.

"Yeah," Starr sighed, "I'm sure he's a cool dude."

Nubee giggled as he grabbed the pillow. "Cool dude. God's cool. Cool God dude."

She shook her head. "Don't you ever think of anything but God?"

He turned to her, breaking into that lopsided grin of his. "I think of you."

She smiled in spite of herself. He could be quite the charmer when he wanted to be. Not that she ever felt any attraction to him or anything. At least not *that* kind. Honestly, how gross would that be. 'Sides, he was in his thirties and she was only fifteen. Well, fifteen in a few months. No, Starr began hanging out with Nubee 'cause she liked his sister, Gita Patekar. More specifically, she liked the fame his dead sister had earned by shutting down the Freak Shop—that place where they experimented on street kids near Hollywood Boulevard.

But, gradually, over the months as the fame faded, Starr still found herself coming to visit Nubee. Not that she was crazy about the facilities. The smell of old people and disinfectant still creeped her out. And the rooms were way too similar to McLaren Hall—the juvee center she'd escaped from a couple times. The point is, she liked hanging with Nubee—though she couldn't exactly figure it out. It's not like he was a novelty or anything. She'd seen retards before, plenty of them. On the streets, in the parks, tucked up in the crannies of freeway overpasses. No, the best she figured, it was probably 'cause he was safe. He was still a man, an older man, but unlike her stepdad (the reason she hit the Boulevard in the first place), this guy had absolutely no interest in sex. Zero. Nada. That meant she could have the best of both worlds—enjoy the pleasure of hanging with an older guy . . . without having to do any of that other junk to earn it.

Course the bus ride out of the city every Saturday wasn't bad, either. If you called Encino "out of the city." That had been Preacher Man's idea. Again Starr smiled. When it came to haranguing you about the Gospel, the big, black old-timer never let up. It was kind of cute the way he'd lock in on the new kids that came to the shelter. I mean, once he got you on his radar, look out. And when he heard that Nubee liked having the Bible read to him and that she had visited him once or twice, he got it in his head to cough up the $4.85 every week for bus fare to send her out.

"If I can't get you to church, I'll leas' expose you to the cleansin' power o' God's Holy Word."

She shook her head. Good ol' Preacher Man. Another piece of work. But another safe port from the storms of the street.

She glanced over to see Nubee sitting in his wheelchair, his pillow resting in his suitcase, patiently waiting. Realizing it was her turn, that it was one of those patterns he loved so much, she reached for the pillow and tossed it back to the head of the bed. But, even then, she sensed this was more than just a game to him. There was something about his insistence. The guy really was serious about leaving.

Once again he rolled to the pillow.

"Hey, Nubes, I got an idea."

He was too focused upon retrieving the pillow to answer.

"What say I read you some Revelation? We haven't read Revelation yet."

Without looking up, he recited, "I like the angels, I like the monsters."

"I know you do." She reached for the worn Bible on his nightstand. "Let's read about them angels and monsters."

Nubee slowed to a stop, holding the pillow midair. He tilted his head, thinking a moment. Then, tossing the pillow back into the suitcase, he repeated, "We go see David."

"Nubee . . ."

"We go see God."

Rachel McPherson caught the badminton birdie on the edge of her racket. It gave a *clunk* and shot out of bounds near the front steps of the lodge.

"That's okay, we're all right!" Albert yelled from her side of the net. "We've got 'em right where we want 'em. Their defenses are down; now we'll go in for the kill!"

Rachel grinned and shook her head. At 0–5, she seriously questioned her teammate's tactics. She crossed to the shuttle and picked it up with a suppressed groan. Thanks to this morning's encounter, her body ached in more places than she could count.

"Okay, Savannah," David called to his own teammate from across the net. "Let's put them out of their misery."

Rachel discretely rubbed her back, musing, *If he only knew . . .*

"Two points and it's a skunk game!" Savannah beamed.

The badminton game had been Rachel's idea. "To help everyone relax," she had said. "To attune themselves to the forces of nature around them." And rightfully so. The morning's events had been frightening. And dangerous. Fortunately, she'd sustained most of the injuries. And that was fine, that's how it should be. After all, she was the expert, the professional. *Professional* . . . how she'd begun to hate that word. More and more she found herself longing for those earlier days, back when she donated her services for free. Granted, it had meant macaroni and cheese a couple nights a week, yet wasn't that why she'd been given her gift in the first place—not to get rich, but to assist others? But now, over the last two years, as her books became best sellers, as her popularity grew, as her TV audience rose, so did her wealth . . . and her overhead. Now she had offices to rent, producers to pay, corporate sponsors to please, and staff members with families to feed. Suddenly she had become Rachel McPherson, acclaimed psychic, national celebrity, woman of the world. And yet, ironically, as each month passed, she thought more and more of their tiny little apartment on Capitol Hill in Seattle, of being the wife to Mr. Jerry McPherson, of being a good and loving mother.

Sadly though, some things were never meant to be.

After the morning's attack, she had offered to end the retreat. There were too many variables, too many unknowns. But to her surprise, no one had taken her up on the offer. Whether it was their devotion to Savannah or just morbid curiosity, she didn't know. Nor did she know if she was particularly pleased with their decision. In all of her years she had never experienced anything close to what had happened this morning. She had read nothing remotely similar in any *Book of Shadows*—those personal journals she and all Wiccans kept to record spells, incantations, and such. What she'd sensed, the raging hatred and violence, went against everything she'd ever learned. There were no evil entities, no evil gods. At least that's what her spirit guides had taught her. Ever since childhood.

Spirit guides . . . She'd met her first in fifth grade, back when Sister Elizabeth Thompson taught them to relax on the classroom floor using yoga and meditation techniques.

"Breathe in . . . ," the nun's airy voice had encouraged them, ". . . and out. Good, good. And in . . . make believe the floor is sun-warmed sand and let your body melt into it . . . and out. Good. In . . . listen only to your breathing, there is only your breath . . . and out. Push all thoughts from your mind. Melting, melting, becoming one with the earth."

Always wanting to be the good student, Rachel did her best to obey—lying on her back, smelling the waxed linoleum, melting into the floor ... and clearing her mind.

"Good, good. No thoughts of your own. Push them aside. And in ... become empty vessels ... and out. One with the earth. No will. No self. In ... you are totally empty, totally open ..."

Mr. Sparks was her first guide. Later, she realized his real name was Osiris, but because of the way he glowed and shimmered, Mr. Sparks seemed a better fit. He had appeared to her at the end of the first week—a glimmering, sparkling presence who stood just outside her consciousness, waiting to be invited inside.

"And in ... no will ... no resistance ..."

And with Sister Elizabeth's careful tutelage, Rachel had made the invitation.

"... and out."

Others followed. Friends of Mr. Sparks. They were distinct personalities whose voices she learned to recognize. Often, they gave her insights that kids her age never had. It was only when she reached puberty that situations occasionally grew unpleasant. That's when one voice in particular asked her to do things with boys she knew were wrong. When she resisted, it began teasing her, taunting her. But what it wanted was not right and she continued resisting. This led to the name-calling—awful, mean names, some she didn't even understand. That's when she finally asked them to leave. All of them. But they argued, promising to control their friend and insisting they had no other place to go. More importantly, they promised they would use their powers to help her do good, to serve others. And, though they occasionally frightened her and made her uneasy, it was that promise, to help and serve others, that finally convinced her to let them stay.

"Hey, Rach, you playing or what?"

"Sorry." Coming to, Rachel popped the birdie over the net to Savannah, who caught it and prepared to serve.

"Five–zero. Ready or not, here it comes!" Savannah hit the shuttle. It sailed high over the net, heading out of bounds.

"Let it go!" Albert shouted. "Let it go!"

Rachel obeyed, resisting the urge to swing. Unfortunately a light gust pushed the shuttle back, dropping it on the line.

"All right!" Albert shouted. "It's out, it's out!"

"No way," Savannah argued.

"It's out by a mile!"

"You're crazy, I can see it from here!"

"Reverend?" Rachel motioned him over.

Reverend Wyatt, who claimed to be too old for the game but agreed to referee, sauntered over to take a look.

"It's in!" Savannah shouted.

"Out! Out!"

The Reverend carefully studied the shuttle.

"It's out, right, Reverend?"

He moved, looking at it from another angle.

Rachel watched, amused at his thoroughness. Anybody else would simply call "do-overs," but not this man. He was a stickler for detail. And after surveying it from yet a third angle, he made the call. "It is in bounds."

"All right!" Savannah cheered.

Albert swore good-naturedly.

The Reverend scowled briefly at the profanity, then called, "The score is 6–0. It is once again Savannah's serve."

"We've been robbed!" Albert complained. "Robbed!"

Rachel threw another look over to David, who chuckled quietly at the antics. He still avoided her, doing his best not to look at her, which she found both challenging and endearing . . . not to mention a bit refreshing—particularly given Albert's full-court leers. The younger computer geek was too smart to make a full-on pass at her, but he'd definitely developed the less-than-subtle art of sneak-a-peek lust.

Even at that, he was less obvious than Savannah. Originally she had appeared decked out in suede knee-high boots, red, pleated miniskirt, and an ultrasnug bustier with lacing up the front—until she caught the Reverend's frown and shaking head. Taking her cue, she excused herself and returned wearing something a bit more modest. But only a bit. Poor Savannah. Rachel wondered if people like her wore such things intentionally or if they'd been advertising so long they simply weren't aware of it.

Rachel scooped up the shuttle, trying not to wince in pain. She popped it under the net only to have it hit David's thigh. "Sorry," she called.

He nodded without looking, and bent down to toss it to Savannah.

Rachel had to admit she was attracted to the man, despite his initial rudeness. He was modest, smart, with a gentle, self-effacing humor. And then, of course, there was his thoughtfulness. That's why he was up here in the first place. He had no interest in being her adversary, she knew that. He was simply committed to helping a grieving widow. Commitment. A vanishing trait among the men of her world. At least those she'd met since reentering the singles scene. Not that she entertained thoughts of him. Heaven forbid. Still, he wasn't hard on the eyes—six foot, dark hair, and just muscular enough to avoid being lanky. She'd heard he was a recent convert to Christianity, which wasn't that big of a deal, particularly since he didn't seem inclined to shove it down people's throats. After all, one of Wicca's greatest attributes was its tolerance.

And what did her voices say about him? Just as they remained strangely silent over the morning's attack, they remained quiet about the man. In fact, Osiris had spoken only two words all morning, back when she'd first greeted

David in the entry hall. Only two words, but they were clear and unmistakable.

Be careful.

That was it. And now, to be honest, she wasn't sure if he'd been referring to David or if he knew what would happen an hour later at the séance.

Be careful. That was all he said.

"Six–zero," Savannah boasted as she prepared to serve. But underneath her shouting, Rachel heard the sound of something else. Crying. A baby. She glanced at the lodge. There were no babies here. Couldn't be. They had the entire place to themselves.

The crying grew louder.

"Ready or not, here comes the skunk point."

It grew more difficult to hear her over the baby. Rachel glanced at the others, but no one else seemed to notice.

Savannah served the shuttle. Once again it flew over the net. Only this time, instead of falling, it continued to rise. And, as it soared higher and higher, the baby's crying grew louder and more urgent. It finally slowed, reaching its apex, and started down. But as it fell, it changed shape. At first Rachel thought it was a trick of the sun. But this was no trick. The thing was growing wings! The cry became a scream—shrill, deafening. The shuttle had become a bird. No, it was too big for a bird. But those were wings, she even saw the feathers. Yet it wasn't a bird, it was ... human! A baby! Falling. Diving straight at her. Screaming, shrieking. A newborn. No, younger than newborn.

Rachel raised her arms to cover her face as it rushed at her, screeching. She closed her eyes and screamed, no longer able to hear her own voice ... until it brushed past, so close, so powerful, that it knocked her to the ground.

"Rachel!" Savannah yelled.

Others ran toward her. "Rachel, are you all right? Rachel?"

The crying had stopped. Now there were only their voices and her own ragged breathing.

"Rachel . . ."

Cautiously, she pulled back her arms. Only the faces stared down at her. There was no bird, no baby. Just the worried, concerned faces.

I t's on the blink again!"

"Mr. Orbolitz . . ."

"One minute it's on, the next off!"

"It's the video link, sir."

"What?"

"Look around the room."

Orbolitz turned from the large projection screen before him to Dr. Lisa Stanton, who sat in the next row. As before she was surrounded in color.

"You see all of the images correctly in here, don't you?"

He craned his neck past her to see the mixing board where the two associates sat, their colors equally as vivid.

"It's in the video link, sir. Not the goggles. The images aren't being picked up by the video feed at the mountain."

Orbolitz made no attempt to hide his anger. "And that's s'pose to make me feel better!"

"Well, no, sir, but—"

"The whole purpose of this little endeavor is to see what happens!"

"Yes, I understand—"

"Every one of them folks has been handpicked. No expense spared!" He turned back to the screen to watch the group helping Rachel McPherson up the steps and into the lodge. "And now you're telling me I won't be able to see their reactions?"

"No, sir, that's not what I—"

"Then what are you saying?"

She swallowed and threw a nervous look to her colleagues. "Let me bring in the video team. Let me see if we—"

"*If?*" Orbolitz was suddenly on his feet, ripping the goggles from his head. "There ain't no *if*, missy! I've invested a ton on this here thing."

"I can appreciate—"

"Now I don't care what you do, or how you do it. Bring in a hundred video teams if you got to, but I want this thing up and runnin'!"

"Sir—"

"You got till noon tomorrow!"

"Tomor—"

"That's nineteen hours!" He threw the goggles at her, crossed to the aisle, and stormed up it. No one spoke. It would have been suicide if they tried. He reached the door and yanked it open, the soundproof seal popping and scraping. Turning back he shouted one last time, "It's already started, girl! The curtain's up! Now just make sure I get to see the show!"

two

uke was not happy. His new cargo pants were wet, soaked up to the thighs from the ferns, salal, and wild huckleberries. Then there was that patch of nettles he'd gotten hold of. Felt like he'd grabbed a handful of bees. The air was wet and heavy, like a foggy day in Southern California, but this was definitely not So Cal. Tall firs rose up all around him like a Christmas tree farm gone berserk. And above them, where the branches thinned from storms or whatever, he was surrounded by looming cliffs and peaks of white-gray rock with traces of snow still clinging to the highest tops. But it wasn't the dampness or the nettles or the view that bothered him. It was the sound.

There was none.

No hum of distant freeways. No droning planes. Not even an occasional passing car. Nothing. Everything was really silent, really still, and really weird. What he wouldn't give for a good tune. Or a bad one. Seriously, he doubted he could ever forgive Dad for making him leave everything behind—his laptop, the DVDs, the iPod. And then to discover there wasn't even Internet up here, or a computer! This was the twenty-first century, for crying out loud. What was he expected to do?

By the looks of things, nothing . . . except be stranded, marooned, and bored out of his skull.

The Reverend, a definite stuffed shirt, though pretty smart compared to the others, suggested he go for a hike.

Said he'd seen a small "pocket glacier" when he'd flown in. It was up a ways, behind the lodge and on the other side of a gulley. He thought Luke might have fun checking it out before nightfall. Not a bad idea. And since everyone had insisted Rachel take the rest of the day off (apparently two attacks per day was the quota), he figured why not. It would at least give him an excuse to get away from the grown-ups. After all, he'd put up with them for most of the day. It was time for a little break—especially from Dad.

It's not that he hated his father. At least he didn't try to. It's just that they never connected anymore. The guy was always underfoot, trying to get him to talk and be all chummy. But everything felt faked, forced. And, those few times Luke did let him in, he always seemed to be worrying about him, judging him and comparing him to Emily. Course he never said anything like that. But he didn't have to. A guy could tell.

Emily had been gone a year and a half now, and in that department things had started to get a little better. Luke still majorly missed her, but at least he and Dad no longer worried about hurting each other by saying stupid things or triggering some memory. Emily's death had gradually become a part of their lives. But deep inside he could tell Dad was still pretty torn up. And still real mad. He tried to keep it under wraps, but there was no missing his hatred toward the Orbolitz dude. And why not? The creep had killed Emily. He'd stolen her eyes. And no amount of churchgoing, or Bible reading, or all the other Christian stuff they'd started doing would change that.

Course there were other people Dad hated too, though he'd never admit it. Guys like Dr. Griffin, who arranged for Emily's death. Or Mom, whose leaving sent Emily over the top and into the hospital in the first place. But the main person Dad hated was himself. You could tell by all the little things he said and did. Mostly, though, you could tell by the things he *didn't* let Luke do. It's like he figured he'd

made all these mistakes with Emily, given her all this free-
dom . . . so now he wasn't going to let his son have *any*.
Seriously, he was lucky to be able to cross the street without getting permission. In fact, it took a major act of nego-
tiation just to be out here alone.

At last he arrived at the gulley Reverend Wyatt had
talked about. It smelled as damp and wet as the rest of the
forest . . . but also a little decayed, like freshly dug dirt or
rotting vegetation. The sides were pretty steep, so he had to
grab different branches to keep from slipping as he made
his way down. When he finally reached the bottom, he
took a moment to catch his breath. Only then did he notice
how dark it was getting. Great, with his luck he'd barely
climb out and get up to the glacier before he'd have to turn
around and race back to the lodge. Cause if he didn't get
back by nightfall, Dad would freak.

When it came to his safety, Dad always freaked.

mr. Kauffman?"
He came to a stop in the red carpeted hallway just
past Rachel McPherson's suite. He'd noticed her door ajar
and was hoping to get past without being noticed. Though
their relationship had thawed somewhat during the day, it
was still better to keep his distance.

"David?"

Sighing slightly, he moved to the door and pushed it
open. She sat on a small sofa, feet curled underneath with
a book on her lap and several others spread around her. She
wore a white terrycloth robe. Nothing about her spoke of
immodesty, which, at least to David, made her all the more
beautiful. The reading light behind her gave a warm glow
to the room, causing the copper highlights in her hair to
shimmer.

"Please come in."

"No, I, uh . . ." He gave a nervous cough and motioned down the hall. "I was just heading for my room. Are you feeling okay now?"

She stretched her long slender neck, moving it from side to side. "Nothing another handful of Tylenol wouldn't help." She reached for a tissue and patted her nose.

He motioned to the open books. "Late night studies?"

"Just trying to figure out what's been going on." She tossed the tissue into a black, wire-meshed basket that was practically full. "What about you, roaming the halls at"— she held her wristwatch to the light—"11:35?"

"I was just outside—trying to get a signal for my cell phone."

"You won't have any luck up here, I'm afraid. It's short-wave radio or nothing."

"Ah."

"Unfortunately that's not working so well either. Some sort of magnetic field from these mountains or something. When we flew in yesterday our helicopter pilot complained how it was messing up his navigational equipment. To be honest, I was surprised he was willing to make the trip again for you and your son."

David cleared his throat. Once again, he noticed how awkward he felt around her. He made a point to keep his feet planted firmly in the hallway with only his head sticking in. "I really do need to apologize for missing yesterday's flight. Sometimes Luke isn't the easiest person to get moving . . . or to do anything else these days."

"Ah." She smiled. "Teenagers."

"In spades." He forced a chuckle. "At least when it comes to dealing with his old man."

"Maybe the time up here will help."

She seemed generally sincere and he replied in kind. "That's what I'm hoping—just as soon as he gets over the fact that there's no radio, no cable, no satellite, and, horror of horrors, no Internet."

They shared another smile, not quite as forced.

"Where is he now?" she asked. "I haven't seen him since he got back from his hike."

"Still up in his room, sulking away."

She nodded.

"You have kids?"

"No, I, uh . . ." She shook her head, glancing away. "I never had the opportunity."

He watched a moment. There was a finality to her tone . . . and a trace of sadness.

"Well . . ." He cleared his throat again. "I'm glad you're feeling okay."

She nodded. "Just a headache." She sniffed, reaching for another tissue. "And this allergy or cold or whatever it is."

"It sounds like everyone is coming down with something."

"Probably just the change in altitude. We're up several thousand feet." She tossed the tissue, this time missing the basket. "You sure you don't want to come in?"

"No, I, uh"—he fidgeted—"I should be getting to bed." Was that a trace of a smile he saw? Could she tell how she was affecting him? Again he cleared his throat. "Well . . . we'll see you tomorrow then."

She nodded as he pulled his head back into the hallway, but not before closing the door on it first, clunking it sharply. Embarrassed, he reopened the door and stole a glance at her. Yes, that was definitely a smile.

"Oh, listen, I was meaning to ask you . . ."

He stopped. "Yes?"

"Rumor has it you knew Gita Patekar."

"Pardon me?"

"Dr. Gita Patekar? They say you knew her?"

"Well, yes, she—you've heard of her?"

"Heard of her? I was her biggest fan."

"Fan? But she—I mean her whole purpose was to, you know—"

"Expose false psychics?"

"Well . . . yes."

"Which meant she was doing me a service by weeding out the fakes from those of us with legitimate gifts."

David frowned. He couldn't remember Gita ever using the terms *legitimate* and *psychic* in the same sentence.

"We were making plans for me to fly down to her lab and run some tests before she . . . well, you know."

David glanced down. He did know. In fact, a day hadn't gone by that he hadn't thought of it. Of her. Of how deeply he missed her—more than he imagined possible. And when he wasn't filled with rage toward the Orbolitz Group for causing her death, he was filled with sorrow for the emptiness she'd left in his heart.

"You knew her well, then?"

He looked back up. "Uh, yes." Then blinking, he added, "She died saving my life."

Rachel registered surprise. "*You* were the one?"

He wasn't sure what that meant or how to respond.

"I'm so sorry."

He gave a half nod.

Slowly, she closed her book. "I'd like to hear about it . . ."

"It's a long story."

"It's only 11:30."

He swallowed. "Maybe another time."

She remained silent. He was grateful she didn't press it.

"Well . . ." He cleared his throat yet again. "I better be going."

She nodded and reopened her book.

"Oh, and thank you for the welcome basket up in the room."

"That's Savannah's doing. Make sure you try her chocolate chip cookies. Homemade by her personally."

"Really?"

Rachel nodded. "She personally hired someone at her home to make them." She glanced up and they shared another smile. "She's got a good heart. And underneath all that pampered princess business is a very lonely and frightened person."

"Frightened?"

"She's terrified at having to face life on her own."

David nodded. Then, almost against his will, he asked, "And thinking she's contacting her husband, you believe that will help?"

She did not miss the inference and answered accordingly. "If we contact him and he encourages her to move on, most definitely."

He did not respond, letting the silence grow between them.

"Listen, David." She lowered the book. "I know you don't trust me. Nor do I expect you to ... at least yet. But you need to know something very wrong happened in that dining room this morning. And later on the badminton court. Things I had no control over."

"Ms. McPherson ..." He was not prepared to discuss the day's events. Although the badminton court was nothing but theatrics, the exhibition down in the dining room had been very impressive. He had no idea how she'd pulled it off. But he'd seen and read of other elaborate hoaxes that, after careful evaluation, had been exposed to be—

"I don't know if Savannah told you, but I'd had two other sessions with her, down in Seattle."

"Uh, no, she—"

"And nothing happened. Absolutely nothing." She paused. "With other psychics, yes. But with me, nothing. To be honest, I had expected the same thing up here."

"Yes, well—"

"In my fifteen years of practice nothing has ever come close to what I experienced, to what *we* experienced."

Refusing to be pulled into the debate, he replied, "Yes, well, I'm sure we'll have plenty of time to discuss it."

She looked at him another moment, then returned to her book. "Right." Once again he felt the cooling.

Preparing to close the door he asked, "Do you want me to lock—" He came to a stop. "That's strange."

"Pardon me?"

"Your door has no lock."

"None of them do."

"How odd."

"It's not the only thing odd up here."

"What do you mean?"

Without looking up, she turned a page, repeating his phrase. "It's a long story. I'm sure we'll have plenty of time to discuss it."

Yes, there was a definite chill in the air.

"Well, then . . . good night, Ms. McPherson."

Still reading, she gave the faintest nod of dismissal. He closed the door, this time careful to pull out his head first. Then turning, he took a deep breath and started down the hall.

david knew it was a dream. But that didn't stop the fear. They were back on the badminton court during Rachel McPherson's "encounter." Only, instead of dropping to the ground, she was fighting and screaming at some giant white bird attacking her—its claws tearing into her hair and scalp, its beak pecking at her eyes. He raced toward her, ducking under the net as she fell to the ground kicking and flailing. But when he arrived and tried to pull the bird off, his hands passed through it as if the thing was mist. He tried again with similar results. Then he looked at his hands and realized the bird wasn't mist . . . his hands were!

Purple, bubbling mist.

He shouted to the others. "Somebody help us!" Spotting his son sitting on the porch, he yelled, "Luke!" But the boy couldn't hear him through his headphones and the portable DVD player he watched.

Savannah raced toward them. "Hang on, sweetheart!" For some reason she was heavier than he remembered. Directly behind her ran Albert Sinclair.

David turned back to Rachel and the bird. Her hands were bleeding. So was her head. Again, he tried to pull the thing off, and again his misty fingers passed through it. He glared at them angry, confused. He glanced at the rest of his body and was astonished to see that it wasn't just his hands, but that all of him was made of the mist!

"Albert!" Savannah screamed. "What are—"

He spun around and saw Albert tackling Savannah to the ground. The sun shone behind them, making it difficult to see anything but silhouettes. Yet, as they fell, Albert's face came into profile, revealing a long, doglike snout. The rest of him appeared gaunt, almost skin and bones.

"Albert!" David yelled.

The young man looked up from Savannah, his lips snarling, his jaws snapping.

Before David could respond, Reverend Wyatt staggered into view. "Get off her! Get off her, you beast!" He wore a black clerical robe with a hood. In his hands was a long broadsword. But it was not made of metal. It was made of letters—glowing letters stacked on top of each other in various shapes and sizes. David knew, he sensed, that the letters formed words, though he did not recognize them. The Reverend raised the sword high over his head and with a shout brought it down into Albert's back. The young man screamed but did not stop attacking. He remained on top of Savannah, tearing at her clothes, ripping and shredding them with his hands and needle-sharp fangs.

Reverend Wyatt raised the weapon and slammed it into Albert's back again.

And again Albert screamed.

Despite her pain, Savannah continued reaching for Rachel. With superhuman effort, she dragged both herself and Albert closer until she was able to take Rachel's hand. But she was not taking it to help. Instead, she grabbed the woman's right wrist and began stripping off the gold Tiffany bracelet.

"Stop it!" David scrambled to them. "What are you doing?" He tried pulling Albert off, pushing Savannah away, but his vapor hands accomplished nothing.

Rachel kept fighting as the bird continued its attack . . . as Albert continued tearing into Savannah . . . as Reverend Wyatt continued hacking into Albert.

"Stop it!" David cried. "Stop it! Stop—"

And then he awoke. He was breathing hard, his face damp with perspiration. But at least he was awake. He rolled onto his side. Luke slept soundly in the other bed. The radio alarm on the nightstand between them read 12:44. He'd been asleep less than an hour.

He lay there several moments as the last of the dream faded. It would be some time before sleep returned, he knew that. Spotting the welcome basket on the table near the window, he threw back his blankets and padded over to it. Earlier he'd emptied it of its grapes and cheese (probably the reason for the dream in the first place). He was grateful to see that Luke had left him at least one of the large chocolate chip cookies. He scooped it up and munched silently as he stared out the window to the trees, their branches dull gray in the shrouded moonlight.

b illy Ray, better known as "Preacher Man" by the folks he harangued from his favorite street corners, was not thrilled about searching the sidewalks of Los Angeles in the wee hours of the morning. He was even less thrilled about the reason.

"I'm sorry it's late." Rosa, a staff member from the nursing home, had called. "I didn't wake you, did I?"

"No," he had lied. "I was just, huh . . . what time is it?"

"Quarter to one in the morning."

"Right, uh ..." He was having a hard time jump-starting his brain into consciousness. "What's ... uh?"

"Nubee's missing."

Suddenly he was wide awake. "When?"

"I'm not sure. You know it is doubtful he left on his own."

"Right." Preacher Man rubbed his temple. "Right, you're right."

"And I think we both know who he's with."

He let out a weary sigh.

"It's not a problem. I mean it is and it isn't. If a responsible adult checks him out, that's fine. But to have him disappear with a minor ... Then, of course, there's his medication."

"Right. I'll get on it."

"Thanks, Billy. And don't be too hard on her. We both know how insistent Nubee can be."

Again, he sighed. "Yes ... we do."

The conversation had been over an hour ago. Since then, Preacher Man had covered every major street between the nursing home in Encino and the 405 Freeway. He knew Starr's MO. And he knew it wouldn't be hard to find a teenager with some guy in a wheelchair trying to hitch a ride at two in the morning. Not hard at all.

In an effort to silence the squeaking AC fan of his ancient Mark IV, he reached up and slapped the cracked vinyl dashboard. The fan had been on the fritz for nearly a year, a long time not to be healed. But it never stopped him from having the faith to believe it was possible. Whether it be lost souls or broken ACs, Preacher Man always had the faith. Not the dead, organized faith of them "cemetery" graduates with their heads full of Scripture and no real understanding of God. No sir, he was talkin' 'bout real faith, the type folks use to move mountains with. The type his sweet Dorothy, bless her departed soul, had practiced when she brought him to the Lord and cured him of his need for drink—goin' on four years now. 'Cept for a misstep or two, he hadn't touched a drop in four years. Glory to God.

A palm branch sailed past the car, thumping on the ground just in front of him. He swerved, barely missing it. The Santa Anas had kicked up early this year—those hot dry winds off the desert that sucked the moisture from the air and made his eyes itch and lips crack. Spiteful thing that put normal folks on edge and made the crazy ones a whole lot crazier.

Off to his left, in the amber glow of a streetlight, he spotted a bag lady. She was bundled in coat and scarf, asleep on a bus bench—her hand draped over the top of a shopping cart preventing anyone from stealing all the earthly possessions she had stacked inside.

He thought back to his conversation with Starr at the shelter yesterday afternoon. He'd made it perfectly clear he wasn't interested in helping. Nor should she be.

"Taking Nubee all the way up there to see David don't make sense, girl. They'll be back in a week. Just tell him to hold his horses."

Starr had been anything but agreeable. "He says we have to see him now. He really believes David's in trouble."

"Just 'cause Nubee believes somethin' don't make it true."

"Like his believing in God and stuff?" It was an obvious stretch, an attempt to manipulate him by playing the God card. He gave her a hard look saying as much, but it didn't stop her from continuing. "Or the Bible?"

"Come on now," he scolded, "you know better than—"

"Or that Jesus is coming soon?"

"Starr—"

"Nubee's always saying stuff like that . . . just like you."

"What we believe about Jesus and the Bible don't got nothin' to do with—"

"Which is too bad, 'cause I was just starting to get into it, if you know what I mean." She gave a dramatic sigh.

"But if I'm not supposed to believe any of the stuff you guys say, then I guess I won't."

Preacher Man shook his head at the memory. It was an amateur stunt at best. But for a kid, she wasn't half bad. Given time, who knows, maybe she could wind up becoming a lawyer ... or even a politician. He gave a shudder realizing here was yet another reason to hurry up and get her saved.

Truth be told, he'd always respected Nubee. His mind and body may not be working up to speed, but the kid always had good instincts. Which is why his concern over David's safety gave Preacher Man pause. So much so that he had called David's mother earlier that evening. He'd been a friend of the family ever since David's little visit to heaven and hell awhile back—something that radically changed all of their lives. So radically that, just six months ago, when he, David, and Luke were in their backyard hot tub, he managed to talk them into a little impromptu baptism right then and there. Preacher Man hated letting any opportunity slip by.

Unfortunately, Mom's answer over the phone hadn't exactly been encouraging.

"No, Billy Ray, I haven't heard a word from him. And that's unusual. He's always so good at checking in."

"You try his cell?"

"He's not answering."

Preacher Man scowled, not liking what he heard.

"And another thing. As far as I can tell, Luke hasn't picked up any of his e-mails. And you know how that boy lives on the Internet."

"They leave you a contact number?"

"Yes, the fashion model's office in Seattle. But they're up at a resort or something in the mountains.

"Maybe she's got some staff or someone who knows. Why don't you give it a call?"

"Good idea."

"Get back to me as soon as you hear somethin'."

"I will."

"Anything at all."

That had been six hours ago. Six hours and not a word. He didn't like the way things were adding up. So, as he continued down the street, he began humming another hymn to calm himself. One of the old standards. Course he couldn't carry a tune in a bucket, but that didn't matter. He figured God listened to the heart, not the voice ... at least that's what he hoped.

He drove through another intersection and spotted something up the street. He backed up, turned the boat of a car around, and approached. Sure enough, it was a wheel-chair pushed by Starr's slouching form. He pulled up beside them and leaned over to call out the passenger window. "A little late for a walk, ain't it?"

Staring ahead, Starr continued pushing the chair. "I was wondering if you were ever gonna show up."

"You knew I was comin'?"

"Be a shame if you didn't."

They continued down the street.

"So are you getting in or what?"

"You taking us to Washington?"

"Girl, that's a twenty-hour drive."

She gave no answer.

"The nursing home, they're all worried 'bout Nubee."

"You can clear that up. Only takes a call."

He sighed in frustration, then directed his attention to the young man in the wheelchair. "Nubee?"

Nubee looked over at him with a grin. "David's in trouble. We go see David."

"Come on, son, you don't know that for certain."

"We go see David; we go see God."

"Nubee—"

Then, taking his cue from Starr, he turned and faced forward.

Preacher Man gave another sigh. "Come on now, you don't want me callin' the cops, do you?"

"We're doing nothing illegal, and you know it."

"Kidnapping's not illegal?"

"Nubee wants to go."

"We go see David, we go see God."

"But he's—"

"He wants to go, and I'm taking him."

"But you're a minor."

Still looking ahead, she replied, "You take us back, we'll just go again ... only next time maybe we won't be so lucky, next time maybe we'll get picked up by some unsavory characters and who knows what will happen to us then."

Preacher Man dropped his head and shook it wearily. She was getting better. Finally he muttered, "All right ... get in."

"You taking us?"

"Get in."

"Not till you promise."

"David's in trouble. We go see David."

He paused one last time. Truth was, she had a pretty good case. Truth was, both Nubee and David's mom might have good cases. Then there was his sister up in Everett, the one always begging for him to come visit her kids ...

He gave another sigh. "All right, I promise. Now get in."

Starr and Nubee noticeably brightened as she brought them to a stop. Preacher Man put the car in park, opened the door, and with a grunt, dragged his tired old bones from the seat. He lumbered to their side, opened the back door, and helped Nubee from his chair into the car.

As he stooped down, helping Starr to figure out how to collapse the wheelchair, he said, "Rosa's worried about his medication."

With a smile of satisfaction, Starr reached into her pocket and produced a baggie of pills.

"That all his?" Preacher Man asked. They found the right combination for the chair and managed to fold it.

"That and then some."

He opened the trunk. "'And then some'?"

She pretended not to hear as she flipped her hair to the side and opened the front passenger door. Preacher Man remained standing, waiting. Finally, she turned to him. "What?"

He stretched out his hand. "I'll be holding the medication."

She gave him a look, but he meant business. With exasperation, she dropped the bag in his hand.

He glanced down at it, then back to her. "And the rest."

"What do you mean?"

He continued holding out his hand.

With another sigh, she stuffed her hand into her jeans pocket and pulled out another fistful, which she dumped into his palm.

He continued waiting.

"That's it," she said.

More waiting.

"Come on!" she whined.

But he did not budge until finally, she reached into her other pocket and emptied it of an equal amount of pills. Without a word she turned, entered the car, and slammed the door.

Billy Ray hoisted the wheelchair into the trunk and shut the lid. He returned to the driver's side humming another hymn. She may be good, he'd grant her that. But he was still the Preacher Man.

three

grab his arms! Hold him!"

David squirmed in his bed, bucking his body, trying to throw them off. He tried to scream, but they'd already covered his mouth.

"Hold his head! Hold it!"

He struggled to raise his arms. They were lead. So were his legs. Hands poured over his face, pushing, pulling. He tried turning his head but they held it tight.

"How many did he eat? You said he had—will you hold him still!"

The grip on his face tightened.

Unable to turn, he watched, wide-eyed. He counted two, no, three of them. Ski masks, navy blue sweats. Two held him down, the third came at him with a gun—a silver gun with a red tip. They were going to kill him! They were going to shoot him in the face! They were going to—

David's eyes exploded open. He rose in the bed on one elbow, searching the room, getting his bearings. It was the lodge. Their bedroom. The same knotty pine paneling, the same view of the forest from his window—only now it was bathed in bright morning sun.

Luke, what about—

He spun to his son on the other bed, not four feet away. The boy was sound asleep. He took a deep breath, forcing himself to relax, then eased back down into the pillow and closed his eyes. It was a dream. Another nightmare. Two in one night. Some type of record. He took another breath. Only then did he notice how stuffy his nose had become. He gave another sniff. Sure enough, like everyone else, he was coming down with something. He rolled over to look at the radio alarm:

9:56

This was no time to sleep in! He sat back up, calling to his son. "Luke! Luke, get up!"

The boy didn't stir.

Still unnerved by the dream, he pulled aside his blankets, threw his feet over the side of the bed, and leaned over to shake him. "Luke, you all right?"

His son gave a muffled moan.

He shook him harder. "Luke."

More incoherency. David stopped. What was he thinking? It wasn't even noon. Did he honestly believe he could wake his son before lunch? Musing at his foolishness, he ran his hands through his hair, trying to clear his spongy thoughts—the price of the cold or sleeping in too late, or both. He gave another sniff, wondering if he still had some of those cold capsules in his shaving kit from the last trip.

He glanced back at Luke. As usual, the boy had twisted his bedding into a giant knot, a war zone of tossing and turning. David wasn't sure when that had started. He never paid attention to that sort of thing until Jacqueline, his wife, left them. That's when Luke's nightmares started. That's when he began his nightly ritual of padding on down the hall and sleeping with Dad. Even then, David hadn't noticed any real problem until after Emily's death. Then, everything Luke did was on his radar. Every friend he made, every time he left the house, every place he went. David had lost one child through his negligence. He wasn't about to lose the other.

Nearly eighteen months had passed since her murder. And, for the most part, they were on the road to recovery—

though the shrinks warned them things would never return to normal. "The pain will fade," they assured him, "but the hole will always remain."

So far they were right. And that was fine with David . . . and with Luke. Emily deserved that much. She deserved to be missed. And she was. Deeply.

Before her death and after Jacqueline had run off, the three of them did everything together. And on those rare occasions when David couldn't be with them, brother and sister looked after each other fiercely—Emily taking the role of mother, Luke keeping a careful eye on a sister who battled with bouts of severe depression. Of course this didn't stop them from fighting. Like cats and dogs. He'd always remember with fondness their river trip in Colorado. They had insisted on sharing their own canoe. Once they were secure in life vests and helmets, he thought it would be fun to watch.

He was not disappointed.

"We're drifting to the right!" Emily had shouted from the front. "Paddle on the left."

"I'm better on my right."

"Change sides and paddle on the—"

"You paddle on the left!"

"Luke!"

"You're not my boss!"

"Listen, genius, you've got to trade sides or we'll—"

"You trade sides!"

And so the argument continued, neither giving in, as they turned lazy circles in the river until—

"Rapids!" Emily shouted. "Luke, there's rapids ahead!"

Now, with their lives on the line (at least in their eyes), it was time to put aside all bullheadedness; it was time to practice maturity and cooperation.

Or not . . .

David, who stayed close in case there was real trouble, continued to watch.

"Turn left!"

"You turn left!"

"Luke!"

"You turn left!"

And so the debate raged until they finally hit the rapids ... broadside.

"LUKE!"

Bouncing and bobbing, they slowly turned until they were actually shooting the rapids backwards.

"EMILY!"

They shouted, they screamed, they hollered. But neither yielded ... until they finally hit a giant boulder more stubborn than even themselves. The canoe tipped, throwing them and all of their gear into the icy water. Fortunately, no one was hurt. And later, when they sat around the campfire shivering and trying to dry out, they were finally able to exercise and appreciate the hard-earned truths of cooperating with one another:

"It's your fault the sleeping bags are soaked!"

"Is not!"

"Is to!"

"Jerk!"

"Moron!"

Or not.

David sat on the bed staring at his son. Eighteen months. And yet in that short time Luke had seemed to age nearly twice that. He suspected much of it had to do with Emily's death. That and his recent entrance into adolescence. David was astonished at how quickly he'd begun irritating and embarrassing his son ... something Luke never hesitated to mention—when he bothered to mention anything at all. Because now, for the most part, David counted himself lucky just to get monosyllabic grunts, interspersed, of course, by hours of brooding silence.

Glancing at the clock, he rose stiffly to his feet. He ran his hand across his face and noticed a slight crustiness on his upper lip. Great, whatever he'd caught was already making his nose run. He gave another sniff and started toward the bathroom.

He shuffled across the hardwood floor into the mirrored room. Motion detectors faded on the lights to reveal two green marble sinks, complete with gold-plated fixtures and a large Grecian tub to his left. He reached for a folded white washcloth on the counter and turned on the water to soak it. But when he looked up to the mirror he came to a stop. He leaned in closer. He touched his right nostril. Tiny flakes fell into his fingers. He pulled back his hand and stared at them. Only then did he realize they were not dried flakes of mucus.

They were dried flakes of blood.

othin'!" Orbolitz shouted at Dr. Lisa Stanton's glowing form. "I got nothin'!"

The woman turned to him. She wore a telephone head-set. "We are talking to the mountain now—checking to see if the problem is in transmission or if it's systemic."

"Systemic?" Orbolitz barked. "This isn't some garden patch, girl! Get 'em on the line."

"Pardon me?"

"Put Dirk on line, I wanna talk to him!"

She spoke into her headset while motioning to the assistants at the back of the screening room.

Orbolitz turned to the large screen before him. Most of the people projected on it sat around a butcher-block table in the kitchen. Apparently no one had an interest in return-ing to the dining room where they'd experienced yesterday's encounter. No problem, who could blame them. What *was* the problem, what infuriated him, were the images on the screen. Unlike the staff surrounding him, the people on the screen still had no glowing color, no halo, no nothing. And if he couldn't see their glow, what made them think he could see their manifestations? That was the word the techies used, *manifestations*. It had a nice supernatural ring to it. Yet what they'd been studying these many, many months was anything but supernatural. According to Dr. Richard Griffin, the first to head the Life After Life Division, it was simply theoretical physics amped up a few degrees.

Griffin had gained his confidence when he helped Orbolitz find donors for his various transplants. (As a diabetic Orbolitz tended to wear out organs faster than most.) Griffin accomplished the near impossible by finding perfect matches which assured minimal complications and virtually no antirejection drug therapy. The fact that it involved killing innocent victims—a college athlete, a mother of three, and of course Emily Kauffman—proved that he not only understood Orbolitz's obsession to live forever, but that he had the lack of conscience necessary to pull it off. Too bad about the accident in the Virtual Reality chamber, the one that left him a mental vegetable. It had been a major setback to the program, and if he were still at the helm Orbolitz knew they would not be scrambling and playing catch-up like this.

He recalled the man sitting across the desk in his massive, windowless office, laying it all out very simply . . .

"We only call things supernatural that we don't understand. Let's face it, a hundred years ago we would have called radio and television supernatural."

"What's your point, Dick?"

"Today cosmologists believe that 96 percent of the universe is made of invisible material."

"You mean stuff that's transparent?"

"No, I mean matter and energy that we can't measure. We know it's here, we can detect it through gravity, but we can't see it, we can't touch it, we can't hear it."

"How's that possible?"

"Most mathematicians believe our universe consists of at least eleven dimensions—some say as many as twenty-two."

"Twenty-two dimensions? What happened to the good ol'-fashioned three?"

"Those are only the ones we can hear, see, and feel."

Orbolitz gave him a look.

"Let me show you." Griffin rose and cleared his boss's desk, a slab of polished redwood carved from a single, giant burl. "The best way to understand higher dimensions that we can't see is by dealing with the dimensions we can see."

"Is this gonna be another one of your brain-bruisin' lectures?"

"No, sir, it's really quite simple. Let's make believe there are people living on the surface of your desk, but that they live in only two dimensions. They understand length"—he motioned across the length of the desk—"and they understand width." He indicated its width. "But they have no concept of depth, there's no up or down in their world. Just length . . . and width."

"Got it."

"Now, how would these people describe you and me standing here in the third dimension?"

Orbolitz shrugged. "Couple o' good-lookin' fellas standin' above 'em who—"

"No, sir. There is no *above*, not in their world. There's only length . . . and width."

"Then I guess they wouldn't see us."

"Precisely. We'd be invisible. But we'd still be here, correct?"

"Yeah."

"Kind of like . . ." He waited for an answer.

"Ghosts?" Orbolitz offered.

Griffin nodded. "Or gods. We'd see them the entire time—wherever they went, whatever they did. They couldn't hide from us."

"'Less they built some sort of roof over 'em."

"No, remember, there's no *up* in their world So there's nothing they could put *over* them."

Orbolitz grinned. "I'm gettin' it."

"Not only could we always see them, but we could view the beginning of their lives"—Griffin pointed at one end of the desk—"just as clearly as we could view their ending."

"Or anytime in between."

"Wherever and whenever we chose."

"To them we'd be, what's the word . . . omnipotent."

"Exactly. And what would happen if we, say, poked our finger into their world?" Griffin placed his finger on the desk.

"They'd get spooked."

"That's right. To them, it would be as if we'd suddenly appeared. And if we removed it . . ." He removed his finger.

"We'd disappear."

"But in reality, we'd always been here."

Orbolitz nodded, quickly piecing it together. "So you're saying all these other dimensions, they're above us—"

"No, you're thinking three dimensions again. They wouldn't be *above*, there is no above."

"So the idea of heaven being above . . . or hell below is . . ."

"—the best primitive man could do to explain a multi-dimensional universe. But in reality, those higher dimensions are not above or below us . . . they are *around* us, sharing our space in worlds we can't see."

Orbolitz nodded, this time a little slower.

"More importantly, part of us is made of those dimensions."

The nodding stopped. "You lost me."

"From what we've witnessed in the VR chambers, there's far more to us than what we see. You and I, we are also made up of more than three dimensions. There appears to be at least one other part of us that—"

"Our souls," Orbolitz interrupted. "The part that leaves our body after death, the part we've been tracking."

"Precisely." Griffin motioned his arm to encompass the room. "Everything around us is made up of more than three dimensions . . ." He lowered his arm and slowly tapped his chest. "So why wouldn't we be as well?"

Orbolitz sat another moment in the screening room, recalling the conversation. It seemed so complex then. And so elementary now. Man is made of more than 3-D, flesh and blood. He is also made of something else—the glow, the halo, that thing that departs the body after death. But what exactly is that glow? How does life affect it? Good. Evil. Our so-called "sins." And, most importantly . . . what happens to it when it reaches its final destination, when it comes face-to-face with that awful, tyrannical Light that no soul they have tracked has been able to avoid?

"Mr. Orbolitz, it's a fine morning to be seeing you again, sir."

He glanced up to the screen and saw Dirk Helgeland, head of operations at the mountain. The heavyset man was all Irish, from his accent to his red hair and beard. But once again, Orbolitz could not see a glow.

"What's happenin' up there, Dirk? We're getting diddly down here."

"I'm thinking it's not the goggles. From what I hear they're working pretty well."

"Down here they're workin' fine, but I'm seein' nothin' at your end."

"As best we can tell, the images refuse to be reduced to any form, either digital or analog, making it impossible to—"

"English, Dirk—talk to me in English."

"For some reason we can't record the images on tape. Nor can we reduce them for transmission, or send them through cable."

Fighting to stay calm, Orbolitz asked, "So what's your take?"

"We'll be needing more time to analyze its properties and—"

"We got time to analyze nothin'!"

Helgeland paused, then nodded in understanding.

"We gotta fire this puppy up and we gotta fire her up now!"

"I understand, sir."

Orbolitz sighed in frustration. "Listen, you and the boys keep workin' to see if you can dream up somethin'. Maybe ratchin' up the grid's power will help. What's she set at now?"

"We're in standby mode. Just under 2 percent."

"We gotta start, son. No more delays. Get them fences turned on, put the pedal to the metal, and let's see what she's got."

"Yes, sir."

"What's our first level?"

"We estimated that 5 percent would be a good place to start."

"Then fire her up to 5 percent."

"Give us twenty minutes and we're good to go."

"You got ten."

"Ten it is."

Well," Albert teased from across the table. "Look who finally climbed out of the sack to join us."

Rachel turned from the grill to see David enter the kitchen. Even at his morning's worst he didn't look half bad. And in the lighting . . . well, there was no missing how some of his features resembled Jerry's.

"Sorry." He gave an embarrassed shrug. "Believe it or not I'm usually a pretty early riser. Must be all this clean mountain air."

"Or the pollen." Savannah sniffed from the other side of the table. "I've never had such allergies." As always she rolled and clicked another sugarless lemon drop in her mouth. But not just any sugarless lemon drop. Earlier, she'd made it clear it was imported from the Netherlands. She pushed out a chair with her rhinestone slippered foot and motioned to David. "Sit. Rachel's about to impress us with her culinary genius."

"You got that right," Rachel said. She slipped a spatula under a row of bacon and lifted it to the platter. "What will it be—bacon, hash browns, and eggs with broken yolks or bacon, hash browns, and eggs with broken yolks?"

"Make mine broken."

"An excellent choice."

"Actually," Reverend Wyatt corrected Savannah, "there is little pollen in the Cascades this time of year."

"Talk to my nose about it," Savannah sniffed, "'cause this sure ain't a cold."

"Tell me about it." Albert sniffed loudly and swore, using the Lord's name. The Reverend cleared his throat. "Sorry, Rev, nasty habit." Turning to David, he asked, "So where's Luke?"

David shrugged. "Should be up before nightfall."

Rachel grabbed a pot holder mitt, opened the door to the stainless steel oven, and pulled out a platter of eggs she'd been keeping warm. Though last night's rebuff had stung slightly, she knew it only came from David's commitment to helping Savannah. And for that he couldn't be blamed. Truth be told, she was glad he'd joined them. His quiet presence gave a certain stability to the group. And if there's one thing she could use a bit more of right now, it was stability.

Earlier, she'd asked Osiris and her guides about the events . . . and about him. Their response was identical to yesterday's. A simple warning:

Be careful.

Over the years, she'd learned to listen to their council. Not only because they were usually right, but because, as they had promised, they used their powers within her to help and comfort others. Still, everything had its price. Sacrifices had to be made.

And for Rachel, it was the baby . . .

She will distract you, Osiris had said. *Prevent you from rising to your highest calling. In time, yes, children will be good. But at this moment you must concentrate upon an even greater good.*

Of course Rachel had refused. All Jerry had ever wanted was to have kids. Lots and lots of kids. And who was she to deprive the man she so deeply loved of something he so deeply desired?

But Osiris and the others persisted in their reasonings . . . which eventually grew into demands . . . throughout the days and finally into the nights. Continual. Incessant. Demands that grew so loud it became difficult to hear her own thoughts. Week after week they continued, giving her no rest. That's when she finally took a stand and insisted they leave. And that's when they knotted her gut into such a cramp that she dropped to her knees and vomited— again and again, until she blacked out—on more than one occasion.

Still she resisted.

Until the beginning of the third trimester.

That's when they entered her unborn child, making the baby kick at their command. That's when they threatened to enter her infant's brain, promising to make the child go insane by torturing it every day of its life. And they could. She knew it. She knew their powers. Only then did Rachel McPherson, the good Catholic girl, go against what she had always believed and held sacred. Only then did she break her husband's heart and her own, by participating in a partial birth abortion, or something they described in more clinical terms as *dilatation and extraction*—a medical procedure where the doctors induced labor and then, piece by piece, crushed and killed little Jessica, the unborn baby they had already named.

But something went wrong. Terribly wrong. Later, as she lay on the crisp, clean sheets, the smell of antiseptic filling the room, her insides gutted, the doctor appeared. The look on the woman's face immediately told Rachel something had happened.

"Mrs. McPherson . . ."

"What is it, what's wrong?"

"There were . . . complications."

"Complications . . ."

The doctor turned to Jerry. "Mr. McPherson, would you mind stepping out of the room for just a—"

"No, he's staying here. What is it, what's wrong?"

"There were complications."

"You said that, what's—"

"You were hemorrhaging—"

"What does that—"

"We were unable to stop it."

"What does that mean?"

"It means we had to perform an emergency hysterectomy."

"Wh . . . what?"

With measured response, the doctor continued. "You will no longer be able to have children, Mrs. McPherson."

"Until I recover."

There was no answer.

"You mean until I recover."

"We had to remove your uterus, Mrs. McPherson. You will never be able to bear children."

The news sucked the air from her lungs. But not just hers. When she turned to Jerry, all color had drained from his face. He tried to hide his emotion, to give her the support and comfort she so desperately needed. But even as he reached out and held her, even as she wept, she could feel his own body trembling.

Of course Osiris and the voices soothed and praised her for her courage—assuring her she'd done the right and noble thing. But no matter what they said, they could not drown out the other voice—the one of her own conscience that made it impossible to look into her husband's eyes.

The one that, despite his insistence that he would always love her, eventually drove her to pack her bags and leave . . . leave the only man she'd ever loved, because she'd killed the only baby she could ever have.

Blowing a tendril of hair from her face, Rachel crossed to the butcher block table with the platter of eggs in one hand and bacon in the other. She could feel David's eyes on her. But, unlike Albert, he watched discretely and professionally. This both pleased and unnerved her . . . at times making her as self-conscious as some schoolgirl. Almost as self-conscious as she knew she made him.

"Here we go." She set the platters on the table beside the toast and hash browns.

"All right," Albert said, reaching for the food and digging in.

"Smells great," Savannah agreed as she snatched a piece of bacon and started munching . . . until Reverend Wyatt cleared his throat and she glanced up. She stopped chewing. "Oh, right." Setting down the bacon, she said, "Okay, everybody, it's time for grace."

"Grace?" Albert asked.

"Yeah, you know—*prayer.*"

"Oh, right . . . sure."

"Reverend," Savannah asked. "Will you do the honors?"

"Certainly." The old gentleman bowed his head and the rest of the group followed. "Dear Lord . . . we thank Thee for the bountiful food which Thou hast provided and ask that Thou bless it and bless the hands that have prepared it. For it is in the name of Thy Son and our Savior that we pray, amen."

One or two amens were quietly repeated as the group raised their heads and reached for the food. As they did, Rachel turned back toward the stove.

"Aren't you joining us?" David asked.

She glanced back. "No, I'm really not that hungry."

"Are you okay?"

She nodded, appreciating his concern and catching herself pushing a strand of hair behind her ear.

"Any more problems?" Albert asked, dishing up the hash browns.

"Nothing other than my embarrassment."

"Why is that?" Reverend Wyatt asked.

She forced a chuckle. "Savannah brought me up here to help contact her brother. But it looks like I'm the one who keeps needing the help."

"Nonsense," Savannah said, rattling a piece of candy in her mouth even as she dabbed a thick layer of marmalade across her toast. "You had no control over those attacks, or whatever they were."

"Just the same"—she started back to the stove—"after a good night's rest I'm looking forward to getting down to business."

"Good night's rest?" Albert mused through a mouthful of hash browns. "Wouldn't that be nice."

"Tell me about it," Savannah agreed as she dished up an egg, then decided on two. "I don't know which is worse, my allergies or my dreams."

"You're having strange dreams?" David asked.

"Not if you call Rachel being attacked by an angel, computer boy here turning into a wolf, and me putting on a few dozen pounds 'normal'."

Rachel slowed to a stop. So did all activity around the table.

Glancing at them, Savannah asked, "What?"

David was the first to speak. "I ... I had a dream exactly like that."

"As did I," the Reverend quietly agreed.

"Ditto," Albert said. "Not only the angel and Savannah's extra tonnage, but," he nodded to Reverend Wyatt, "you had this giant sword in your hand that you were hacking everybody up with." He turned to David. "And you, you were all misty and foggy."

Rachel's heart beat faster. He'd just described her own dream. Slowly, one pair of eyes after another turned to her as her mind raced, trying to comprehend.

"Has anything like this happened before?" Savannah asked.

Rachel shook her head. "No. Not that I'm aware . . ." She looked up and slowed to a stop. A purple, bubbling mist was forming around David.

The Reverend saw it, too. "What on earth?"

David frowned, not understanding, apparently not even seeing. But before Rachel could comment, she noticed the Reverend's image waver until he was surrounded by what appeared to be dark clerical robes.

"What's going on?" Savannah demanded. "Why are you dressed like that?"

Reverend Wyatt turned to her and caught his breath. So did Rachel. For suddenly, Savannah's face glowed large and puffy with giant sagging jowls and a neck swollen to twice its size.

Seeing their expressions, Savannah raised her hands to her face. As she did, Rachel spotted the model's left wrist. It had swollen disproportionately to the other. But not swollen as in sprained or fat. No, it had swollen into the exact size of her Tiffany chain bracelet. Only it was not *around* Savannah's wrist, it was *under* it—each link, even the ropelike texture was clearly visible—all outlined and tightly wrapped *under* her skin.

Albert swore in concern as a shadowy snout began extending from his face.

Rachel closed her eyes, forcing the sight out of her mind. When she reopened them she was grateful to see that everything had returned to normal—every*one* had returned to normal. David, Reverend Wyatt, Savannah, Albert— exactly as they had been . . . except for the silence and the shock on each of their faces.

"Tell me ..." Savannah crunched her candy. "Tell me I didn't see what I just saw."

bring 'em up, too."

"You're not serious?"

"Course I'm serious."

Lisa Stanton fidgeted before the massive desk. "That's three additional people."

"I can count. If they're fixin' to stir up trouble, let's bring 'em all in. We got the space, right? Extra equipment?"

"Well, yes, but—"

Orbolitz leaned back in his calfskin chair, grinning at the idea. "Skanky white trash, a retard, and a religious fanatic. I'd say that's more diverse than even we could dream up."

"It could make for some intriguing interaction."

"Got that right. And all friends of Kauffman. Should be kinda fun to see what they do to his head."

"Or soul."

Orbolitz smiled. "Or soul." He swiveled to the bank of plasma screens filling the left wall of his office. Four rows of twenty-seven-inch monitors, each viewing a specific room, hallway, or gathering place in and about the lodge. Above the rows, dead center, was a crimson digital display reading:

09.00%

"How much time we got?"

"She postponed again."

"She what?"

"She was concerned about last night's dreams and this morning's manifestations. Felt the group hadn't fully 'attuned to their surroundings'."

Orbolitz shook his head. "What does that do to my little video meet and greet?"

"I suggest you have your video conference with them immediately afterwards."

He nodded.

"I'll make sure we have the camera crew present and standing by."

"And those?" He motioned to the goggles behind him on the bureau below the mounted head of a eight-point buck. The glasses had been greatly streamlined from the last pair and made mobile with a self-contained battery belt. She glanced to them, and he noticed her normally tense body grow even tenser. He had his answer and erupted, "When are we going to get some results?"

"Mr. Orbolitz . . . they function perfectly. Better than we had expected."

"Here!" he barked. "They function here! But what good does that do me?"

As always Stanton was careful to choose her words. "Dr. Helgeland assures us that all aspects of the mountain are working as expected. Everything is up to speed."

"Except these!" He reached back and swept the goggles to the floor.

Stanton looked down, waiting for his temper to cool. With measured words she replied, "Sir, we're trying everything—at the moment we're experimenting with long-distance telephoto. But so far the manifestations refuse to be captured on any medium."

"Useless," he fumed. "Totally useless."

"Down here, yes. The only way to successfully utilize them would be . . ." She hesitated, then tried again. "The only way they can serve the purpose for which we intended would be—"

"—for me to go up there." She started to respond but he cut her off. "For me to go there and watch everything close-up and in person."

She nodded. "Which, of course, would be too risky."

"Not as risky as blowing all my money on some experiment that's half-baked!"

The woman remained silent—which gave Orbolitz a moment to consider. He leaned back in his chair. "Then again, I really wouldn't be the one in danger, would I? I mean, it's not like I'm packin' one of those receiver thingies. I'd just be an innocent observer."

"Not so innocent, I'm afraid."

He looked at her, then smiled. "You reckon they'd take my presence kinda personally? Might want to do me some bodily harm?"

"I'd say the odds are rather high."

"But even those reactions would be interestin', wouldn't they? 'Specially in Kauffman's case." Before she could reply, he concluded. "Well, let's see what happens at the séance . . . and how they respond to my little greetin'."

"Yes, sir."

He gave her a wave of dismissal and she turned to leave. "Oh, and Lisa."

She turned back. "Sir?"

"Get them makeup and hair people here early. I wanna look my best for the lab rats."

"Yes, sir." She headed back toward the towering pair of wooden doors with the giant oak trees carved in them. He watched, marveling at how all those brains could be wrapped in such a beautiful package dressed so poorly. Dressed poorly and wired far too tightly. No matter. She got the job done, and for Orbolitz that's all that counted.

Once she'd stepped outside he reached for the intercom and buzzed his secretary. "Mrs. Halton, call the fellas over at the hangar. Tell 'em to start preppin' the Gulfstream."

The voice on the other end was thin and melodious. "Are you planning a trip, sir?"

"You know me, I always like to be prepared."

"I'll tell them, sir."

"Thank ya, darlin'." With that, he leaned back, propped his boots up on the desk, and thought.

n o, no, no," Rachel chuckled. "It's not like we run around the woods naked looking for trees to worship."

David gave a nervous cough. "I'm sorry, I didn't mean to suggest that, it's just—" He held back a fir branch, letting her pass along the path. "I guess I really don't understand that much about Wicca."

"Most people don't. And you can't blame them. With so many offshoots and homegrown varieties, it's hard to know what's real." She paused, waiting for David to join her side.

The walk through the forest had been her idea—another attempt, she said, to calm and center the group for the upcoming session. David couldn't have agreed more. After this morning's mass hysteria, or whatever it was they'd experienced at the breakfast counter, along with the group dream, a little *centering* wasn't a bad idea. Albert and Savannah had fallen back, slowing their pace for Reverend Wyatt to keep up, while David and Rachel had somehow paired off to take the lead. It hadn't been David's intention . . . at least that's what he told himself. And, though being alone with her both pleased and made him nervous, he wasn't about to let any type of attraction interfere with his purpose . . . at least that's what he told himself.

They'd just crested a ridge to the north of the lodge and were working their way through ferns and over fallen trees toward a small stream below.

"Actually," Rachel continued, "when all is said and done, our beliefs are quite simple. They can be reduced to three basic principles."

"Which are?"

"First, we must worship at least one god and one goddess. We can worship more if we choose, but two is mandatory—one male, the other female."

The statement almost brought him to a stop. "And you believe that? You believe in these . . . multiple gods?"

"I not only believe in them—but I speak with them and they speak with me . . . on a regular basis."

He shot her a look.

"Ever since I was twelve."

He had no idea how to respond. "And . . . this . . . 'gift' you have, in talking to the dead—"

"Comes from my gods, yes."

"Do all Wiccans have this ability?"

She shook her head. "No, almost none. In fact, I actually started communicating with my deities long before I knew what they were. At first I thought they were angels."

David nodded.

"But these are definitely not the dead."

"Actually . . ." David cleared his throat. "The dead aren't angels, either."

"Really?"

"Separate creatures altogether. At least from what I've read in the Bible."

"Hmm." Her answer was noncommittal, but he could tell she was thinking.

As they continued down the slope toward the stream, he grew more and more certain she really believed in what she said. And over the last day and a half it had become obvious that something legitimate and unusual was indeed happening. But not necessarily in the terms she thought. This "communicating with her gods" was certainly a new angle. But, whatever was going on, he was positive they were not helping her speak with the dead. From what he'd seen in both heaven and hell, the barriers could not be crossed. And, from what he'd read in the Bible, God gave clear warnings that no attempts should ever be made to do so.

Still, if it wasn't the dead she was contacting, then who? "Please," he said, "tell me more."

She laughed. "I don't want to keep rattling on about myself." Once again, she pushed her hair behind her ear, a nervous habit she seemed to be doing a lot of lately. "I'd really like to hear more about you and your family. And, if you don't mind, your relationship with Gita Patekar?"

He looked down. "Maybe a little later." He felt her eyes watching him and pressed on. "What are some other, you know, misconceptions about Wicca?"

"I suppose the biggest is that we're worshippers of nature."

"You're not?"

She shrugged at his surprise. "Sorry. Though it wouldn't be hard with all this beauty." She nodded to the trees around them and the soaring peaks above. "The gods and goddesses may choose to infuse themselves into this splendor, but we worship very specific deities, not nature."

David gave a nod, though he didn't entirely see the difference. "And what about Jesus Christ? What's your take on Him?"

She looked at him again. Then, somewhat gently, she replied, "It sounds as though Gita may have touched more than your heart."

He glanced away, embarrassed. "She was a good woman."

Silence grew between them. Again, he felt her watching him. After all this time, were his feelings about Gita still so obvious? Of course they were to him. He'd never met a woman so . . . pure. Knew he never would again. But surely he was capable of keeping his feelings more hidden than this.

"Yes," Rachel quietly repeated, "she was a good woman. They don't come any more honest and straightforward. A bit opinionated, perhaps, especially in the religious department, but definitely good."

David looked at her. "You knew of her faith?"

"She shared it with me." Then with a smile added, "More than once. And you?"

Again, David looked down, unsure how to respond.

Rachel responded with the slightest surprise. "You became a Christian because of her."

He nodded, still feeling a little uncomfortable with the label. Not because he was ashamed of Christ—after what he'd seen in heaven, after *Who* he'd seen, the Man with the holes in His hands, he could never be ashamed. It was just the idea of being so quickly categorized—especially with the media broad-stroking Christians as narrow-minded, intolerant, card-carrying Republicans.

Another moment passed before Rachel finally came around to answering his question. "We believe Jesus was a great man, a good teacher—but as far as Savior of the world . . ." She shook her head. "We really don't believe the world is an evil place that needs to be saved."

"And yet," he pointed out, "isn't that exactly what Jesus taught? Didn't He say again and again that His purpose for coming was to die for our sins?"

"I suppose . . ."

"But if you believe He was a great teacher and disagree with His purpose of coming to save the world—well, you really can't have it both ways, can you?" He hoped he didn't sound too argumentative.

She paused, then slowly nodded. "Then I would have to say he was a great teacher . . . but not infallible."

David resisted the need to continue. He'd made his point. Besides, the day was too perfect, the mountains and air too beautiful to turn everything into confrontation. Especially with her.

They walked in the silence, savoring the moment, until Rachel spoke again. "There is something else we believe."

"What's that?"

"Not only is nature a beautiful thing to celebrate, but we believe all of its pleasures and desires are to be enjoyed."

He glanced at her, but she would not look at him. He swallowed, noticing how dry his mouth had become. In an effort to change the subject, he asked, "You, uh, you mentioned three beliefs. What are the other two?"

"We also believe in the Wiccan Rede: *'If ye harm none, do what ye will'*."

"I'm sorry, what does that—"

"We may enjoy whatever we wish, as long as we don't harm others. There are no rules, no sins. If we enjoy something, we may abandon all restraint and indulge in it."

The phrase did little to relieve David's tension. Was she making a pass at him? He couldn't tell. When it came to women there wasn't much he could tell—a point his daughter had never hesitated to point out to him.

"And uh . . ." Again he cleared his throat. "The third?"

"We call it the Law of Return. If a person does evil, it comes back to them. If they do good, it also returns."

"Sort of like karma?"

"Sort of. It's called the Rule of Three:

" 'Be always mindful of the rule of three,
Three times thy actions return to thee.
This is the lesson which thou must learn,
Thou receives only what thou dost earn.' "

They finally arrived at the stream. It was shallow but six or seven feet across.

"Now what?" she asked.

He spotted some larger stones and started toward them. "Over here."

Rachel sounded less sure. "Listen, you need to know, I'm a bit of a klutz."

"You'll be fine." His take-charge attitude surprised him, and he wondered if he might be showing off a bit. They arrived at the stones, and he crossed them effortlessly and with a bit of flair. Yes, he was definitely showing off. He turned back to her and motioned. "Come on."

"You sure?"

"A piece of cake."

She looked down, tentative. Then, ever so carefully, she stepped onto the first slick stone. Then to the next. But she was already losing her balance. She squealed, taking the next two in rapid succession. "David!"

He moved to catch her just as she fell into his arms— warm and beautiful and lovely and—He quickly released her. A gallant idea, except that she was still clinging to him for balance.

Well, she *had* been clinging to him for balance. Now she was splashing into the water, rear-first, shrieking at the icy cold.

He was there in a second but far too late.

"What are you doing?" she demanded.

He reached for her, but she slapped his hands away. "What is wrong with you?"

"Here, let me—"

"What is wrong with you!" On her own effort, she struggled to her feet, until they slipped out from under her, sending her splashing back into the water with another yelp.

"Rachel—"

Looking up at him, she cried, "Do you really hate me that much!" She blew the wet hair from her face.

"I don't—"

"Do you?"

Before he could answer, she turned over and crawled on her hands and knees through the frigid water back to the bank.

four

What's wrong, why are we slowing?"

Preacher Man squinted into the setting sun as it struck his dirty windshield. Not far ahead a car sat along the side of the road with a red flare burning. "Looks like somebody needs our help."

"Oh, please," Starr mumbled. "Let them find some other good-deeder." She plopped her face back into the balled-up sweatshirt shoved against the door.

He thought of saying something about their responsibility to others, but after sixteen hours (seventeen if you count the times they'd stopped so she could have smokes) she was wearing him out. Lord have mercy, could that girl argue. She didn't always make sense, but she always had the answers . . .

"Soon as I get enough saved, I'm getting some head shots taken and find me an agent."

"Are you now?" Preacher Man had asked. They were just north of Medford when she had launched into her life plans.

"Yeah, I'll probably do a few commercials first, then once I get experienced, land a series."

He'd heard similar scenarios a hundred times from the kids at the shelter. "And then what?"

"Movies, of course."

"Of course."

"Eddie, he's always saying I'm pretty enough for his videos and all, but—"

"Whoa, whoa, who's Eddie?"

"Relax, he's already been married—a couple times. Got a bunch of kids."

The thought gave Preacher Man little comfort.

"He's always saying I'm pretty enough for his videos and everything. But I'd never stoop to nothing like that, I mean I got my pride. Not that Momma would think so, but I do. A lot." Turning toward the window, she concluded, "Who cares what she thinks, anyways."

He threw her a look. "You talk to her much, your momma?"

"Not lately. I mean, it's not like I haven't tried, a bunch of times. But every time I call, *he* picks up."

"He? Your dad?"

"*Step*dad. And then when she does answer, I mean it isn't long before she gets all teary eyed and starts bawling like some baby. Bag that, who needs it." She gave a sniff and swallowed.

Preacher Man stole another look. She continued staring out the window, briefly touching her eyes. Apparently her mother wasn't the only one feeling the emotions.

He was jarred from his thoughts by a woman alongside the parked car, waving her arms, shouting for him to stop. And for good reason. As he slowed and pulled in front of the car, he saw another body lying on the ground.

Stirred from his sleep, Nubee called from the back, "We go see David; we go see God?"

"Soon, brother, we're just 'bout there." Coming to a stop, he added more quietly, "Wherever 'there' is."

The truth is, he'd expected to hear something from David's mother by now. Some clue of his location. They'd soon be in Washington, and so far, he'd heard nothing. He'd even started calling the number himself, but the results were equally in vain.

The woman raced to his side of the car shouting, "Help us! Help us!" She was blonde and, for the record, not one bit attractive. At least to Preacher Man's experienced eye. "You've got to help us!"

He pushed open the door and with effort pulled himself out of the car. The air was warm with the roasted oat smell of dried grass.

"You've got to help us!"

"What's the problem?"

"It's my sister!" She started back to the body. Preacher Man followed. "She was having a hard time breathing. She couldn't breathe, and then she started having a seizure or something!"

"Do you have a cell phone? Did you call 911?"

"I tried, but it's not working. My battery's dead. What do we do? What do we do?"

They arrived and he kneeled down on the warm asphalt next to the body. She was even uglier than her sister. "Ma'am, can you hear me? Ma'am, can you—"

But that was as far as he got before Sister One threw a choke hold around him from behind.

"What are you—"

He managed to rise, but Sister Two suddenly came alive, scrambling to her feet—so fast that her wig slipped to the side. Angrily, she ripped it off, revealing a black crew cut. In her hand was a gun. No, not a gun. It looked like a gun but—

"What are you doing?" Preacher Man coughed, trying to wrench free. For a woman the first sister was incredibly strong. "Let go of me, let—"

Sister Two grabbed his arm, and in one continuous move, pulled up his shirtsleeve and fired the gun into his bare skin. He felt the pressure, the burn, then realized it wasn't a gun at all, but some sort of injection. She released his arm and turned for his car. He continued struggling with Sister One. "Let go of me!" He turned his head, which had suddenly grown wobbly. He caught a glimpse of the woman arriving at his car and throwing open Starr's door. He heard a muffled scream, took a step forward, noticing how slow his body moved, how his legs were turning to rubber—until they gave out altogether and he floated toward the pavement down, down ... never knowing if he hit.

everybody nice and relaxed now? We've put the day's events out of our minds?"

The group nodded.

David hoped that was true—especially the part involving his performance down at the stream. Though, somehow, he had his doubts.

"Nice, deep breaths now ... in ... and out ..."

The five of them sat in the conversation pit near a stone fireplace at the end of a large living room. Less than an hour ago, they'd finished an excellent dinner. Well, maybe *excellent* wasn't the right word. More like *intriguing*. Albert had insisted it was his turn to ply his culinary skills. And, though David was a big fan of spaghetti, he'd never had the opportunity to eat such scorched noodles—or as Reverend Wyatt diplomatically put it ... "charbroiled pasta."

After they'd finished, David had just enough time to head upstairs and go another round with his son. He'd made it clear that Luke would not be allowed to attend the next session. Given their last encounter, it was far too dangerous. This, of course led to the usual tug of wills ...

"You're treating me like a kid again."

"Nobody's treating you like a kid."

"Yeah, right."

"I just don't think it's a good idea for—"

"Why drag me all the way up here if you're going to make me a prisoner?"

"Nobody's making you a prisoner."

"Yeah, right. All that's missing is the ball and chain."

"Things have changed. It's not like I thought it was."

"Yeah, right."

David was growing a bit weary of that response. "Look, I'm not so sure we're dealing with a hoax anymore."

"Duhh . . ."

The response may have been different; the attitude wasn't. And so the debate raged—Luke ducking and weaving, trying every tactic known to teenhood, while jettisoning most common sense and all common courtesy. Still, somehow, David had won . . . at least the battle . . . at least for now . . . at least he hoped.

The séance had started ten minutes earlier. Savannah, Albert, Reverend Wyatt, Rachel, and David sat in comfortable sofas and overstuffed chairs in a conversation pit around a large square coffee table. A crackling fire filled the air with the sweet smell of burning cedar.

"Breathe in . . ."

"You hear that?" Albert asked.

"Shh," Savannah admonished. She'd switched from clicking sugarless candy to snapping sugarless gum.

" . . . and out . . ."

"No, listen. It sounds like . . . Is that somebody crying? Don't you guys hear that?"

David glanced up. Savannah and the Reverend sat with their eyes closed, straining to listen. And Rachel? Though her eyes remained shut, he could see them darting under her lids.

"Yeah . . . ," Savannah softly agreed. "I do hear something."

Now David heard it too. It was very distant but very clear. Some sort of hypnotic suggestion? Maybe, but he had his doubts.

"A child," Reverend Wyatt whispered. "It's a crying child."

Savannah nodded. "A baby."

David glanced at her. For the briefest second he thought he saw the heavier Savannah, the one in his dream. Then it was gone.

With her eyes still closed she turned to Rachel. "Do you hear that?"

Rachel did not answer.

"Rachel . . . sweetheart?" Savannah opened her eyes. "Rachel?!"

David turned back to see Rachel's left arm rising into the air. A frown had creased her face; perspiration appeared on her upper lip.

"Rachel, honey, are you all right?"

At last she opened her eyes, blinking as if coming to. She followed their gaze to her arm and gave a start.

"What's going on?" Albert asked.

She tried answering, but no words came. Scowling in concentration, she attempted to lower her arm. It did not cooperate but continued rising until it was at right angles to her body. She reached to it with her other hand, struggling to pull it down, but with no success—until suddenly, her right hand flew back, sticking out in the opposite direction. She gasped but still could not speak.

The baby's cries grew louder, so distinct David could pinpoint their location—directly in the center of the coffee table. But of course no baby was there, only its cries. He turned back to Rachel. She also stared at the table, the tendons in her neck tightening as if she was trying to look away. But like her arms, she could not move her head. She could only stare forward in growing fear.

"Rachel?!" Savannah shouted. "Rachel, what's going on? What do you see?"

"No . . . ," she whimpered. "Please . . ."

Albert sat up on the sofa beside her. He reached for her arms but was suddenly thrown back into his seat.

"Rachel?" David rose. Cautiously he moved around the table toward her. "Rachel?"

But she didn't seem to hear. She could only stare at the table, her face wet with perspiration, her eyes filled with terror . . . and something else.

"I'm sorry . . . ," she whispered.

Albert saw it first and swore. As he did the air seemed to shimmer. On Rachel's left arm four white stripes appeared around her wrist.

"What is that?" the Reverend whispered.

An identical set of stripes were also forming on her right wrist. And the more she struggled, the more defined they grew.

"Someone's . . . holding her," Savannah shuddered. "Those are finger marks!"

She was right. It was as if someone had grabbed both of Rachel's wrists—their fingers pressing deeply into her flesh.

"I'm so sorry . . ." Her voice quivered as she whispered to the table. "I didn't . . ." Her eyes welled with moisture. "I didn't know . . ."

Deliberately, David stepped into her line of vision. If she couldn't lower her arms or move her head, then he could at least block her sight.

But she continued staring, as if looking through him, the moisture spilling onto her cheeks. "Please . . . I didn't—" Suddenly her eyes widened. "No! Stay away! Stay—" Her face twisted and she screamed as something struck David from behind—so powerful it sent him flying headfirst toward the stone fireplace. But, just before he struck, he felt pressure against his head, as if he was being turned, deflected. His shoulder slammed hard into the stones, but that was all. The impact knocked the wind from him, but he quickly scrambled to his feet. To his surprise, he saw Rachel's arms had dropped to her sides. She was still covered in sweat and trembling, but she'd regained control of her body. And, except for her gasps of breath, the room had become completely silent. The crying baby was gone.

"Rachel, sweetheart." Savannah joined her side. "Are you okay?"

Still breathing hard, Rachel looked up at her.

"What was going on?"

"Your husband never did contact you, did he?"

"I—what?"

"That's not why we're up here, is it? He's never contacted you."

"Well, of course he has. Why else would we be here?"

Rachel remained unconvinced.

"Of course he has," Savannah repeated. "I mean, just ask David here. He saw the locket. When he was in hell he saw the locket. He knows what Ashton's been telling me. Isn't that right, David?"

David nodded. "I did see that locket . . . and I am the only one who saw him in hell."

"That ain't exactly correct, son."

The voice startled everyone.

"If you recall, ya'll had a little company out there on that Lake of Fire."

David grew cold. It had been over a year since he'd heard the voice, but he recognized it instantly.

The group exchanged glances, looking for the source.

"Over here, folks." It came from behind them—around the corner, over in the TV area. Blue-green light flickered against the walls, across the furniture. "Over here."

Slowly they rose to their feet, stepping up and out of the conversation pit.

"Over this a way."

They eased across the room. David was the first to see the large TV screen on the wall. And there, in all of his high-definition glory, grinned Norman E. Orbolitz—the man who had murdered his daughter.

I t was weird how the silence didn't bug Luke like before. He figured one of the reasons was because there really wasn't that much of it. I mean, there was and there wasn't. In one sense there was even more silence now, during the night, than during the day. Maybe it was the lack of a breeze, or the lack of birds. Or maybe it was the way the clouds had come in and wrapped the mountain up in a gray, sound-absorbent blanket. The point is, it was so quiet that he heard everything—every snap of a twig under his tennis shoes, every rustle of undergrowth as he moved through it, even the tapping of water as it condensed and dripped from the overhead fir needles.

But it wasn't just nature that he heard. Because the more time he spent out here, the more he heard something else as well. His thoughts. Not the surface ones that were always there—the ones nagging at him to study his algebra, or impress some girl, or show up some jerk. No, these were other thoughts. Thoughts he barely knew were there. About himself. About life.

Of course he always wondered why he'd survived and not Emily. And he always felt crummy for the mean stuff he'd pulled on her . . . like the little train of toilet paper he'd slipped into the back of her skirt on her way to her first dance . . . or videotaping her kiss on the porch and digitally replacing the boyfriend with a fat pig.

But this was different. These thoughts were . . . deeper. It was as if he was stepping back and seeing parts of a giant puzzle, an awesome pattern. "Wheels within wheels," that's how Dad had put it. Like there really was a plan. Maybe even a plan Maker.

Weird.

And with that hearing and thinking, came the seeing. Thanks to the Reverend's battery-powered lantern he noticed thousands of details—the purple-black berries of the salal, the millions of little feathery tentacles that actually made up the moss; or, when he walked, how the shadows of the lower branches twisted and darted against the higher ones. It was all very cool. He also saw the drama. It was everywhere, all around him. Like the dozen fallen trees from the winter storms, their upturned roots stretching toward him like monster arms. Or the rock slides rising high over his head, disappearing into the darkness—rocks that could just as easily begin sliding again, burying him within seconds.

There was life up here—sights, sounds, drama. Subtle yet powerful. Beautiful yet deadly. Not prechewed by someone else for a make-believe video game or the big screen. But life in the raw. Life without a net. He smiled, pleased with the phrase, thinking it was something his dad could have dreamed up.

Of course he didn't bother telling the guy that he'd be sneaking out. Not that he was really sneaking; he just didn't bother telling. Ever since Em's death he'd learned that was the only way to handle Dad. Otherwise he wouldn't let him do anything. Not that he blamed him. With Mom's running off and Emily's death, family membership was down 50 percent. But it did mean Luke had to implement some new strategies.

First, there was his Don't Ask, Don't Tell policy. That way if he got busted, he really hadn't disobeyed, 'cause he'd never really been told no. This led to a second and equally important rule: It is easier to get forgiveness than permission. With the help of these and other tactics, Luke soon found himself able to live a remotely bearable life.

Earlier, he'd climbed the tree-covered ridge in front of the lodge. He'd traveled up it and then down to a plateau and a long bluff that overlooked a bank of clouds. The Reverend said there was a river down there, hundreds of feet below. Luke would have to take his word for it, because all he'd seen were clouds. Eventually he doubled back and returned to the gulley, the one he'd crossed to the pocket glacier. He had just started down into it when the whine filled his ears.

He slowed, tilting his head to the left, then the right. He took another step, then another. The whine grew louder. He continued moving down until it became so loud he winced and had to stop. He tried taking another step, but the pain was too great and he stepped back up. As he did, it eased slightly. He paused, frowning, then took another step up and another. With each step it grew less. How strange. Maybe it had something to do with the altitude. He stepped down again, and again the pain increased. Then he stepped up and up . . . until it had completely stopped, until there was only the sound. A few more steps and even that disappeared.

Okay fine, if he couldn't go to the glacier, he'd go around the lodge and back to the bluff. If it was some sort of altitude thing, he'd just check with Reverend Wyatt and try again tomorrow.

He turned his back on the gulley and circled the lodge, climbing over fallen trees and across moss-covered boulders. He had started up the ridge and was moving at a pretty good clip when a rotting log gave way. It crumbled under his feet and he fell two or three yards before hitting the ground and rolling back down the slope. He had no idea how long he tumbled, but he certainly knew when he slammed into the fir tree and stopped.

He wasn't sure which was worst, the tumbling or the stopping. He lay on his back catching his breath, grateful he'd not let go of the lantern and that it was still working. He stared up at the tree as it disappeared into the fog. For a moment he stayed there, enjoying the absolute silence of the forest, and his breathing . . . and the hum.

Hum? Great, more weirdness. Either that or he'd smacked his head too hard in the fall. Whatever the reason, he seemed to feel it as much as hear it. He lay another moment trying to understand, until he rolled onto his stomach, grabbed the tree for support, and rose. Only then did he notice that the tree wasn't really a tree.

Oh, it looked like a tree—same black and brown bark, same moss-covered branches. But it didn't feel like a tree. It felt . . . softer, spongier. Like hard foam. He leaned in closer to examine it. That's when the buzzing grew louder. He pulled away and frowned. He tilted his head and gazed back up the tree. Like so many others, the top was jagged—spindly, branches broken off from past storms. But there was something else. Just below the fog there was a series of long skinny panels circling the tree. They'd been painted, camouflaged to look like the tree, but there was no disguising their shape. Four to five inches wide, they stretched into the fog and out of sight. It many ways they reminded him of the panels on the cell phone towers back home. But there were no cell phones. Not up here.

hey, Dave, it's great to see you again, buddy."
David stared at the TV, unable to speak.

"And, Savannah—I tell you, gal, you just keep lookin' better and better."

Savannah gave a tentative nod. With a nervous cough, she replied, "Norman."

Rachel turned to them. "You two know this man?"

David barely heard. All he could do was stare at Orbolitz's eyes. Those beautiful, violet-blue eyes that had belonged to his daughter, until the man had stolen them for his own.

"Oh, yeah, me and Dave, we go way back. Got somethin' in common, the two of us, don't we, son?"

David's coldness turned to ice.

"And Savannah, she helped me set up this whole little get-together. Nice work, gal."

Savannah nervously snapped her gum.

"Who are you?" Reverend Wyatt took a step closer to the screen. "How can you see us?"

"Norman E. Orbolitz," Albert replied in quiet awe, staring. "Head of the Orbolitz Group. One of the largest communication empires in the world."

"You got that right, Al. Though I gotta take issue with you—we're not *one* of the largest, we *are* the largest. And, as far as how I can see you—we got cameras all over this place."

The group glanced around.

Orbolitz laughed. "You won't be able to see 'em. They're built in. Everywhere. Well, 'cept the privies—everyone's entitled to a little privacy, wouldn't you agree?"

"Why are you here?" the Reverend demanded.

"Actually, the real question is, 'Why are *you*?' You and the rest of your friends—which I might point out have been carefully screened and hand-selected over thousands of potential subjects."

"Subjects?" Rachel asked.

"Yes, ma'am."

"How are we subjects?"

"That's what we're 'bout to clear up. Now listen carefully, 'cause I'm a little busy and don't have time for repeatin' myself." Without waiting for a reply he began. "It goes somethin' like this ... It takes the brain twelve minutes to shut down after the body dies. Me and a few science fellows, we've recorded those twelve minutes of brain activity from over thirteen hundred volunteers who have died. From this data we've built a computer model of everything folks experience in those first twelve minutes—the tunnel, the light, the Garden, heaven, and of course hell—which is where me and Dave first met up, ain't that right, son."

David reached out and steadied himself against the back of a chair, recalling all too well his experiences at the Lake of Fire.

"That's when we saw Savannah's husband, remember? The rock 'n' roller wearing that gold tiger-tooth pendant?"

David scowled, remembering. Of course. He wasn't the only one who had seen the man. So had Orbolitz.

"Pretty genius, don't you agree? Using that as bait to get you up here? And as you'll see, you're a vital part of this here experiment."

"Subjects ... experiments?" Albert moved toward the screen. "What are we, your guinea pigs?"

Orbolitz smiled. "'Fraid so, Al. You see, me and God, we got like this grudge match goin'. I hate Him and He hates me. Only problem is, He gets to play the final card—when I die it's all His show."

"But ..." David's voice was dry and unsteady. "You've been working *not* to die. That's why you harvested those organs. That's why you had my daughter killed ... for her eyes."

"Diabetic retinopathy, terrible condition. But thanks to these peepers"—he tapped the side of his head—"so far, so good. Doctors weren't sure they'd take, it being a new procedure and all. But they have. Must be all them good genes I inherited from you. Thanks, buddy."

David felt himself starting to tremble.

"But living forever—well, scientifically it just don't seem to be an option, least yet. So, if I'm going to beat God, I gotta figure out how to do it on the other side."

"Beat God?" the Reverend repeated. "That's sacrilege."

"Yup."

"You will die and face His judgment like everyone else. Nobody can beat God and His laws."

"Not necessarily. We beat gravity, didn't we? We're beatin' His laws every day—science, medicine, technology. And if those are the laws God runs His universe by, then just like gravity, we oughta be able to find a way to beat Him at the big one."

"How?" Rachel asked.

Orbolitz looked over to her and grinned. "This is where it gets interesting. To beat your enemy, you have to know your enemy. Remember them thirteen hundred death experiences? Well, we've been able to reduce them all down to just the God part."

"The what?" Albert asked.

"Each and every one of them people had some sort of contact with God. So what we've done is combine all thirteen hundred pieces of their God experiences into one full, concentrated program. Now, all we gotta do is see what happens to folks who get exposed to that program, who get fully exposed to the Presence of God."

"That's . . . ," the Reverend sputtered, "that's not possible!"

"Oh, but it is. And by analyzing them results, we'll know beforehand what we're gonna face. We'll study the effects on select individuals, see what His Presence does to them, how it does it, and if possible . . . figure how to beat the Almighty at His own game."

"And we're . . . ," Albert spoke in awe, ". . . we're those selected individuals."

"Bingo. We got thirteen hundred bits and pieces of scattered info—but we've never seen what happens when all those experiences are combined and concentrated into one big enchilada. That's where you come in. Over the next seventy-two hours we'll be exposing you to as much of His recorded Presence as we got, to see what happens. But it's gotta be gradual. See, a while back we exposed a couple volunteers to it all at once, and well, they kinda blew up on us."

"So why all the way up here?" Albert asked. "Why not just kidnap us and take us to your lab?"

"Good question. First we need to see how folks respond in more realistic situations outside a lab—you know, people interactin' with one another and such. And the more remote you are, the less RF interference we get. And believe me, folks, you are remote."

"Why us?" Savannah asked. "Why me? I've done everything you've asked."

"Yes, you have, darlin', and you'll be rewarded handsomely. But you, along with each of your friends, have some very specific traits. And we want to see how them traits will react to His Presence as we increase it."

"How do you do that?" Savannah asked. "How do we experience this . . . Presence?"

"It's already started."

"Those weird things we've been seeing?" Albert asked. "Our dreams?"

"For starters, yup. And facilitated nicely, I might add, by Ms. McPherson's gifts."

The group turned to Rachel.

"That's why my experiences have been so intense, so unpredictable?" she asked.

Orbolitz grinned. "And we've only just begun. Right now we're at, let's see here . . ." He peered above his camera. "Twelve percent. Kid's stuff. For now it mostly means you'll be seeing each other from God's perspective, kinda the way He sees you. But things should really start poppin' as we increase it a few percentage points every hour or so."

"But"—Albert frowned—"how do we actually experience it, this . . . God Presence?"

"What do you mean?"

"I mean, it's not like you have us hooked up to some machine or transmitter or anything."

"Actually, this house, the entire grounds are the machine. A very expensive one, I might add. And them sniffles you been havin'? They're not exactly allergies. You see, there's this little place in the front of our brains that's sensitive to God stuff."

"The *God Spot*," Rachel replied. "The part science has proven to be most active during spiritual experiences. The location of our soul."

"Whatever you call it, it seems to be the place God does most of His communicating. So all we did was insert these itty-bitty receivers up your nose and into that spot to—"

"Wait a minute," Albert interrupted. "Receivers? Into our nose? When was that?"

"First night you were here. A bit of sedation to help you sleep, courtesy of Savannah's chocolate chips, and a little night visit by our medical team. The procedure took less than a minute apiece."

Instinctively, David and the others reached to their noses.

Orbolitz chuckled. "Don't worry, far as we can tell there's no side effects. And your bodies will reject 'em in a week or so. They'll work their way back out—provided, of course, you survive."

"I'm sorry." Albert shook his head. "This is just plain nuts."

"How's that?"

Moving closer to the screen beside Savannah, he explained, "You may be Norman E. Orbolitz, you may not be—but the idea of exposing us to the actual Presence of God—"

"The *recorded* Presence," Orbolitz corrected. "As experienced by thirteen hundred—"

"Whatever. The point is, it's absurd. No one can do that."

"Al, I'm surprised at you. How can someone so creative have such little imagination?"

"Imagination is one thing; what you're proposing . . . I mean, surely you've got some evidence to show us, some proof that—"

"Ah, proof. Of course. That's the scientist in you talking. Well, Al, what's the ol' saying, 'The proof's in the pudding'?" Orbolitz leaned forward and spoke into what appeared to be an intercom. "Dr. Helgeland?"

A voice replied. "Sir?"

"We got some puddin' to serve our guests."

"Sir?"

Turning back to the screen, Orbolitz explained, "Everybody, this here is Dr. Dirk Helgeland. He'll be your host for the next three days."

"And a good day to you folks. How are you this fine autumn evening?"

The cheeriness of his Irish brogue was more than unnerving.

"Dirk, let's start increasin' the power."

"Yes, sir. Folks, we'll be bringing you up to 17 percent."

"Actually, let's make that 20 percent."

"Twenty percent?"

"Yes, we got ourselves a couple skeptics."

"Twenty percent it is."

Orbolitz turned back to the group. "Now, by nearly doubling the Presence you should be experiencing . . . well, actually we aren't sure what you'll be experiencing." With another chuckle he added, "Which is the whole purpose of this little get-together." Speaking back into the intercom, he asked, "How we doin', Dirk?"

"Approaching 20 percent now."

"Good . . . good. And now let's bring down the lights, please."

Suddenly every light in the room dropped to a dim glow.

The group stood in the silence, exchanging concerned looks. There was nothing. No sounds, no feelings, no sensations, until—

Rachel was the first to spot it and she caught her breath. David turned to see her staring at Savannah. A tiny patch of color had begun glowing near the center of Savannah's chest.

Savannah looked at them blankly. "What?"

No one spoke as the color continued growing.

"What's wrong? What are you looking at?" She finally glanced down at herself and gasped. The glow, mostly oranges and reds, continued to grow, stretching down her stomach, then to her thighs and legs . . . while at the same time spreading into her arms and up her neck toward her face.

"What's going on?" she cried. She reached for the light, trying to touch it, but her hands passed through it. "What's happening?" Within moments it had filled her entire body. More than filled. The glow actually extended beyond her body two or three inches—except for her left wrist. There, it was much thicker, nearly doubled . . . and deformed . . .

taking the shape of the Tiffany gold-chained bracelet she had admired. She grew more panicked. "Somebody tell me what's going on!"

But hers was not the only glow. Directly beside her, Albert's chest had been filling with the faint light, a light that rapidly spread through his own body ... until it reached his head. Here, it not only covered his face but began to extend slightly, growing into ... well, what appeared to be some sort of animal snout.

David looked on, speechless. There was something strangely familiar about these glows. They were the same colors he'd seen in the Garden when he was in the Virtual Reality chamber. They were less vibrant and vivid, but somehow the same. He turned to Rachel. She was also glowing. But hers was more uneven than the others, almost lumpy. Instead of a single glow like Albert's and Savannah's, hers were multiple, overlapping one another.

"What is happening?" Reverend Wyatt demanded. David turned to see the man slapping at his sweater and slacks. A glow was coming from him as well, creating a type of outer garment, like a cloak, with something strapped to his side.

"David?"

He turned to Rachel, who stared at him. He glanced down and saw he was also glowing. But instead of cloaks, or snouts, or bracelets, his colors were churning and swirling.

"Well," Orbolitz chuckled, "by the looks on your faces I'd say you're definitely getting a taste of the pudding. Good ... good." As he spoke a loud thumping filled the air. But it didn't come from the screen's speakers. It came from overhead, outside the lodge. The group traded alarmed looks.

Orbolitz smiled. "It's nothin' but a little helicopter, folks. Why don't you go see who's at the door. I'll be checkin' in a bit later." With that he reached forward, hit a switch, and the screen went dark.

The thumping grew louder and David broke from the group, heading for the nearest window. Pushing aside the curtain he saw that it was indeed a helicopter, the one he and Luke had arrived in the day before. It had just touched down on the lawn outside, its bright landing lights bouncing off the grass and illuminating a shiny blue door that slid open. Two men emerged from it carrying a body.

David turned and raced to the entry hall, where he threw open the door. The pounding was deafening. He headed outside, running down the porch steps, as the men laid the body on the grass and returned to the chopper. He raised his arm, squinting against the wind and light. The men reappeared with a smaller body, a girl, her hair flying in the rotor's downdraft.

"What's going on?" Albert shouted from behind him. "Who are they?"

David gave no answer as he continued forward, instinctively ducking from the beating blades. Any glow that had been around him or Albert was lost in the bright light. The crew disappeared and reappeared with the third and final passenger. Someone in a wheelchair.

As he arrived, David shouted, "Who are you? Who are these people?"

Neither crew member gave an answer but turned and reentered the chopper. Albert ran toward them, arriving just as they slid the door shut in his face. He banged on the window but they did not respond. The turbines whined louder and the craft started to rise. Its skids slammed into Albert's shins and he shouted an oath. As he swore, the air once again seemed to ripple.

But David barely noticed. Because there, in the wheelchair, passed out or dead, was Gita's little brother. David moved to him and dropped to his knees. "Nubee! Nubee, can you hear me?" Only then did he notice a faint smear of blood just below the young man's nose. And an even fainter smile flickering across his lips. "Nubee!"

"Dad! Dad, what's going on?"

He turned to see his son running from the woods. What was he doing outside? It didn't matter, not now. He looked at the other two bodies. An old black fellow who—*Preacher Man*! It was Preacher Man! And the girl lying beside him with the flying blonde air. What was her name? The girl from the shelter?

The chopper continued to rise, the noise and pounding downdraft starting to fade. He caught movement out of the corner of his eye and turned back to the wheelchair. Nubee's lips were moving. He leaned in. "Nubee, can you hear me? Nubee!"

Again the lips moved. He pressed his ears closer until he finally heard the words:

"We go see David, we go see God . . ."

part two

five

"No way am I sitting around being this guy's lab rat." Once again Albert was on his feet pacing. Like the others, the light radiating from him had acquired some darker hues and had grown more defined. Darker, in that the outside edges of his orange-red glow had turned blue, almost violet. More defined, in that the aura about his head, particularly his face, had clearly formed into what appeared to be the snout of a dog or wolf. Some of the glow was still blurry and nebulous, but at night and inside where the lights could still not be brought back up, it grew clearer with every passing hour.

"So what do you suggest?" Savannah demanded. She'd quit her gum and returned to the sugarless candy. Checking out her reflection in the window, she gave another sigh. Unlike Albert's glow, which had seemed to shrink slightly in size, hers continued to expand, at some places a good foot to eighteen inches beyond her body.

Albert continued pacing. "We either resist this stuff or we—"

"Resist it?" she scorned. "We don't even know what it is!"

Albert continued in measured tones. "We either resist it, or at the crack of dawn we hightail it out of here!"

"How?" she demanded. "Where?"

"We turn around, we walk through those doors, and we don't stop until we—"

"We don't even know where we are!"

Frustrated, unable to reason with the woman, Albert turned to Reverend Wyatt.

Like the others, the old man's glow had grown more defined, outlined by his own thin, violet-blue shell. What had appeared as a glowing cloak was now clearly a robe, complete with what looked like a hood over his head and some sort of a sword strapped to his side. He sighed wearily. "As I have said before, everything was overcast when we arrived. I only caught a glimpse of Mount Baker, and that was at the beginning."

"You're the expert on these mountains; can't you at least take an educated guess?"

It was the Reverend's turn to exercise patience. "Even if I were to choose the correct route, it may still take several days and nights to hike out."

"I'm not spending a single day or night out there!" Savannah declared.

Albert spun to her. "Did it ever dawn on you we might not have a choice?"

The group was testy, to say the least. And for good reason. The best David figured it had been six hours since Orbolitz's little talk and the helicopter's visit. Six hours of fear, anxiety, and growing desperation. By now the sedative had pretty much worn off of Preacher Man, Nubee, and the girl from the shelter (Starr was her name, "with two r's," she'd reminded him)—though they helped it by nursing their third or fourth cup of coffee. Like the others, they also glowed with the orange-red light and outer violet shell . . . as did Luke, who slouched off in the corner. Oddly enough, his shell had formed only in patches, mostly around his eyes, his ears, and the part of his chest closest to his heart. David wasn't surprised. It many ways it was exactly how he pictured his son's emotions—toward himself and others. Cut off. Isolated. Aloof.

"I agree with the Reverend," Rachel spoke from across the room. The lumpy glows encircling her had also grown more defined. "Provided this is not an elaborate hoax, there's no way he's going to just let us stroll out of here. He's invested too much; he's bound to have guards or something."

The thought made sense, and David turned to his son. "What about it, Luke? You've been all around outside."

"No, there's—" The boy's voice cracked and he tried again. "There's no guards."

"What about a fence?"

"Nothing I could see."

"You don't have to see it." Albert turned to him. "It could be electrical wires, or an electrical field, or just about anything."

Luke shook his head. "I didn't see anything." Then, frowning slightly, he added, "Least I don't think so."

David knew there was more. "What's up, son?"

The boy hesitated, then looked at Albert. "You said electrical field?"

"Or magnetic or anything, given his money and technology."

"What about . . ." Luke glanced down, then back up. "You know those electronic thingies they shock dogs with if they leave your yard?"

"Electronic leashes?"

"Yeah. There's this gully behind the lodge. The first time I crossed it everything was fine. But tonight I couldn't. It's like everytime I tried, I'd get this whining thing in my head. And if I kept going it felt like my whole brain was gonna explode."

David turned to Albert. "Does that mean anything?"

"If the guy's implanted some sort of receiver in us, there's no reason it couldn't also act as a leash. He sets up an electrical field around the property, we try to cross it, we get zapped. Pretty simple, really." Albert shook his head, swearing, once again using God's name in vain, when suddenly the air shimmered and he grabbed his jaw yelling, "Ahhh!"

"What's wrong?" Savannah cried.

"My mouth!" He reached up to feel his lips, his gums. "Just then, when I—" He stuck out his tongue, looking for the source of the pain, testing it with his fingers.

"Albert?"

"It felt like I'd bitten into a mouthful of razors." He licked his lips, checking them again.

"Are you all right now?" the Reverend asked.

"Yeah . . . I guess. How weird was that?"

But it wasn't entirely weird. At least to David. Wasn't that exactly what he'd felt in the Garden, when he'd visited his daughter in heaven, when he'd eaten the glowing fruit from the tree? And what had she said? *"Its reality is too great for you, Daddy."* He didn't understand it then and he didn't understand it now, but—when Albert swore, had he inadvertently said something too real for him?

Rachel repeated her thought. "How do we know this isn't just some elaborate hoax?"

"It's no hoax." Savannah sighed, adjusting her skimpy halter top. "The guy's been planning this for years."

"And you've been in on it?" Albert demanded.

"Just the last few months. You know, getting you guys up here and everything."

"Why?"

She shrugged. "The money." Her response was so candid, it nearly defused his anger. "When Ashton died, I was penniless. Broke. Norman offered to help . . . a lot."

"But why us?"

"Don't know. He said you all had the right profiles, the 'limps', he called them."

"Limps?" Reverend Wyatt asked.

"Yeah, character flaws."

"Hm ..." The Reverend frowned, obviously trying to think it through.

"What?" Albert asked. "What's on your mind?"

The Reverend turned to him. "Orbolitz stated that in the beginning we would be seeing ourselves as God sees us. And if he's referring to our character flaws, then he's obviously referring to the errors of our way, the sins of our flesh."

"Sins of our flesh?"

"Yes. Our imperfections, our ... limps."

David glanced down at his hands, his arms, his torso. Although his glow had also formed a violet shell, it was wavering. No, not wavering ... boiling. Tiny bubbles were rising to its surface, their activity growing stronger as the evening wore on.

"So you're saying this is how God sees us?" Savannah asked. "On the inside with all our junk and stuff?"

For the first time Nubee spoke up. "'I am he who searches hearts and minds ...'"

The group turned to him in surprise.

"What's that?" Albert asked. "What did you say?"

Nubee tilted his head and gave a lopsided grin.

The Reverend quietly replied, "Revelation 2:23."

"He likes the Bible," Starr answered drolly.

David smiled. Of all the glowing colors, Nubee's outside darkness was the thinnest. His inner oranges and reds had grown brighter and more defined while his outer violet-blue border was nearly nonexistent. And, though he sat hunched over in his wheelchair with his head cocked to the side, his glowing colors seemed to sit just a little straighter and more erect.

"If that's true ...," Albert mused, "I mean, if whatever he's transmitting into our heads is making us see ourselves like God sees us, these sins of the flesh, then—"

"Whoa, whoa, what are you saying?" Savannah tossed back her hair. It was a small gesture, but done so provocatively that it left Albert staring. "What about our good stuff?"

The Reverend turned to her and quoted: "'But we are all as an unclean thing, and all our righteousnesses are as filthy rags.'"

She looked at him a bit stunned. "Are you serious?"

"It's in His holy Word."

Savannah glanced at the rest of the group. It was obvious she wanted to say more, but equally obvious she was outclassed in the theology department.

Turning back to Albert, the Reverend continued. "So, if what we are experiencing, if what we are observing are indeed the sins of our flesh, than we must find a way to fight and overcome them."

"Overcome them?" Rachel asked.

He nodded. "Otherwise I fear they shall destroy us— much as they did with Orbolitz's first experimental group." The Reverend continued, growing more convinced of his theory as he spoke. "We need only look at poor Savannah here. She grows larger by the moment. And David with his increased bubbling. And Albert, who knows what is occurring with your face? And Rachel, and the list continues."

"But how?" Savannah asked. "I mean, if we don't even know what they are?"

"We'll know," Rachel quietly replied. "As he cranks up that Presence, these glows or whatever they are will get stronger. We'll figure them out, trust me."

"And then?" David asked.

Reverend Wyatt took a breath for resolve. "And then through prayer, discipline, and self-control, we shall overcome them. We shall fight against these failures and we shall prevail. We shall 'resist the devil, and he shall flee.'"

The group remained silent, weighing their thoughts. Once again Savannah tossed back her hair, nervously running her hands along the thighs of her form-fitting low risers—another gesture not lost on Albert.

Seconds passed. Nobody had a better theory. And since Reverend Wyatt was the apparent expert, no one felt inclined to disagree. Well, almost no one. For the first time that evening, Preacher Man spoke up:

"'Scuse me, Reverend. I don't mean to be disrespectful."

Reverend Wyatt turned to him. "Yes?"

"It's just—I mean if these glowy things are really how the Lord sees us, with our sins and all . . . well, I ain't so sure we can really beat 'em. I mean with just prayer and self-control. We may be needin' somethin' a bit stronger."

Reverend Wyatt blinked. "Something stronger?" Suddenly understanding filled his face. "Yes, of course, of course." He reached into the breast pocket of his sports coat. "With prayer, self-control, and"—he pulled out a small Bible—"the Sword of the Lord. With these we shall prevail."

"Sword?" Albert asked.

Once again Nubee quoted, "'For the word of God is living and active. Sharper than any double-edged sword.'"

The Reverend grinned at him. "You are correct, my friend." He motioned to the book in his hand. "*This* is our weapon, *this* is our sword."

"The Bible?" Starr asked skeptically.

"When the Devil and Jesus did battle on the Mount of Temptation"—he raised the book—"this is the only weapon our Lord fought with, the holy Word of God."

"Uh . . ." Preacher Man cleared his throat. "That ain't exactly what I meant."

Reverend Wyatt turned to him, puzzled.

Preacher Man explained. "The Word of God . . . ain't that what the Devil fought with too?"

Irritation briefly flickered across the Reverend's face. "What are you implying?"

"Don't get me wrong, I know it's real important. But if we're gonna beat this stuff, I'm figurin' we'll need more."

"More than God's Holy Word?"

"It's a good place to start, but—"

"Prayer, discipline, the Sword of the Lord—what more could we possibly—"

He was interrupted by a roaring *whoosh* . . .

David spun around just in time to see Albert's glow flying across the room. Only the smallest portion remained attached to the man's feet, stretching across the floor—the rest headed straight for Savannah. She screamed, raising her arms, but it did little good. The glow was on her in a second; its translucent hands gripping her own light, tearing aside the darker shell, plunging its luminous jaws deep into her orange glow, ripping at it with its teeth.

"Get it off!" she screamed. "Get it away! Get it away!"

"Albert!" Rachel cried. "What are you doing? Stop it!"

"I'm not doing anything!" Albert shouted from across the room. "I'm over here. I'm not—"

"Get it off of me! Get it off!"

The glow continued snapping, shredding, until it actually began gulping down portions of Savannah's glow.

"Get it off! Get it off!"

"Stop it!" the Reverend shouted as he strode toward Savannah. "Stop it this instant!"

"Get off her!" Starr yelled.

"I'm not doing anything!"

"You are lusting in your heart!" the Reverend cried. "You are having lascivious thoughts!"

"I'm *what*?"

The Reverend arrived at Savannah's side. Bible still in hand, he shouted at the glow. "'Thou shalt not commit adultery'!" As he yelled, his own outer shell grew darker, denser. Not only around his hooded robe, but around the sword at his side. Suddenly, a glowing pair of arms appeared from under the robe and reached for the sword. It gave a metallic ring as they drew it from its scabbard and raised it high over his head. "'And if thy right hand offend thee, cut it off'!" As he quoted the verse, his glowing arms brought down the sword, slamming it hard into Albert's luminous snout.

The snout threw back its head as if to howl . . . but the cry came from Albert, across the room, doubling over, grabbing his face in pain. "What are you doing?"

Again the Reverend shouted, "'Whosoever looketh on a woman to lust after her hath committed adultery with her'!"

"*What?*"

"Stop thinking them thoughts about her!" Starr yelled.

"I'm not—"

The Reverend's glowing form raised its sword again, and again he shouted, "'It is profitable for thee that one of thy members should perish, and not that thy whole body should be cast into hell'!" The weapon came down onto one of Albert's glowing arms, completely severing it. It fell to the floor with a hiss as Albert, grabbing his own shoulder, writhed and screamed from across the room . . . as the crippled glow withdrew, streaming back across the floor to join him.

The group stood in stunned silence as Albert gasped, rubbing his face, his shoulder, trying to understand. "What . . . what was that?"

Rachel moved to help Savannah. "Are you okay?"

She tried to speak but was still catching her breath.

"What happened?" Albert repeated.

Reverend Wyatt turned to him. "It's as the little girl here stated. You were lusting after Savannah in your heart."

"Lusting in my heart?" Albert scoffed. "What are you talking about?"

Starr stepped toward him, making it clearer. "You wanted to have sex with her, moron."

He could not have looked more startled. "No way. Why would I—I mean how could, even if I wanted . . ." But the look on Savannah's face slowed him to a stop.

"We seen you scoping her out," Starr scorned. "Like all night."

Reverend Wyatt repeated, more quietly, "'Whosoever looketh on a woman to lust after her hath committed adultery with her already in his heart.'"

"I . . ."

"You were lusting, son. No need to deny it."

Albert looked from the Reverend, to Savannah, then back to the Reverend.

"But we were able to stop it," the Reverend continued. He looked to Preacher Man, raising the Bible in his hand. "With the Word of God, we were able to put an end to it." Then, turning back to Albert, he quietly added, "And now you must repent."

"Repent?"

The Reverend nodded. "You must promise never to entertain such thoughts about her again."

Scowling, rubbing his shoulder, he answered, "Yes, yes, of course." He turned to Savannah. "I'm ... the last thing I had in mind was to hurt you. I mean that. I never would have, you know ..."

"It's okay." She was still breathing hard. "Lots of things are happening 'round here we don't understand."

Albert nodded, then looked to the floor, obviously embarrassed. But more than embarrassed. It appeared that he was clearly sorry.

Seeing his sincerity, Reverend Wyatt slowly turned to the group. When he spoke it was with deep earnestness. "Now we know with what we are dealing. More importantly"—he indicated the Bible in his hand—"we know how to defeat it."

David looked on, slowly nodding with the others. No one seemed to disagree.

No one but Preacher Man.

With dawn's growing light everyone's glows faded. They were still there, Luke was sure of it. In fact, if you stood in the darkest shadows you could catch glimmers of them. But even in the morning fog and heavy drizzle there was enough daylight to wash them away—a relief for everyone involved.

The group was outside now—bundled up, traipsing through the wet undergrowth as they searched the woods along the gulley for the electronic fence or whatever it was that Luke had described. They may or may not have to battle the Reverend's *sins of the flesh*; they didn't know. But they did know that if there was a way to get out of there, nothing would stop them.

"Over here!" David shouted. "I'm getting something over here."

"Me too!" Savannah yelled, farther ahead. "I got something down here!"

And on it went—someone shouting about a whine or headache, then tying a rag or cloth napkin around the nearest tree. Albert, who was a lot less of a showboat after the thing with Savannah, finally figured it was a buried cable. He couldn't get close enough to know the details, but with everyone's help, he hoped to have the whole parameter mapped out by nightfall. And then what? Who knew.

Luke stood, watching in silent contempt. What difference did it make? If they were trapped, they were trapped. Who cared how. But the fake tree he'd discovered last night, well now, that was a different story. If he could figure what was up with that, then maybe it would do some good, maybe he would wind up saving them all. Not a bad idea. It'd sure make everyone see him in a different light—even Dad.

He had dropped back, lagging behind the group. Then, when it was safe, he peeled off and headed back to the lodge and up the slope in front of it. Things looked different in the daylight, but he was sure he could find it. Of course it would help if he could hear the buzz again, but he couldn't hear anything with everyone's shouts echoing all over the place.

He shook his head. What a weird group. Weirder still were their glows. Could it really be their souls or whatever Reverend Wyatt had said? How cool would that be—the old guy with his Sword of God, Albert getting busted for lust.

Course there was plenty he didn't get, like Savannah's glow growing fatter and fatter, or Rachel's darkening clumps ... or Dad's outer covering that kept getting thicker and bubbling more and more.

Then there was Preacher Man and Nubee. Course, it was cool to see them again. And their glows? Nubee kept the same red and orange colors he had at the first, except they were a lot brighter. The same was true with Preacher Man, though he did have a few darker spots. He also had this big disc, a couple feet in diameter, hanging from his waist. No one knew what it was. Not Preacher Man, not even the Reverend. Still, any way you looked at it, he and Nubee definitely had the brightest glows.

"I guess that pretty much makes you perfect," Luke had teased the big guy earlier.

Preacher Man broke into one of his throaty chuckles. "Perfect?" He shook his head. "If you only knew." Then, slapping him on the back, he added, "No, son, any goodness you see in me ain't me. It's only Jesus. It's all about Jesus."

Somehow Luke wasn't surprised at the answer. For Preacher Man everything was about Jesus ... only Jesus.

He slowed to a stop. Up ahead was the rotten cedar he'd fallen through, the pink, crumbled wood freshly exposed. He turned, trying to picture the route he'd tumbled last night. It was impossible to tell for certain—maybe some broken twigs, maybe some scuffed moss—nothing really stood out. He headed up to the log, then half walked, half slid down what he imagined to be his route.

The first tree he approached wasn't even an evergreen. And he definitely remembered hitting an evergreen. He continued to slide, passing another. The bark was right— brown and black, covered with some of that dry fungus stuff. But when he looked up he saw the top was full, not at all like the one just past it. The one whose top was completely bare ... except for the half dozen panels around it.

He stopped his slide by catching the tree. The bark felt spongy and fake like last night. He leaned his face closer and listened. As before, he didn't hear the buzz as much as he felt it. Strong and clear. He looked up, wondering if he could climb the thing. Ten or so feet above him were some dead (or fake dead) branches complete with the mandatory hanging moss. No way could he reach them by jumping. But maybe he could shinny up to them. He glanced around to make sure no one had joined him. When he was sure the coast was clear, he gave it a try.

By squeezing the trunk with his knees and hugging it with his arms, he made quick progress. The fungus and stuff were just glued on, and they quickly came off, giving him an even better grip. And since the tree was a bit rubbery, it provided more than enough traction. In seconds, he reached the first branch, tested it, and pulled himself up to it. So far, so good. He rested a moment, then rose to his feet, staying as close to the trunk as possible. He reached for the next branch, pulled himself up to it, sat, then stood. Then he reached for the next, pulling, sitting, standing . . . and then the next, developing a rhythm.

At about thirty feet he noticed his joints beginning to ache. Not his muscles, at least not his legs or arms, just his joints—hips, knees, shoulders. What was that about? He continued to the next branch and the next. Soon his head began to ache. But not like before, not like with that electronic leash thing. This was a deeper ache, a throbbing at the base of the skull. With it came an incredibly bad taste in his mouth, like aluminum.

He paused, trying to get his bearings. Bearings? He was only climbing a tree, how do you lose your bearings climbing a tree? But he was. And it grew worse by the second. He looked up to the panels some twenty feet away. Or was it ten? He couldn't tell anymore. He took a breath to clear his head and started again. He reached for the next branch but missed it. He tried again and missed again. He squinted. It didn't help. He tried a third time and somehow got it. He pulled himself up. He spat, trying to get the taste out of his mouth. And now with the taste came the nausea.

He sat on the branch and closed his eyes. That's when the tree moved. His eyes exploded open and he grabbed the trunk. It shifted again. He clung tighter. Maybe it was his headache, or the nausea, or the fogging vision. Whatever it was, he forced himself to take another breath. He'd have to concentrate on every move now. He rose unsteadily and reached for the next branch. But it wasn't there. Well, it was until it blurred and moved. He reached again, it moved again, so did the tree—so much that he leaned back to keep his balance and lost it. He lunged forward, grabbing the trunk, hugging it for all he was worth. It turned, then turned back, then turned and turned, everything moving, the branches, the sky, the tree twisting free of his grasp and slipping away. He was slipping away. Slipping away and falling . . .

So with Wicca you get lots of power and stuff, right?"

"Power?" Rachel asked.

"Yeah, you know, like control?" Starr took a drag from her cigarette and flipped her stringy hair to the side.

Rachel stole another glance at her. Ever since they'd met, her heart had gone out to the child. Underneath the baggy clothes and layers of makeup, the fourteen-year-old could almost be attractive—if someone would just take a little time to help and guide her. Starr must have sensed her feelings, because the moment they'd left the lodge to mark out the parameter, she'd attached herself to Rachel's side. Some of it may have been Rachel's celebrity status; Starr claimed to have seen her TV show more than once. Whatever the reason, the girl had joined Rachel and soon began a constant stream of questions.

Rachel saw her neediness almost immediately, when the auras first appeared. Unlike the others, Starr's was not complete. Bits and pieces of her glow had not formed and connected. Random areas were missing, like holes. Holes Rachel instinctively knew were the areas yet to be formed in the girl's life—elements of character everyone else had, but that she had never entirely developed. And it was these gaps that so moved Rachel, that brought out the mothering instincts in her. As best she could tell it had been a long time since the child had been around a female's influence. Because it wasn't just her clothes, her makeup, or even her glow. Everything about the little waif cried out for love and nurturing. Everything about her begged for guidance as she was entering the strange and baffling world of womanhood.

You are right, the voice in her head had agreed. *She needs us. She needs our truth.*

That, of course, was Osiris. As a Wiccan, she did not believe in proselytizing. Actually, they honored all faiths. But for some reason Osiris felt it was different with this child. Apparently, he sensed the same neediness that Rachel did.

Starr continued chattering away. "And you think the Reverend is wrong, at least for you? You're pretty sure those light thingies that were around you, you're pretty sure that they're your gods?"

"I think so, yes."

"How many do you have?"

"I've never known the exact number. Eight, maybe nine."

"But they all have the power to kick butt, right?" Starr took another drag from her cigarette and blew it out.

Go ahead, dear.

Rachel hesitated. There was power ... and then there was power.

She wants the truth.

After a moment she answered. "Yes ... there is power. But you must understand that I'm really an exception."

"Right, you told me. Wiccans usually don't have their gods inside or around them. But there are others, right. Out here in these trees, in these mountains."

"Yes, that's true."

"And if I joined up or whatever, I could call upon them to do stuff?"

"Yes, but more importantly, you could worship them and use their powers to help others."

"And cast spells?"

"Lots of Wiccans cast spells, yes. But not for evil. As I said—"

"I know, I know. 'If ye harm none—do what ye will.'"

Rachel was impressed at how quickly the girl grasped the few concepts she'd already shared. Then again, the young were always the most open. Particularly the young who looked for some control over their life—the outcast, the shunned, the abused.

"But if you wanted, you could get David to fall in love with you, right?"

Rachel looked up, startled. "What? Why would I want—"

"Pleeease, everyone knows you got a thing for him. I mean, you don't have to be psychic to see that."

Rachel felt her face warming. "I really don't—"

"Could you, you know, like cast a spell on him for that?"

"There are some groups of people that are more difficult to influence than—"

"You mean 'cause he's a Christian."

Be careful.

Rachel had already suspected that was one of the reasons for Osiris's silence regarding David. It wasn't that he was afraid of the man. He was just ... wary. She chose her words carefully. "Some of the Christian faith are more difficult to influence, yes—but not all."

"And what about sky clad?"

Rachel almost laughed. "And where did you hear of that?"

"Girls at the shelter. Is it what I think it is?"

Rachel smiled. Of course this was another big attraction for the curious—at least for younger adolescents, those getting in touch with their bodies . . . and desires. "It means being dressed only in sky."

"Yeah," Starr giggled, "like totally naked."

"Yes." Rachel nodded. "Lots of Wiccans worship that way. It's simply coming before the gods and goddesses as ourselves, with no pretension . . . and, of course, no shame."

"How cool is that!"

"Yes, it is very cool." Rachel smiled. "Listen, if you'd like, I've got some books up in my room that you're welcome to look at."

"Really?" There was no missing the eagerness in her voice.

Rachel couldn't help smiling at her excitement. "Sure. And later, if you want, I'll be happy to answer any questions you might have."

"You'd do that for me?"

"Of course I would."

"Wow. That would be so cool. Thanks. Thanks a lot."

be still and know.

Luke woke up to the words.

Be still and know that I am God.

But they really weren't words. More like thoughts. Not his thoughts, though. Well, they were and they weren't. Why would he think up something weird like that? And what was it supposed to mean?

Be still.

He lay on the damp fir needles, his eyes closed. Silently, he took inventory of his body. As best he could tell nothing was hurt too badly. His left side was a little sore, especially the ribs just under his left arm. But for falling out of a tree, he wasn't doing half bad. He noticed the buzz was still there in his head. It didn't bother him, though. Not like the awful aluminum taste that was still in his mouth. And, of course, the phrase he couldn't get out of his head.

Be still and know.

He tried opening his eyes. They felt like lead. He tried again, using all of his will, until he finally pried them apart and saw . . . nothing. Nothing but blotches of light and shadow. He closed and reopened them. Same thing. No shapes or outlines, just blotches.

One more time.

Double ditto.

Concerned, he sat up too quickly and winced at the pain stabbing his head. He rubbed his eyes. Still nothing but light and shadow. Slowly, tentatively, he reached out to the darkest shadow . . . until his hand struck a tree. The fake tree. He could feel its hard sponginess. He grabbed it and with effort pulled himself to his feet. Another wince. Apparently he could add a sprained ankle to the list. Balancing on the other foot, he kept blinking, trying to clear his vision as he dropped his head, attempting to spit the aluminum taste from his mouth.

He failed on both accounts.

He turned, facing down the ridge. The lodge was there somewhere. He stepped out, leading with his bad foot. He yelped in pain and crumpled back to the ground, rolling a half dozen feet before finally stopping by hitting, what else, but another tree.

Okay, fine. If he couldn't walk, then he'd crawl back to the lodge—on his hands and knees if he had to, it wasn't that far. He thought of shouting for help, but a guy had his pride. Besides, he hadn't heard a soul since he'd woke up. Come to think of it, the buzz had suddenly disappeared as well.

He started off. He reached his hand into the shadows, touching wet undergrowth, then dropped it lower to the fir needles below. He did the same with the next hand, then the next. It was a slow process, sometimes painful when his knees caught shards of broken granite, but he continued. He convinced himself that the loss of vision was temporary. Like a concussion or something. At least that's what he hoped. At least that's what he prayed. Why he'd fallen out of the tree in the first place was beyond him. So was the taste he couldn't get out of his mouth.

A few dozen more steps and he noticed the buzz had returned. How weird. He'd left the fake tree far behind, but the sensation was coming back. In a moment it was as loud as ever. But only for a moment. As he moved, it faded again . . . until he heard the snap of twigs behind him and the rustling of undergrowth. Someone had found him. By the sound of it, lots of someones. Spotting the nearest tree shadow, he grabbed it and, doing his best to appear calm and in control, pulled himself back to his feet.

"Well, well, well, lookee here, boys."

He couldn't place the voice. As he turned toward it, the rustling stopped.

"Luke, ol' buddy. How ya doin'?"

"Fine," Luke said, scowling at his cracking voice. "I, uh, I had a little fall."

"What's wrong with them eyes? Can't you see?"

He shrugged. "Just a little concussion or something. I'll be fine."

Shadows flickered, wind brushed against his face. Someone was waving a hand in front of him.

Still trying to stay calm, he asked, "Do I know you guys?"

"Just a few visitors come to say howdy."

"Visitors? From where?" Again his voice broke and he coughed, trying to cover it. "I mean, how did you happen to—"

"Boys," the voice interrupted, "why don't one of you give Luke a hand gettin' back to the lodge. We got plenty of work to do."

Before he could react, a giant pair of hands grabbed him around the waist, lifted him from the ground, and threw him across some very broad shoulders.

"What are you doing? Put me down! Put me down!"

He heard laughter and the voice ordering, "You be careful now. One drop on the head per day is enough."

"Yes, Mr. Orbolitz, I'll be careful."

six

reacher Man grabbed another handful of chips and turned to David on the sofa beside him. "You sure you feelin' okay?"

"Why's that?"

"No offense"—he motioned to David's chest—"but you're not lookin' so good."

David glanced down at himself. They were out of the direct sun and back in the lodge with its dimmed lights. As a result his glow had become more visible. Not only visible, but as the Presence increased, each of their glows had grown more distinct and defined. In David's case, his violet-blue shell was boiling so furiously that it had actually deepened and grown some into his orange-red glow, making it more difficult to see the warmer color underneath.

He sighed wearily and looked across the room to the others. Rachel and Starr were together as they had been all day—whispering, giggling, sharing secrets like old friends. Their shells had also thickened and darkened—Rachel with her swirling, shifting lumps and Starr with her scattered bits and pieces.

Over by the fireplace, Savannah, Reverend Wyatt, and Albert were hunched over the coffee table mapping out the parameter from the information they'd gathered. Savannah's darkening shell bulged two, sometimes three feet beyond her body, while the outline of Albert's canine snout had grown so dense it was becoming difficult to see his face. The same was true with Reverend Wyatt and his hooded robe.

And Luke? It had been a couple of hours since David had seen the boy. No surprise there. But that didn't stop him from worrying, from checking their room (more than once), and from strolling outside in the off chance they'd bump into each other. He'd give him another ten minutes or so before starting the process all over again.

"You're sure you're okay?" Preacher Man repeated.

David turned back to him. In marked contrast to the others, both Preacher Man and Nubee, who sat on his other side, glowed the brightest. And while the older man had a few violet, shadowy spots, Nubee's oranges and reds glowed brighter and brighter, sometimes making it difficult to see his body underneath.

David gave a shrug. "I'm a little shaky. Probably all the emotion."

Preacher Man nodded and reached for more chips. "Fear's a powerful thing."

"Who said anything about fear?"

Preacher Man looked at him as he bit into the chip and began munching.

"I'm talking hate."

The munching stopped. He waited for more.

David obliged. "You ever hate somebody so much that you want to kill them? That you'd do anything you could to destroy them?"

"Orbolitz?"

"Who else."

Preacher Man looked away, then quietly conceded. "He's put you through a load of grief."

Just as quietly, David replied. "It doesn't look like he's stopping anytime soon."

"And that is your problem, David Kauffman." It was Nubee.

Both men turned to him in surprise.

"What'd you say?" David asked.

"Your hatred." Nubee nodded toward David's boiling shell. "I am certain that is your problem." It was Nubee's voice—the same accent, the same tone, but clearer and far more lucid than David had ever heard.

He traded looks with Preacher Man, who replied, "Nubee, you're talking."

"I have always talked." Although the words didn't perfectly match what little of Nubee's lips David could see through the glow, they were definitely coming from him. "I am simply making more sense now."

Preacher Man chuckled. "You got that right, son."

"How . . . how are you doing that?" David asked.

"I do not know. But it is certainly fun."

"Fun?" Preacher Man exclaimed. "Praise God, it's a miracle!"

"You're not doing anything different?" David asked.

"Not that I can tell." He broke into his cockeyed grin and giggled. "I am just being me."

"Praise the Lord!" Preacher Man repeated. As he spoke, his light shimmered just a little brighter. "And you think David's hatred, you think his unforgiveness, that's what's making him thicken and bubble like that?"

Nubee quoted, "'Forgive and you will be forgiven.'"

"What?" David asked.

"'If you do not forgive men their sins, your Father will not forgive your sins.'"

"You don't think I have a right to hate Orbolitz? After what he's done?"

"I think you have every right."

"But . . ."

"But it is still destroying you."

"You mean the way this darker light keeps boiling and getting thicker?"

"It is boiling and getting thicker because it is feeding upon your inner glow. I believe it is eating into it . . . just as it is eating into you."

David turned to Preacher Man but received only a shrug. "Not sure 'bout all that, but the boy's got a point." He reached for another chip. "We *are* supposed to love our enemies."

David turned back to Nubee. "After what he did to your sister? To my daughter?"

He did not answer.

"Nubee?"

Still no answer.

With growing frustration David turned back to the preacher. The man continued munching.

He tried again. "Look . . . I know what you're saying. And believe me, I've tried. For over a year now, I've been trying. But there are some things a man just cannot do."

"Cannot?" Nubee asked. "Or will not?"

David felt his jaw tighten.

"There is a big difference."

He tried to hold the young man's gaze but could not.

"He's right," Preacher Man agreed. "If you don't want to forgive him, it'll never happen. But if you do want to . . . or *want* to want to, well then, that's another matter."

"Yeah, right," David scorned.

Preacher Man gave him a look.

"Those are easy words, but you tell me *how*." David nodded toward Reverend Wyatt. "What am I supposed to do, go around spouting Bible verses like him? Judging every-body's thoughts and actions?" He heard his voice beginning to tremble, surprised at his intensity. "Because I'll tell you something . . . it's one thing to know what you're *supposed* to think and do . . . it's quite another to be able to do it!"

Neither man gave an answer. And for that, David was grateful.

"After a moment, Preacher Man sat back on the sofa and motioned to Reverend Wyatt. "What do you s'pose our friends hood is all about?"

"What do you mean?"

"I mean, we've already seen the purpose of that sword. But what about his hood?"

David looked on. "I imagine it's like a monk's robe or something."

"Maybe . . . or maybe it's somethin' else."

"Like what?"

"Like an executioner's hood."

"A what?"

Preacher Man said nothing. Once again Nubee quoted, " 'The letter kills, but the Spirit gives life.' "

The old-timer turned to him with amusement. "The boy's a walkin' concordance."

Nubee grinned.

"He's right, though. The good Reverend may be wielding God's Sword, but he doesn't know the first thing about His Spirit."

"I'm not sure I know what that means."

"It means he ain't a bad man, probably doin' the best he can."

"But?"

"He knows all about God, but . . ." Preacher Man hesitated.

"But what?"

"I don't believe he really knows Him."

David frowned, trying to comprehend.

"And if you don't really know Him, if you ain't abiding in the arms of His great Love, then you'll never know how to wield Love's great weapon."

"And knowing Him, 'abiding' in that Love . . ." David pieced it together. "You're telling me that's the key to all my problems?"

Preacher Man turned back to him. "You saw Him, son. When you was in heaven, you saw Him face-to-face."

"Yes, I did."

"Did it change you?"

"Forever."

Preacher Man nodded. "How can anyone live in His presence without gettin' changed?" Holding his look, he added, "And how can anyone who wants to get changed not keep livin' in His presence?"

"You still haven't answered my question. If this is my hatred"—David angrily motioned to the bubbling light around him—"how do I get rid of it? How am I supposed to feel anything good about a monster like Orbolitz?"

"Who said anything about feeling?"

"What?"

"Love ain't about feelin'. And it certainly ain't about feelin' good. Would you say Jesus was feelin' good when He went to that cross for you?"

"Of course not, but—"

"But He did it anyway, didn't He. Out of love."

David started to give an answer but realized he had none.

"Don't get me wrong. Feelin' warm fuzzies is nice. But it sure ain't mandatory."

Once again David's jaw clenched. Unfortunately, he knew Preacher Man was right.

"You just keep abiding in His presence. Just keep rememberin' how much He's forgiven you."

"And then what?"

"And then ... well, sometimes His holiness just sorta sneaks up on you."

Before David could respond, the front door opened and a familiar voice shouted: "Got a special delivery here for a Mr. David Kauffman."

David spun around to see three men enter the room. The largest, a huge brute with a black receding crew cut, was carrying his son across his shoulders.

"Luke!" David sprang to his feet and started toward them.

The big man spotted him and approached, dumping the boy onto a nearby sofa. Luke winced in pain but didn't cry out.

David dropped to his side. "Are you okay? Are you all right? What happened?"

"Yeah." Luke winced again, testing his side. "I'm okay."

David gave him a quick once-over—rumpled clothes, disheveled hair, but other than that he—

"Don't worry none 'bout his eyes, Dad."

David looked over his shoulder to see Norman E. Orbolitz. Although much of the man was covered in a layer of violet light, there was no missing his thin, translucent skin stretched over sharp jaw and cheekbones, as well as the cablelike tendons in his neck. Fortunately, he wore a pair of high-tech goggles that spared David from seeing his eyes.

He spun back to his son. "Can't you see? What happened to your eyes?"

"Not a problem," Orbolitz answered. "Comes from a little too much electromagnetic energy—*RF* they call it."

David continued examining his eyes, moving his hand in front of them, trying not to panic . . . as they looked but did not see.

"Kinda fried himself a bit up on one of our towers. Wouldn't worry none. Should be better in a day or so."

"I'm all right, Dad," Luke insisted, embarrassed at the attention. "I'm okay."

"Kid's tellin' the truth, Dave. He'll be better in no time. But you folks . . ." Orbolitz turned to the rest of the group and adjusted his goggles. "Whoo-wee, ya'll glowin' really pretty now, aren't ya?"

Albert stepped in front of the coffee table, obviously trying to block Orbolitz's view of the map they'd been making. "What . . . what are you doing here?"

"No need to be so secretive, Al. We got cameras all around, remember. 'Sides, it makes no difference to me you figurin' out where our little fence is. You're still not gettin' out."

"What do you want from us?" Rachel demanded.

Once again adjusting his goggles, Orbolitz grinned. "Evenin', Ms. McPherson. I think we've already established what I want. I just come over to see what I got. And I got to tell you folks, you are everything I hoped for . . . and worse."

David rose back to his feet. Not only was he shaking, but he literally felt his violet-blue shell bubbling harder.

Orbolitz turned to him and smiled. "Son, you best get some Rolaids. Looks like you got a major case of acid indigestion."

David opened his mouth, but the rage caught in his throat.

Still grinning, Orbolitz turned back to the group. "Savannah? Got a little somethin' here for you."

He motioned to his second companion, a tall bulldog of a man who stepped forward and slipped off his blue nylon knapsack. She stiffened, preparing for the worst as he approached. He stopped several feet short, unzipped the sack, and dropped it to the floor. Multiple stacks of money spilled out.

The group stared.

"That would be the rest of your payment," Orbolitz explained. He motioned to the bulldog, who pulled a necklace from his coat pocket with sapphires as big as any David had ever seen. "Plus a little bonus for a job well done." The big man stooped down and carefully draped the necklace across the knapsack.

Savannah stared down at the fortune, then up to the group around her. It was obvious she was embarrassed, even afraid. It was equally obvious she wanted what she saw.

"Go ahead," Orbolitz encouraged.

She looked back at the treasure.

Orbolitz chuckled. "Girl, if you don't want it, I might get my feelin's hurt and take it back."

Her eyes darted to him, then to the group, then back to the knapsack. Finally, with a breath for courage, she took a tentative step toward it. And another.

"Savannah . . ." Reverend Wyatt scowled.

She looked to him.

As he quoted, his glow reached toward its sword. "'For the love of money is the root of all evil.'"

Frightened by what she saw, and glancing nervously to her comrades, she came to a stop. But her glow did not. The violet shell continued growing, stretching forward.

"Savannah!" The Reverend raised his sword.

"It's not me!" she protested from deep inside her light. "I'm here, I'm not moving!"

It was true. Her physical body remained stationary as her outer glow continued stretching toward the treasure.

The Reverend's own glow gripped its sword.

And still her light stretched, until it reached the money and necklace. Then, with a sickening *slurp*, it encompassed them, absorbing their mass, the violet glow bulging and darkening to where it nearly blotted out whatever was left of her.

"Savannah!" Rachel raced to her.

"No need to fret, Ms. McPherson," Orbolitz said.

Rachel looked to him.

"She's still in there . . . somewhere. Actually, what you're seein' of her now is a lot more accurate than what you've seen before." He shook his head, marveling at the spectacle. "Amazing, simply amazing." He called out, "Dirk, you recordin' all this?"

The voice with the Irish accent filled the air, "That we are, Mr. Orbolitz. Least what we can see of it."

"Excellent. Excellent."

David scanned the room. Savannah's actions had drawn everyone's attention, including Orbolitz and his two thugs. The one to the man's left stood several steps ahead of him, leaving that side of Orbolitz, the one closest to David, wide open. If David moved quickly, he could reach him and take him down. He'd only have a second before the guards would pull him off, so he'd have to be fast . . . and thorough. He glanced about for some type of weapon—a lamp, a vase, a—

wait, he had one. Luke had ridiculed him for picking it up in Seattle, but what was a wilderness trip without a Swiss Army knife? He slipped his hand into his front pocket, felt the smooth plastic case.

It would have to be in one instant move—racing forward, pulling out the knife, opening the blade, and stabbing it deep into . . . what? His throat? No, his heart. It would have to be his—David felt a hand on his arm. He looked over to see it belonged to Nubee, who silently shook his head.

Rachel took a tentative step forward. "Why are you doing this?" she demanded.

"Observation and evaluation, Ms. McPherson. Just seein' how you folks tick. Oh, and Al . . ." He turned toward Albert. "Brought a little somethin' for you as well."

The other bodyguard, the one with the receding crew cut, stepped forward and unlatched a leather satchel he'd been carrying. He reached inside and pulled out a dozen 8 x 10 full-color photos. One by one he dropped them onto the floor in front of Albert. Pornography. But with poses so vile and explicit that many in the group stared slack-jawed. Others, like David, managed to look away. So did Albert. He would not be so easily manipulated. At least in the beginning.

But as the pictures continued falling before him, he eventually took another glance, a bit longer, and another longer still. As he did, his shell shimmered, growing thicker, his canine snout becoming nearly solid. But not just one snout. As he stared, several muzzles appeared—about his head, his neck—multiple mouths with multiple fangs poking and pushing against their violet border. David watched, repulsed at the spectacle . . . and at how somebody with all of Albert's money, who could purchase any sex material he ever wanted (or person for that matter), could be so easily controlled.

"Albert!" Reverend Wyatt's voice boomed. He stepped forward to face the young man, blocking his path as he raised his sword.

Albert looked at the Reverend, then up to the sword, obviously remembering their last encounter. His muzzles pushed against their shell, their snarling forms straining and pushing, but they proceeded no further. The fear of the weapon kept them at bay. What few glimpses David managed to catch of Albert showed the young man was under incredible pressure. But somehow he was able to resist. Despite the temptation, and to his great credit, Albert was able to muster up the needed self-control.

Orbolitz smiled. "Nicely done, Al. Nicely done. Course, we also brought along a DVD player and several movies that we made specifically for your unique tastes."

The crew cut bodyguard produced a portable player and a large bundle of DVDs, setting them beside the photos.

Both bodyguards now stood in front of Orbolitz, though one a bit closer than David preferred. Nevertheless, he gripped the knife firmly, pulled it to the edge of his pocket. He was already breathing hard, could feel his heart pounding. If he was going to make his move, it had to be now.

"David," Nubee whispered. But David did not turn to him.

Orbolitz was grinning, calling out to Dirk, saying more to Albert. But David only heard his breathing, his thumping heart, the boiling of his shell.

Orbolitz reached up, again adjusting his goggles, exposing his entire left side.

David leaped to action.

Pulling the knife from his pocket with his right hand, he yanked open the blade with his left. Everything turned to slow motion as he lunged, the shiny blade eight feet from the man's chest, then five, Orbolitz turning toward him, eyes widening, mouth opening to yell. But David heard nothing, just the pounding and bubbling as he focused all his hatred upon the man's heart, as he turned the blade so it would slip between the ribs, as he ... Suddenly, he was hit from the side, a flying tackle from the closest bodyguard.

The two of them fell, the bodyguard wrenching back his arm. They'd barely hit the floor before the second man arrived with a swift kick to David's face, throwing his head so far back he thought it would fly off. He saw stars and searing light. He did not remember feeling pain.

Nor did he remember hitting the ground for the second time.

seven

Rachel sat on the green chintz sofa staring at David, who slept in his bed across the room. He'd received some pretty powerful blows, especially to the head, and the group felt they should keep a careful eye on him. Rachel agreed to take the first watch. Though they'd not hit it off by any stretch of the imagination, she still couldn't rid herself of the attraction. Maybe it was his quiet strength of character, his thoughtfulness. Of course she could tell she had a similar effect upon him, but she got that vibe from lots of guys. Yet with David it was different. The others reminded her of dogs in heat, as if feeling the attraction gave them the right to satisfy it. But not with this man. Maybe it was the courtesy and respect he showed her ... when he wasn't busy throwing her into icy streams. The fact is, she might have deserved that, coming on as strong as she had. But trying to relearn the whole singles' scene was new to her, and she was bound to make a few mistakes.

The bottom line: there was a depth to this man. A sensitivity. Very much like Jerry. Dear, sweet Jerry ...

"We can get through this. Together we can—"

"She's our baby, I killed our—"

"Lots of women have abortions."

"It's not the same. You didn't want to. From the start you said—"

"I'll get over it." He had reached out to her. "We'll get over it." She let him take her into his arms. Even with her suitcase packed and standing beside the door, even as she was leaving, he insisted upon holding her. "We'll get over it," he repeated. Against her will, she felt herself melting into his chest, feeling his favorite flannel against her cheek, smelling his Old Spice, believing it might actually work, until . . .

"We'll have another and in time we won't even remember—"

She stiffened.

"What? What's wrong?"

She pulled her face away. "We can't have another."

"Right. I meant adoption."

She closed her eyes, then took a step back.

"Rach, I meant adoption, you know what I meant."

But she did know. She knew that no matter what he said, no matter how he tried to hide it, the disappointment would never fully leave.

"We'll adopt a big family . . . a huge family." He reached back for her. "We'll—"

But she would have none of it. "No."

"Rach—"

Using what little strength she had left, she reached down and grabbed her suitcase.

"Rachel . . ."

She pulled open the door and pushed the screen. It gave a mournful groan. Hot tears spilled onto her cheeks. "I'll get the rest of the stuff when you're at work."

"Rachel . . . I love you." The catch in his voice tore her heart, but she would not turn to face him. "We can get through this. I swear we can, if you would just—"

But she knew they couldn't. After what she'd done to him. To them. He could say the words now, but in a month, a year, the truth would surface. He was saddled with damaged goods and could never have what he really wanted. The truth would return and it would break their hearts all over again, and then again, and again . . .

"Rachel."

She stepped off the porch. It was cold and damp, a typical Seattle spring.

"Rachel, please . . ."

She headed down the cracked sidewalk to the taxi, uneven puffs of breath visible in the predawn air. Jerry kept calling after her, but she barely heard over her stifled sobs.

"Luke . . ."

She blinked away the memories to see David stirring in bed. She rose from the sofa and approached. Orbolitz still kept all lights in the lodge set low, and she could easily see David's violet cloak continue to bubble and thicken, eating into his orange-red glow underneath. But its progress had slowed. At least for David. Over the last few hours, as the Presence increased, something else had begun to appear—a hollow pocket, no bigger than a fist, in the center of each of their chests. Well, hollow for Savannah, Albert, Starr, and herself. But for the others, including David, the pocket was filled with a very small but intense light. So white that it could clearly be seen underneath the other colors. So bright that, in David's case, it seemed to give energy to his inner, orange-red glow—replenishing it, replacing from the inside what the darker, bubbling shell had been eating from the outside.

But that wasn't the only addition. For as Orbolitz increased the Presence, Rachel began to hear the crying. It had begun two, three hours ago, and she recognized it immediately—from their session near the fireplace, on the badminton court, and, of course, from the dreams that had plagued her these many, many months.

"Luke . . ."

She moved closer. "David, it's Rachel."

His eyes fluttered open, searching the room until they focused on her. "Where's my . . ." He coughed and tried again. "Where's Luke?"

"He's okay." She gave a reassuring smile. "The last I saw he was out on the porch swatting mosquitoes. 'Enjoying the silence,' I think he said." Trying to keep things light, she forced a chuckle. "Weird, huh? At least for a kid that age."

David broke into another raspy cough. She turned for the pitcher of ice water on the bureau.

"What . . . time is it?" he asked.

"Almost seven."

"At night?"

She poured the water into a glass. "You got beat up pretty bad." She turned to see him struggling to sit up. "Take it easy. Not so fast."

"Where . . . where is . . ." He coughed again.

"Orbolitz?" she asked, handing him the glass.

He nodded, drinking greedily.

"End of the hall. The bridal suite, I think."

He practically choked. "He's here? You let him stay?"

She motioned to his injuries. "He's sort of calling the shots, if you hadn't noticed. Says he wants to stay and see what's happening firsthand—now that we've passed the first third of his little experiment. Last I heard we'd reached 36 percent."

"Doesn't he know we'll go after him?"

"Considering his playmates, I doubt he's given it much thought." She noticed his shell beginning to bubble harder.

"There's three times as many of us. We could band together, figure out a plan."

"Except for all those video cameras."

"No one's even trying?" he asked incredulously. "No one's leading?"

"I'm afraid you were the only taker. And I wouldn't be planning for a rematch anytime soon."

He sighed in frustration, then glanced down at himself and groaned. "It's still here."

She nodded. "Same for all of us. The darker light, the violet part, is a lot thicker. If you ask me, instead of getting rid of him, we'd do better finding a way to get rid of *it*."

He looked back at her, frowning at what she knew were the dark multiple colors encircling her. "I'm all right," she replied. "I know what they are. We've been together for a long time." She took his glass and refilled it. "You, on the other hand ..." She nodded at his violet shell. "Any idea what that's all about?" She handed him the glass and he sighed wearily.

"Yes."

She waited for more.

"It's my hatred."

"Your what?"

He closed his eyes. "My unforgiveness."

"Unforgiveness?"

"Toward Orbolitz."

"But ... you have the right. You have more than enough reasons to—"

"I have every reason." He opened his eyes, then continued, a bit sadder, "But I don't have the right."

"What does that mean?"

He thought a moment. "The whole basis of my faith, I mean everything I believe ... it's based on forgiveness."

"I understand that, but Orbolitz ... the man killed your daughter, he's holding you prisoner. He could kill all of us."

"I know, I know." Again he closed his eyes. "But if I don't forgive him ... I won't be forgiven."

"What?"

Quietly, he quoted, "'Forgive us our debts, as we forgive our debtors.'"

It is time to leave.

Rachel was surprised to hear Osiris's voice. It was only the second time he'd spoken in David's presence. He sounded agitated. And with the voice, the baby's cries, which had been in the background, suddenly grew louder.

David continued. "That's what Christ tells us to pray, 'Forgive us our debts as we forgive our debtors.'"

Leave now.

Ignoring the voice, Rachel answered, "But how does that apply to you? The man's a murderer ... I don't understand."

Glancing at his bubbling shell, he gave another sigh. "Apparently neither do I. But as much as God forgives me ... He expects me to forgive others."

You must leave now!

She felt pressure underneath her breastbone, the type she always felt when Osiris insisted upon having his way. But she ignored it and continued. "What do you have to be forgiven of? Compared to Orbolitz, you're a choirboy."

David shook his head. "It's all the same. Sin is sin. In the long run, we're all equally as guilty."

She almost laughed at the absurdity. "I wouldn't be so sure of that." Osiris pressed harder. She turned her head so David couldn't see her wince.

"What do you mean?"

"I mean ..." She worked to keep her voice even through the pain. "You have no idea what others have done. Albert, Savannah ... me."

"That's just it ... it doesn't matter—"

The baby's cries grew louder, turning into screams, making it more difficult to hear David.

"He will forgive anybody of anything."

LEAVE! NOW!

Osiris's intensity startled her. So did his sudden accusation.

MURDERER!

She caught her breath at the word, strained to hear David through the screams.

"Remember I said that was the whole purpose of Christ's coming, so He could—"

TORTURER!

She gasped, leaning over, the pressure in her chest nearly unbearable.

"Are you all right?"

KILLER OF BABIES!

The pain rose from her chest into her throat. Her eyes began burning with moisture. But not from the pain. From David's words. Was it possible? What he was saying? She shook her head. No. Fairy tales. Wishful thinking. She gasped again, her thoughts escaping. "No."

"What?"

"There are some things—" She had to speak louder to hear over the screams. "There are some things that can never be forgiven."

"But that was His whole purpose—"

She shook her head, giving a quick swipe at her eyes. "Some things cannot be forgiven."

GO!

"But we can work at them. We can make them better."

"No, that's just it. Christ came to—"

She spoke even louder, quoting from the Rule of Three: "'This is the lesson which thou must learn, Thou receives only what thou dost earn.'"

"What's going on? Rachel, are you—"

TORTURER! BABY KILLER! GO!

Scowling, trying to persuade herself as much as David, she continued, nearly shouting. "You make mistakes, you make them right. The law of nature. Reciprocation." She took a ragged breath, her mind racing. Wasn't that exactly what she was doing with Starr? She couldn't help her baby, but she could help Starr. And the others, like Savannah, like the thousands across the country desperate to reach their deceased loved ones. Making their life better, wasn't that her purpose? Dedicating her life to their welfare meant fixing what she had ruined, erasing her actions, removing her own vile and unspeakable—

SLAUGHTERER OF INNOCENTS!

The phrase sucked all breath from her.

"Rachel?" David's voice was far away. "Here, you'd better sit—"

DESTROYER! KILLER OF CHILDREN! GO! NOW!

She doubled over, grabbing her stomach, unable to breathe.
NOOOW . . . !

She turned and started for the door, nausea rising into
her mouth.

"Rachel!"

She stumbled into the hallway, caught a glimpse of
David trying to climb from his bed. She knew he was calling but she could no longer hear—not over the screams,
the accusations, the all-consuming guilt.

t hank you for dropping me off."

"No prob," Starr chirped as she wheeled Nubee into his
room. It was cool hearing him talk so clearly. It was also cool
seeing the way his glowing, orange-red light was solidifying
into this lean, muscular man. It was hard to explain, but it
looked exactly like she'd pictured him on the inside—strong,
smart, intriguing. And, yes, attractive. Very attractive. The
light didn't freak her out, not like at the beginning. In fact,
by now she was getting pretty used to it. And in Nubee's
case, she was actually liking it. "Want me to help you into
bed?"

"No, thank you. Simply roll the chair beside it and lock
the wheels. I shall do the rest."

She nodded. But as she pushed the chair toward the bed
an idea came to mind. At first she ignored it, thinking it
was just plain stupid. But it wasn't stupid. Not really. I
mean, they'd been hanging together all these months—she
a budding young woman, he a wiser, older man. And now,
now that he was all together, now that he was becoming
so cool, and since they had grown so close . . .

She shook her head at the thought. But it would not leave.

Besides, what had Rachel said about Wicca celebrating sensual pleasures? "If you enjoy something, you do it"? It's not like they were sex fiends, Rachel had made that real clear. Rachel had made a lot clear. But the books she'd loaned her, the ones she'd been reading all evening, they *did* talk about sex. And they *did* say that if it was something you wanted, you were totally allowed to go for it . . . and enjoy it.

Enjoy it? Who was she kidding? She didn't even know what she was supposed to enjoy. It's not like she was ignorant; she'd seen plenty of people doing it in the movies and TV and stuff. And her friends were always talking about it. But the sad fact was, she was already fourteen, almost fifteen, and she still hadn't done it. Course she wouldn't admit that to anybody; but still, it's not like she could stay dumb and naive her whole life. She had to grow up sometime. And since Nubee was a man, a real man now, and since he was older and more experienced, and since she'd have to do it sometime . . .

She looked down at him, watching as he unbuttoned his shirt. All right, fine. But how to begin? She didn't want to come off sounding like some bad TV show or being all stupid and corny. She swallowed, noticing how dry her mouth had become. She thought of lighting up, but the movies always showed them doing that afterwards, not before.

Well . . . it was now or never.

She crossed in front of him and eased herself down onto his bed. "So . . . you got the room all to yourself, huh?" She pulled her legs under herself like she'd seen in the magazines and smiled in a way she hoped was suggestive.

"Yes."

She watched as he worked to slip his right arm out of his shirt.

"Kinda lonely, isn't it?"

"Not really."

Her smile tightened. "I mean, having a big room like this all to *yourself*?"

He shrugged, finishing his right sleeve and starting on his left.

She frowned, then lowered her voice. "A wonderful bed like this, that's so soft and comfortable."

"It's okay."

She pursed her lips. What'd she have to do, spell it out for him?

He pulled off his shirt and dropped it to the floor before reaching past her for his pajamas. She gently touched his arm.

He glanced up.

In her most mature voice she replied, "I could make it so things aren't so lonely."

He looked at her.

Why was he making this so hard? She held his eyes, doing her best to appear sultry, whatever that was. It must have worked, because he suddenly froze.

She gave him a knowing, encouraging smile . . . trying to hide her fear.

He glanced away, avoiding her eyes.

Poor guy, he must be nervous too. Okay, now what? Well, *his* shirt was off; it must be her turn. Unfortunately, she had several layers to go. First, she reached for the zipper of her sweatshirt. As she pulled it down, she noticed how thick and clumsy her fingers became. But she succeeded. Next, she reached for the top button of her shirt.

"No."

She looked up at him, surprised.

He slowly shook his head. His eyes were filled with sadness, but something more.

She understood and forced another smile "You don't have to be afraid, dear. I'm plenty experienced." She unfastened the first button.

Again he shook his head. "No."

"What?"

He swallowed, his eyes soulful, glistening with moisture.

"What?" she repeated.

Quietly, he quoted, "'Avoid sexual immorality.'"

She slowed to a stop.

"'That each of you should learn to control his own body in a way that is holy and honorable.'" Of course. He was quoting the Bible again. But he wasn't finished. He licked his lips, looking more than a little nervous. "'—not in passionate lust like the heathen, who do not know God.'"

She watched as he swallowed, his forehead now having a slight sheen.

"'Flee sexual immorality.'"

She smiled, pleased at the effect she was having on him. "Oh, sweetie, there's nothing immoral about this. This is only natural and—"

"'Flee sexual immorality.'" His words were strangely forceful. Stranger still was the mist that accompanied them. Silver puffs of breath came from his mouth with each syllable. For the briefest moment they joined together, forming a larger cloud, so shiny that Starr could actually see a reflection of herself. And what she saw made her gasp.

In the reflection she was having sex with another man. She blinked, not believing her eyes. The reflection changed, showing her with a different man. Then again with yet another. And another. Multiple images flickered past, in fractions of seconds, so vivid, so lurid.

"What are you doing?" she demanded. "That's gross! Stop it!"

The cloud broke up, returning to a mist which quickly disappeared.

She stared, speechless, then looked back at Nubee.

He appeared equally as stunned.

She closed her eyes, shaking off the images, taking a purging breath. Everything about this place just kept getting weirder and weirder. But she'd put herself on the line this far; she couldn't back down now. With more than a little trepidation, she started her next shirt button. It stuck and she had to glance down to undo it. Then, looking back at Nubee with pretend confidence, she started the next.

Again he opened his mouth. And again he spoke:

"'All other sins a man commits are outside his body...'"

The silver puffs came and again formed into a larger, mirrored cloud.

"'... but he who sins sexually sins against his own body.'"

Different images appeared this time ... a sweaty, terrified Starr in hospital stirrups, a doctor with a suction hose. She was having an abortion.

She stared at the scene, horrified.

... another image, older Starr, giving birth, screaming in pain ...

"Nubee, stop it!"

... now she's slouching, dirt poor, trying to quiet a screaming baby in her arms with two ragged toddlers shrieking at her feet ...

"Stop it!"

... another hospital bed, her left cheek with a grotesque purple lesion, *Kaposi Sarcoma*—she's seen it on other AIDS victims. Weakly, she turns to her newborn baby, his face covered with the identical sore.

"Stop it! *Stop it!*" Tears spilled onto her face as she grabbed her sweatshirt, breaking up the cloud and its images. "Why are you doing this to me?!"

He gave no answer.

"Why?" Her nose was running as she rose, stumbling away from the bed, wiping her face. She did not wait for an answer but headed for the door. She threw it open and raced into the hall, running down the corridor, wanting to scream, wanting to cry, wanting to be anywhere but there ...

Who are you?" Preacher Man fumbled for his glasses on the nightstand. "What's going on?"

"Hey there, Billy Ray."

He pulled on his glasses and squinted. Orbolitz and his two thugs stood just inside the room. "What do you want? What time is it?"

"Just past midnight."

Taking a chair from the desk, Orbolitz dragged it to the bed and calmly sat on it. Behind him, his assistants placed two briefcases on the dresser and began unpacking them. All three were cloaked in such dark, thick light that it was nearly impossible to see their expressions. Orbolitz's goggles made it even more difficult. Still, there was no missing his good-ol'-boy grin.

"And as far as what I want, I reckon that's not real important, least for now. What is important, my friend, is what *you* want."

The clinking of glass drew Preacher Man's attention back to the dresser. The men were bringing out bottles of booze. They were setting up a bar!

A cold knot formed in his stomach.

Orbolitz glanced over his shoulder. "Just wanna make sure you got all the comforts of home. Or"—he turned back to him and grinned—"what you wish home had."

"I don't drink. I ain't a drinker."

"Not my understandin', Billy Ray. I always heard 'once an alchy, always an alchy.'"

"I been sober nearly four years now."

"And that's very commendable. I'm bettin' God's real happy with you."

Preacher Man stole another glance to the dresser and saw the clear, amber, and chocolate-brown bottles. Scotch, bourbon, whisky, rum—they had them all.

"Which brings me to my question. How happy would He be if you didn't?"

"Didn't what?"

"Stay on the wagon."

The knot grew bigger.

"A great man o' God like you, one of His boys . . . what would happen if you suddenly turned back to your old ways. Back to the disgusting sins of your past?"

"I ain't goin' back."

Orbolitz laughed. "Nice words, Billy." He tapped his goggles. "But you're not seein' what I'm seein'."

"What do you mean?"

"I mean your glow, the outer part of it. It's stretchin' every way it can to take a gander at our little collection over there."

"I ain't goin' back."

"And should me and the fellas happen to leave it here overnight . . . well, what's the ol' saying, 'The spirit is willin' but the flesh is weak'? Or is it, 'A dog returns to his vomit'?" He turned to the men. "Mr. Jefferson, get our boy some ice, will you? I hear he hates his screwdrivers warm."

One of the men nodded and disappeared into the hall.

Turning back to Preacher Man, Orbolitz continued. "Things are gettin' kinda exciting around here, wouldn't you say? His Presence just keeps gettin' hotter and hotter."

"Brother . . . you don't have to do this."

"I don't?"

"You can know what'll happen when you die. You can go heaven without even worryin' 'bout it—all you gotta do is repent and accept Jesus."

Orbolitz laughed. "And then what? Expect Him to throw His arms around me, say all is forgiven?"

"Yes . . . exactly."

"You ever think maybe I don't want to be forgiven?"

"Everyone wants to—"

"That I don't need His handouts?"

"We all need—"

"I need nothing!" The outburst surprised them both. Covering it with a smile, Orbolitz continued. "Least not from Him." He glanced over his shoulder. "Where is that boy? Jefferson!" There was no answer and he turned back to Preacher Man. "Let me tell you a little bit about me, son. My momma, she was a novice, goin' to be a nun. Did you know that? Not even out of her teens 'fore she was molested by one of God's holy servants. And when they didn't buy 'immaculate conception,' they swept us both under the rug like a pair of cockroaches, off to some back-woods monastery, hopin' we'd be forgotten."

"I'm sorry to—"

"But I wasn't forgotten." His intensity grew. "Not by the sisters of charity ... or their brothers. See, I became a symbol to them. A symbol of the world's sin and immorality. And if they couldn't stomp it out of the world, they could sure try to beat it out o' me."

Preacher Man lowered his eyes. But Orbolitz wasn't done, not by a long shot.

"I used to hide under the altar, the last place Mother Superior would ever look for the Devil's spawn. And I would sit there, sometimes for hours, just staring up at that bloody crucifix. We had so much in common, the two of us—rejected by our daddies, rejected by men." His voice hardened. "And if that's how God Almighty treated His own son, well, I sure wasn't interested in joinin' the family."

Preacher Man felt his compassion rise. "But that was for you. The love of Jesus up on that cross, that was all for—"

"I don't want His love! I want nothin' from Him!" Then, a little softer, he added, "'Cept to beat Him at His own game."

"But if you'd pray to Him. If you'd just ask—"

"Oh, I prayed, Preacher. All the time. 'Dear God, please ... *please* make me the Antichrist. Please make me Your enemy. Please, let me be the one to show the world the truth and turn 'em against You."

Preacher Man looked on. He could find no words.

Orbolitz answered the silence. "But like all my other prayers, it was ignored."

The bodyguard entered the room with a bucket of ice.

Orbolitz smiled and turned. "Here we go. Pour this man a little vodka and orange juice, will you, Franklin. Heavy on the vodka." He turned back to Preacher Man. "That is how you like it?"

"I ain't goin' to drink."

"But you want to, don't you?"

Preacher Man heard the seal breaking, his eyes involuntarily shooting to the bottle as its cap was unscrewed, its contents poured over the ice. He glanced away, but Orbolitz caught the look and smiled. "Once an alchy, always an alchy."

Preacher Man took a breath. "It ain't gonna happen." As he spoke, the large flat disk beside his bed, the one that had remained at his side since he first began to glow, flickered, increasing in brightness.

He heard more liquid pouring, looked over to see freshly squeezed orange juice spilling from the sparkling cut-glass decanter. Memories began to surface. Warm, pleasant.

Orbolitz chuckled, again tapping his goggles. "Yes, sir, you're becomin' quite a sight."

Preacher Man swallowed. "I ain't gonna drink."

"Actually, you won't have a choice in the matter. Not in the beginning. How we comin' there, gentlemen?"

Jefferson approached and handed Orbolitz the drink. The man took it and rose, motioning for both guards to accompany him.

Preacher Man stiffened as they approached. "No . . ." He pulled back until Jefferson took his shoulders and pinned them down on the mattress. He kicked and squirmed until the other man grabbed his legs, laying over his waist and thighs.

"No . . . I will not—"

"You misunderstand." Orbolitz approached, hovering over him in his goggles. "Nobody's askin'."

He brought the glass forward. Preacher Man tried to turn, to kick—but they held him tight. Jefferson grabbed his face, digging his fingers into the nerves just below his ears—so hard, that Preacher Man cried out until a plastic mouthpiece was suddenly shoved between his teeth. He tried spitting it out, but it was too big. He pushed at it with his tongue, but it would not budge. Orbolitz brought the glass to the edge of his lips and began to pour. The liquid burned. Preacher Man closed the back of his throat and it flooded out of his mouth until Orbolitz pinched his nose and he gasped for breath. He choked, he gagged, but Orbolitz continued pouring, filling his mouth with the burning liquid that he so hated, that tasted so sweet and familiar and—

"First one's on the house," Orbolitz laughed.

He continued choking and gagging, fighting not to drown, the only solution being to drink, to swallow the burn, to gulp the heat, feeling it warm his throat . . .

"Maybe the first couple—"

. . . the soothing, comforting warmth . . .

"—after that, you're on your own."

. . . the warmth that had brought such peace in the past, so many pleasures, warming his gut and, very shortly, his mind.

eight

It was another fitful night's sleep for Rachel McPherson ... if you could call it sleep. First there was the conversation with David—the words chasing and tumbling upon themselves inside her head:

"You have no idea what I've done."
Murderer!
"He will forgive ..."
Baby killer!
"That was the whole purpose of His coming."
" 'This is the lesson which thou must learn—'"
"Christ will forgive anything ..."
" '—Thou receives only what thou dost earn.'"

Then there was the baby's screaming. For the most part, it had quieted down. If not quieted down, then at least it was drowned out by the fighting and arguing of her spirit guides ... the gods whose forms now surrounded her on the bed. As Orbolitz continued increasing the Presence throughout the night, her gods had become more and more visible. In fact, for the first time since they'd taken up residence inside her so many years before, Rachel could actually see their features. Granted, part of it may have been her forty-eight hours with no sleep. Maybe they were just fragments of dreams, hallucinations. But somehow she had her doubts. They were just too real.

For the most part they looked like gargoyles, three to four feet tall with froglike faces. Their skin glistened in murky browns, greens, and blotches of black. None of them had hair, but many were covered with knobby, wartlike growths. Their feet and hands were webbed and several had long, razor-sharp claws. Nearly all sported protruding teeth and fangs.

Not only had they become visible, but as the Presence increased, they became more agitated . . .

It's only getting worse, a smaller one at the foot of her bed sulked. Rachel had heard its voice before, though not often. It was one of the weaker ones that was seldom given the opportunity to speak.

You know nothing, a larger brown one snarled from atop her headboard. Rachel looked up, startled at its close proximity.

I've felt the burn of His Light, the first one argued. *I know when His —*

Silence! the larger one commanded.

I know when His beloved invite Him to—

I order you to be silent!

I know how He sears us with His approaching—

The larger one streaked off the headboard and hit the smaller one, throwing it onto its back, ripping at its throat and belly with its talons. The little one shrieked and Rachel screamed, pulling up her feet, distancing herself as far from them as possible.

Enough! another voiced boomed.

She instantly recognized it. Osiris. Mr. Sparks. She turned to her left and saw the largest of the group, his face longer, more reptilian. He looked nothing like the Mr. Sparks she had first invited inside. No grand, towering figure. No majestic form clothed in sparkling white light. But she knew it was him.

The fighting continued until, with a shout, he darted to the foot of her bed and entered it. With a series of lightning-fast slashes, he cut deep into the attacker's face. The recipient shrieked and howled, staggering backwards, away from Osiris and his whimpering victim.

Others on the bed appeared unfazed, as if the action wasn't that unusual. Maybe it wasn't. Rachel had certainly heard them arguing before. Heard, but never seen.

It's only going to get worse, a hunch-backed one to her right whined. Rachel recognized that voice as well ... Miss Priss. She had been the strongest during Rachel's adolescent years, at times almost paralyzing her with self-criticism. But eventually Rachel had learned to circumvent and overcome that voice. Yet, there were times, if Rachel wasn't careful, that Miss Priss would still try to control and dominate.

She's right, another one near her shoulder agreed. *Each hour this Presence grows, our situation worsens.*

But it's not Him, a shiny black one by her knee insisted. *It's only this thing's perception of Him.* By the way it pointed and sneered at her, Rachel knew she was the "thing" it referred to.

It makes no difference, Osiris growled. *If she experiences it, we experience it.*

As long as we remain within her, the one by her shoulder hissed ... *as long as she remains alive.* It bared its teeth at Rachel, causing her to shudder. She had no idea they could be full of such hate.

That is precisely my point, the attacker argued. *Whatever she experiences, we experience. That is why we must leave.*

And go where? the black one demanded. *The thing has been ours for years; I will not go looking for another.*

You will if I so order, Osiris snarled.

The creature bared its fangs and hissed at Osiris, while taking a defensive step backwards.

Perhaps one of the others would be a more suitable host. Rachel felt this creature as much as heard it. It had entered her not long after Mr. Sparks. It was the one that drove and hounded her to have sex with the boys. *What of the young girl?*

I do like girls, the smaller one agreed.

Young girls mean young men . . . virile young men.

You are a fool! Miss Priss scorned. *Every host's experience will be the same.*

Except His Beloved, the black one argued.

We dare not approach the Beloved!

They are only men.

They are His *men. And growing wiser every hour.*

Silence!

We must remain!

The decision is not yours!

What of the girl?

He is right, it is safer to—

I do like girls.

And so the argument raged throughout the night as Rachel drifted in and out of fitful sleep—each hour the creatures growing more and more visible—each hour, Rachel becoming more and more frightened and dismayed over the decision she had made so many years before.

Orbolitz stood just inside Preacher Man's door watching as Reverend Wyatt quoted Scripture to the man:

"'Let us walk honestly, as in the day; not in rioting and drunkenness, not in chambering and wantonness, not in strife and envying—'"

Through his goggles he saw Reverend Wyatt's hooded figure raise its sword. The blade hovered directly over Preacher Man, who leaned against his dresser, staring at a recently emptied glass. From his side hung the faint remains of the round disk, all but disappeared.

"'—But put ye on the Lord Jesus Christ, and make not provision for the flesh.'" With the last word, he brought the sword down hard into the old-timer.

Preacher Man screamed as the blade severed a large piece of the violet darkness from his shoulder. It fell to the floor where it hissed, then quickly shriveled and evaporated.

It was quite a spectacle. But Orbolitz, who stood at the doorway between his bodyguards, watched with mixed feelings.

"Leave me be!" Preacher Man roared at the Reverend. "It ain't none of your business!" Filled with anger and self-loathing, he poured himself another glass, brought it to his lips, and drank. As he did, the dark, glowing shoulder regrew, replacing what had been lost.

Orbolitz sighed impatiently. It was nearly morning. Helgeland had just contacted him, saying the Presence was at 44 percent. Everything was on schedule. And from what he was able to observe through the goggles, each member of the group responded exactly as their fifteen-teraflops supercomputer had projected.

Save for one exception.

By now all three layers of each of the subjects were clearly visible . . .

First, there was the thickening violet shell, or "sins of the flesh," as the Reverend called it. Although some of its growth came from outside sources like Albert's porn or Preacher Man's booze, much of its increase came from eating into the second layer—the orange-red glow. And the degree that it ate and thickened determined the amount of the orange-red glow that remained.

Except . . . and this was the part that irritated Orbolitz . . . except when it came to the third level—the nucleus—that tiny, hollow pocket in the center of each of the participants. Well, hollow for half of them—Albert, Savannah, Rachel, and that trampy girl from the streets. But for the others— the Reverend, Preacher Man, Nubee, David, and the boy— it was a different story. Because inside each of their pockets was an intense, white brightness. In Nubee, it was dazzling, nearly impossible to look at. In David and Reverend Wyatt, it was dimmed by the thickness of their outer shell. But regardless of its brightness, it seemed to provide sustenance to the surrounding orange-red glow—replacing to one degree or another whatever the darker outer shell ate and devoured.

And that was Orbolitz's frustration, his sense of injustice. Why did those with the core brightness have their orange-red glows constantly replenished . . . while those without that light simply have theirs eaten away by their outer shell?

"Come on now, Reverend!" Orbolitz taunted. "He can't keep on sinnin'! He's a man o' God, like yourself. You can't let him get away with that!"

Reverend Wyatt looked over to Orbolitz. It was clear he agreed. It was equally clear he didn't want to—especially if it meant inflicting more pain. Turning back to Preacher Man, he pleaded. "You must stop this, my friend. Exercise discipline, use self-control."

Staring at the glass, Preacher Man gave no response.

"I understand that it must be difficult, but I assure you if you would try harder, if you would practice just a bit more self-restraint, you would—"

"You can assure me nothin'!" Preacher Man shouted.

"Friend—"

"Nothin' can help me! Not your formulas, not your high-falutin knowledge o' Scripture!"

"You must—"

"Leave me alone!"

Grieved, but seeing no alternative, Reverend Wyatt prepared to raise his sword again. "'Wine is a mocker, strong drink is raging: and whosoever is deceived thereby is not wise.'"

"You think I want this?" Preacher Man's voice cracked with emotion. "Don't you think I'd stop if I could?"

"You know the Word of God! You know His commands!"

Preacher Man shook his head and reached for the bottle.

Reverend Wyatt quoted: "'Now the works of the flesh are manifest, which are these; adultery, fornication, uncleanness, lasciviousness, idolatry, witchcraft ...'" He raised the sword high over his head. "'... hatred, variance, emulations, wrath, strife, seditions, heresies, envyings, murders, drunkenness, revellings, and such like: of the which I tell you before, as I have also told you in time past ...'" Gripping it firmly, he took aim, preparing to strike. "'... that they which do such things shall *not* inherit the kingdom of God.'"

With the final phrase he brought the sword down, once again hacking deeply into Preacher Man's shoulder. Again, Preacher Man screamed as a large slab of his violet light fell to the floor.

"Please," Reverend Wyatt begged. "You must end this."

But the self-hatred, the guilt, and the pain were more than Preacher Man could bear. As soon as he was able, he resumed pouring his drink. As he did, the darker light regrew.

Orbolitz watched in disgust. For as the darkness regrew, as it devoured the orange-red glow for much of its power, that orange-red glow barely decreased in size or brightness. As in every other occasion, it was replenished by the man's blazing center core.

"Unfair!" Orbolitz shouted. "That is so unfair!"

Neither Preacher Man nor Orbolitz seemed to hear as Wyatt again raised his sword and again recited, "'And be not drunk with wine, wherein is excess ...'"

But Orbolitz had seen enough. He turned to leave. The two could go on like that forever—the Reverend hacking away at Preacher Man's darker shell, Preacher Man constantly regrowing it by feeding upon the orange-red glow ... that was constantly feeding upon the blazing light. It was a perpetual tug-of-war to which there appeared no winner.

rachel had not seen David since she'd fled his room last night. But their conversation had never left her thoughts—

even now as she walked through the forest trying to quiet the voices, trying to quiet her soul. How was it possible? The forgiveness he spoke of? Everything else in the universe was cause and effect. If you jump off a cliff, you fall. If you hurt someone, you pay. "Sowing and reaping," "an eye for an eye." Wasn't that in the Bible? And yet, according to David, there was something greater than this principle. *Someone* greater.

Funny, over the years she'd learned never to say His name out loud—not even to swear—a lesson Albert was apparently learning as well. Saying the name *Jesus Christ* had always brought a gentle correction from Mr. Sparks. Nor was he particularly fond of those who practiced Christ's teachings. He said Jesus' original instruction had been good, but that it had been twisted and perverted until it made today's followers self-righteous, unloving, and intolerant.

But now, after spending time with David, she had her doubts. How could someone who was encouraged to admit his mistakes and ask for forgiveness be considered self-righteous? And Christ's command to extend that forgiveness to others, regardless of their actions . . . well, that sounded anything but unloving or intolerant. Unbelievable, yes. Illogical, of course. But not something her gods should be so uncomfortable with.

Then there was her other concern. As Orbolitz continued increasing the Presence, things continued to grow more disturbing and uncomfortable . . . for everyone.

Savannah's violet shell had become so thick and bulky that it was difficult for her to pass through doorways, let alone move up and down the stairs. It pained Rachel to see the woman eye something in the lodge, or even in magazines, then watch her darker light suddenly absorb its shape. It was one thing to take in the Tiffany bracelet or the Fabergé egg on the fireplace mantel, but there were much larger items—pieces of clothing, Native American artwork, the silver serving trays from the kitchen, even the hand-carved beaver and the crouching bobcat in the entry hall. It wasn't always clear what she had absorbed, but the bulging angles and increasing size made it obvious she could not stop.

The same could be said for Albert. Shadow snouts and snapping fangs stretched and poked in every direction. And not just around his head and neck, but in his chest, his abdomen, even his back. Rachel had thought the pornography Orbolitz supplied would have curbed his appetite, but surprisingly, it only seemed to make it worse.

Word had also reached her of Preacher Man's struggle up in his room. And David's. And Starr's. Dear, vulnerable Starr. She was glad they'd become friends so quickly. And she was grateful the child trusted her enough to be taken under her wing. But now . . .

Earlier she had knocked on her door, but Starr had already left the lodge. No breakfast. No word to anyone. Only when Rachel ran into Luke and Nubee outside did she learn what had happened the night before in Nubee's room. He'd tried his best to be delicate in the explanation, but there was no doubt what had occurred.

And it broke Rachel's heart.

How had the girl misunderstood what she'd been so careful to explain? Worse than that, had she inadvertently encouraged her?

Then there were the voices . . .

The thing is getting old.

It will continue to serve us.

What about the young girl?

I do like young girls.

Young girls mean young men . . . virile young men.

Were they planning something with Starr? She wasn't sure. She hoped it was only their agitation from the increasing Presence. The good news was she no longer saw them. Not like last night. The bad news was, as the Presence increased, she was able to see their dark, swirling shadows more and more clearly ... even in daylight.

The girl is not our solution.

She too is under the influence. Everyone here is under the—

Not everyone—

So young, so luscious.

What of those in the mountain —

No.

—they have not received—

I said, no!

Young girls mean young men ...

And so the argument continued—a schism forming. Some wanted to take flight and depart their host, the "thing," the "it," the "her." Others wanted to take their chances and remain. Of course, she would have liked to weigh in, but she knew it made no difference what she thought. It never had in the past. So, with a weary sigh, she continued up the steep, fern-covered ridge searching for Starr ... and a little peace.

That's when she heard the clapping.

She picked up her pace and crested the ridge. Down below, where it flattened out near the bluff, she saw Albert and Starr. Albert sat in the shadows on a fallen tree, encased in his dark, luminous shell. He was clapping as Starr leaped and spun, skipping around him in what she must have thought to be a dance of seduction. But it was seductive only because she had stripped down to her underwear.

Albert loved it. Rachel could tell, not only by his clapping and the way he followed her every move, but by his outer darkness. The snarling, snapping jaws, pushing at the edges, hungrily stretching toward the dancing child.

Beautiful, isn't she?

Luscious.

Ignoring the voices, Rachel shouted, "What are you doing?"

Albert looked up, startled.

She headed down the slope, slipping, sliding. "Get away from her!"

He rose to his feet.

"Get away!"

"I didn't—"

"Get away!"

It was clear she meant business, and Albert quickly scurried around a fallen tree for protection. As he did, he briefly stepped into a shaft of sunlight, nearly erasing his dark glow. "It was her idea!"

Rachel slipped and fell. But the rage kept her going. She was back on her feet, heading directly toward him.

"Don't blame me!" He backed away into the shadows, his glow returning. "It was her!" He pointed at Starr. "It was her idea!" The girl had come to a stop, suddenly looking very self-conscious.

Rachel continued toward him, not slowing.

He hesitated, glancing to one side then the other, before turning and starting to run.

"Get out of here! Go on! Get out!"

He stumbled once, twice, but continued running. Rachel thought of pursuing but knew she couldn't catch him. She slowed to a stop, breathing hard. "Go on! Get out!"

He stumbled again and continued.

"If I ever see you around her again, so help me, I'll—"

"What are you doing?" Starr shouted.

Rachel turned to her. "What am *I* doing? What were *you* doing?"

Starr nervously scooped up her clothes. "I was celebrating my ... femininity. I was empowering myself by ..."

"By what? Parading around naked in front of that ... pervert!"

Holding her clothes against her nakedness, Starr argued, "I was not parading. I was starting to *sky clad*. The books say that—"

"I know what the books say. And they don't say anything about doing it in front of dirty old—"

"I can do it where and when I want!"

"Starr—"

"'Do what ye will and if it harm not—'"

"Yes, but you have to practice a little wisdom. You can't
just foolishly—"

"I am not a fool!"

"Nobody said you—"

"You ruined it!" Starr's voice broke. "You ruined
everything!"

Rachel started toward her. "I'm only trying to protect
you from—"

"I don't need your protection. I've got the gods!"

"You . . ." The phrase brought Rachel to a stop. "Starr,
listen, you don't understand—"

"I understand everything! It's in the books!"

"Yes, but . . . you're not even initiated. You've not even—"

"I'm doing it myself. The books say I can."

"Not by sky cladding in front of some sicko! There are
ways—"

"I don't need your ways!" Tears streamed down her
cheeks.

"Starr—"

"And I don't need some old . . . cow to tell me—"

Again Rachel started toward her. "I'm just saying—"

"Leave me alone!" The girl turned, wiping her face,
then suddenly bolted.

"Starr!"

She stumbled but caught her balance and continued
into the woods. "Leave me alone!"

"Starr!"

She kept running, threading her way through the undergrowth, clutching her clothes.

"Starr!" Rachel took several more steps before she
slowed. "Starr . . ."

wonder though, if the same problem your father has, if it is not similar to your own."

"What does that mean?"

"It means some of your outer shell, it is boiling much as your father's."

Luke glanced down to his chest. His vision had improved from the day before, but it was still hard to see anything clearly. "No way."

"Yes, I am afraid way. We are approaching the forest now. We must turn to the right."

Luke continued, half walking, half limping, while angling Nubee's wheelchair off to the right. His ankle was only a little better, but it felt great to be outside again . . . even if it was only the lawn in front of the lodge . . . even if it did mean using Nubee as a seeing-eye chair. He'd take what he could get. Anything to get away from the grownups and the weirdness of their lights.

"May I make another observation?"

"Do I have a choice?"

"Most likely not."

Luke hid his amusement with a sigh. "Go ahead, Nubee, observe away." He'd always liked the guy, even when he couldn't speak. And now that he could communicate like a regular person, like a regular *smart* person, well, he liked him even better.

"I do not think your anger is directed entirely toward Orbolitz."

"If you're going to say I'm not crazy about my dad, save your breath. We already know that. And we're trying. We're not doing great, but we're trying."

"Orbolitz and your father are only part of the problem. A bit more to the right, please."

"Who else is there?"

"Everybody."

"What?"

"Nobody meets your expectations."

"Meaning?"

"Nobody meets your expectations, because *you* do not meet your expectations."

Luke remained silent.

"'As you judge, so will you be judged.'"

"You lost me."

"Your anger at everybody, it is because you are angry with yourself."

"You learn that watching Oprah or Dr. Phil?"

"I learned it by watching myself. I hated myself for my failures so much that I began hating others."

Luke said nothing.

"Because you hold an impossible standard for yourself, you hold it for others. And when they fail to meet that standard, especially those closest to you, such as your father, then you are critical and angry at them as well."

"Nubee?"

"Yes, Luke."

"Shut up."

"I am sorry. I am only trying to—"

"No, I mean it. Be quiet."

"I am only—"

"Listen." Luke slowed the chair to a stop. There it was again, the buzz he'd heard by the fake tree. But there was no fake tree here. "Don't you hear that?"

"Hear what?"

"That humming sound, that buzz."

"No, I don't. And if you are trying to change the subject—"

"Shh . . ."

Luke moved them forward. The buzz continued a moment or two then started to fade. He stopped. He backed up a step and it increased. Angling the chair slightly, he continued forward. The buzz continued. He stopped again.

"Luke?"

"Quiet."

He kneeled and the buzz grew still louder. Just as he expected. It was coming from the ground. "There's some sort of current or something running under here."

"Are you certain?"

He rose and slowly pushed them forward. The buzz continued a bit longer before it started to fade again. He continued, adjusting their angle slightly, and the buzz returned. He kept going, slowly, carefully. Whenever the buzz faded he veered to the left or the right until it returned.

"Nubee, do you see anything on the ground? Any marks or anything?"

"I see nothing."

"I can't believe you don't hear that."

"Maybe your impaired sight has helped your hearing."

"Up ahead. If we keep going straight, do you see anything?"

"Just trees."

"What do they look like?"

"The trees."

"Yes."

"They look like ... trees."

"Are they all the same?"

"Luke, I fail to see—"

"If we go in a straight line, the first tree we hit, is it like all the others?"

"Yes. We are nearly there now."

"What about its top?"

He could see Nubee's head tilting back, looking up. "It is similar to many of the others. Its branches are broken off from the wind and it ..." He stopped.

"What? 'And it,' what?"

"That is odd."

"What, Nubee?"

"Closer please."

Luke continued pushing. They were starting to hit some undergrowth. "Nubee?"

"The top. It appears to have long panels."

The undergrowth grew thicker, making the chair harder to push. Luke could see a tall shadow looming just ahead. "Is that the tree in front of us?"

"Yes. You may stop anytime, please."

He kept pushing.

"Luke, you may—"

Klunk. They came to a jarring stop. Moving around the chair, holding on to Nubee for support, Luke reached out until he touched the tree. He pressed with his fingertips, dug in with his nails. Just as he thought. It was like the other. It was also fake.

You should be ashamed of yourself." Rachel nailed Albert with a glare. "She's just a girl!"

"It wasn't my idea." Albert turned to the rest of the group. "It was hers. It's what *she* wanted."

"You're the adult . . . or hadn't you noticed?"

"It's not my fault." Albert swore again, and again the air rippled. "Oww!" He gripped his mouth but continued shouting through the pain. "I'm trying! Why do you think I was out there? I was trying to get away, to control it. But the harder I try, the worse it gets. You can't blame me; it's the way I'm wired." He motioned to the others around the fireplace. "Just like you can't blame the preacher here for his issues—"

Preacher Man straightened, trying his best to appear sober . . . with minimal success.

"—or David with all his junk, or Savannah . . . or anybody else in this room." Turning back to Rachel, he added, "Including you."

She glanced down, very much aware of her own baggage.

"We're not puppets," David muttered. He eased himself down on the sofa beside her. His violet light thicker, boiling more intensely. "We have free will."

"Precisely," Reverend Wyatt agreed from the opposite chair. His hood was so dense that Rachel could no longer see his face. "And it is that free will, along with God's Word, that can liberate us all from—"

"No," Preacher Man interrupted.

Wyatt stopped and looked at him.

"There's more." The old man's voice was clogged and exhausted, but he pressed on. "There's more than God's Word ... and our will."

Rachel watched, waiting with the others.

"And prayer," Nubee reminded him.

"There's more than prayer."

With strained patience Reverend Wyatt replied, "And you still say this, even in your condition?"

Preacher Man looked up, holding him with red, watery eyes. "I say it, 'cause you keep leavin' out the other ingredient."

"Which is?" David asked.

Preacher Man turned to him, licking his dry, parched lips. "His love ..." He swallowed and continued. "His love for us ... and our love for Him. It's not just the doing. It's the abiding."

A moment passed before Savannah spoke from within her bloated light. "Doesn't look like it's helping you much, old-timer."

Preacher Man turned to her, wanting to give an answer, then looked down, obviously having none.

"What about Starr?" Rachel asked, adjusting her cardigan sweater and bringing them back on topic. "Has anyone seen her?"

"She can't be far," Albert said. "Not with the electronic leash."

"You have it all mapped out?" Reverend Wyatt asked.

"All three sides."

"And the fourth?"

"The bluff. A sheer drop, eight hundred feet to the valley below. No way she could climb down that. But there's something else." He looked at David. "Don't know if it'll help, but your boy here, he may have found something."

All eyes turned to Luke, who slouched further.

"Go ahead," Albert encouraged. "Tell them."

"Tell us what, boy?" Tension swept the room as they turned to see Orbolitz making his entrance down the stairway, accompanied by his two bodyguards. "So how's everybody doin' this afternoon?"

No one responded.

"I gotta tell you"—he tapped his goggles which could barely be seen underneath his dark shell—"every hour you folks keep lookin' more and more interestin'."

Rachel felt movement on the sofa and glanced over to David as he shifted his weight. It was obvious he was struggling to contain his rage, but his glow's churning made it equally obvious he was failing.

"Just a little over a day, folks. Thirty more hours and we'll be at maximum power."

David shifted again. She reached down to his hand, a gesture of caution.

"Thirty more hours and God Almighty, or at least his recorded Presence, will be at 100 percent. Then, provided any of you survive the ordeal, you'll be—"

A roaring *whoosh* filled the room. Rachel turned to see David's glow break loose from his body and race toward the stairs. Orbolitz saw it too and tried to duck, raising his arms with a cry, but it did no good. The impact sent him staggering backwards into the steps. David's light continued its attack, tearing into the man's dark shell, ripping through it, trying to reach the body inside.

"Get it off me!" Orbolitz shouted. "Get it off!"

His bodyguards traded confused looks. Without goggles they apparently saw nothing.

"Get it off!"

Reluctantly, they moved into action—reaching in vain to where they guessed David's light might be.

Orbolitz wrestled and squirmed, pointing at David, "It's *him*! Stop *him*!"

They leaped up and lumbered across the room toward David as he rose from the sofa. He tried to run but only managed a couple steps before they tackled him to the ground and began their assault.

Rachel dropped to her knees, trying to pull them off. "Stop it! Leave him alone!" They flung her aside, but she leaped back in. "David, stop it! Stop attacking!"

But of course he did not stop. She doubted he could.

"Dad!" Luke joined the mix, pounding on the back of the crew cut bodyguard. The big man barely noticed.

"Get him off!" Orbolitz cried, continuing his struggle at the stairs. "Get him off!"

Others joined in, yelling, shouting.

The man in the crew cut turned and struck Luke in the face, so hard the boy flew backwards onto the floor.

David saw it. "Luke!"

"Get him off! Get him—"

"David, stop it! You must try to—"

And then, through the bedlam . . . a voice began to sing:

"O Lord my God, when I in awesome wonder . . ."

Rachel turned to see Preacher Man. He struggled to rise to his feet. With his big, gravelly voice, his consonants softened by the alcohol, he continued singing:

"Consider all the works Thy hands have made . . ."

Others turned, surprised.

"I see the stars, I hear the rolling thunder,
Thy power throughout the universe displayed."

At first Rachel thought it was her imagination. But, as he sang, Preacher Man's core light, that tiny pocket of burning whiteness at his center, began growing brighter.

*"Then sings my soul, my Savior God, to Thee:
how great Thou art, how great Thou art!"*

From across the room, Nubee joined in.

*"Then sings my soul, my Savior God, to Thee:
how great Thou art, how great Thou art!"*

The group exchanged looks, obviously as perplexed as Rachel.

Without missing a beat, Preacher Man began the second verse. Nubee followed. As they sang, both of their center cores grew brighter. And, as their cores intensified, so did the orange-red glows around those cores. But not just theirs—all the cores that were illuminated grew brighter. And, as the cores grew brighter, the orange-red glows followed. Even David's.

Rachel stared as the glows continued to increase until they actually began pushing back and dissolving the darker, outer shells. Not through any struggle or conflict, but simply by being brighter. Even David's attacking darkness on the stairs grew less.

But his diminishing shadow did little to comfort Orbolitz. Suddenly the old man grabbed his goggles and screamed. "What is happening? What are you doing?"

Preacher Man and Nubee continued singing. Their voices growing stronger, more confident.

"But when I think that God, His Son not sparing . . ."

Then, all at once, both of their orange-red glows exploded, bursting from their bodies, and reaching across the room to others. Not just to those with the blazing cores, but to all the orange-red glows, feeding them, joining with them, filling the entire room with their beautiful brightness.

Rachel turned to Reverend Wyatt in astonishment. He looked as baffled as she did. But he also saw the singing's power. And, apparently knowing the words, he joined in. Tentatively at first, but with growing conviction:

"Sent Him to die, I scarce can take it in . . ."

But there was more. Besides the growing glows, Rachel heard other voices. Other singers. She searched the room. Only the three men sang, but there were others. A dozen. No, more. Their number increasing.

"That on the Cross my burden gladly bearing . . ."

Then there were her voices:
Stop them!
The burning!
And with the voices came the sudden cramps and nausea—so quickly, she doubled over as if she'd been hit.
We must go!
No!
The searing!
No!
And still the singing continued:

"He bled and died to take away my sin."

Now Orbolitz was screaming. "Get away! Get them away from me!"

The room filled with brightness as all the glows joined into one. More voices sang—lifting, soaring. And . . . was that incense? Rachel couldn't be sure. She was sure of nothing but the cramps and the nausea—so intense she could no longer stand but dropped to her knees.

We must leave. Now!
No, I forbid—
Now!
Where?

She looked up, nearly blinded by the room's brightness. Everyone stood in awe. Everyone but Orbolitz, who remained by the steps, swatting madly at the air. "Get away! I need more filters! Helgeland, increase the filters!"

"Then sings my soul, my Savior God, to Thee . . ."

Rachel clenched her eyes against the pain, her face cold with sweat.

The young girl . . .
I like girls.
I order you to stay!
Now, we must leave, now!
No, I order you to—
We must leave!
Where?
Outside. The girl is outside!

Suddenly she understood. Filled with horror, Rachel protested, but was rewarded with gut-wrenching convulsions—

"How great Thou art, how great Thou art."

—so powerful she could not catch her breath. She began to vomit. Not food. She hadn't eaten all day. Dry heaves. Empty, but not empty. For with each gagging contraction, she felt something leave, something exit through her mouth. Not visible, at least not in this light, but she knew what they were. More terrifying, she knew where they were going.

"No," she gasped, "no!"

"Then sings my soul, my Savior God, to Thee . . ."

The gagging stopped as quickly as it began. That's when she heard the rattling. Windowpanes shaking.

"Earthquake!" Albert shouted.

She struggled to her feet, barely able to stand. Weakened, dizzy, soaked in sweat, she started for the door. She had to stop them.

The rattling grew to a roar, like a train.

But Rachel barely heard. She reached the door and stumbled outside. "Not the girl!" She cried. "No! Not the girl!"

nine

david wasn't sure when the blows stopped. Nor did he know when the room had filled with so much light. One minute he was on the floor, having the stuffing beaten out of him; the next he was surrounded by blinding brightness and being pulled to his feet by Reverend Wyatt.

"Earthquake!" The man shouted over the roar. He glowed with the same light as the rest of the room. "Outside! Hurry!"

David fought to keep his balance, unsure which was spinning more, the floor or his vision. Either way he was grateful for the Reverend's help as they staggered for the door, as windows exploded around them and pictures slid to the floor, shattering. They stumbled onto the porch just as the pitching came to an end and the thundering roar faded.

"Rachel!" Preacher Man shouted. "Starr!" He was out on the lawn helping Luke walk, or maybe it was the other way around. Together they were racing toward the woods.

"What's wrong?" Reverend Wyatt called.

"They need our help!"

David looked up the slope, unable to see anything but trees.

"Demons!" Preacher Man cried.

"What?"

"Demons!" Preacher Man lost his footing and Luke caught him. "She needs our help!"

The Reverend hesitated.

"Hurry!" The two disappeared into the trees. "'Fore it's too late, hurry!"

rachel ran through the woods, the undergrowth catching her legs, a branch slapping her eye, making it water. She didn't know where Starr had gone—"outside" was all she'd heard from her voices before the quake—but she had a good idea. "Starr!" She breathed hard as she climbed the slope she'd scaled just hours earlier. She didn't know where the girl had gone, but she did know what had happened. Some of her gods had left. Not all of them, not Osiris, not his allies. But the others, the ones who had argued about leaving when they were back at the lodge, and last night on her bed. Now she understood . . . perfectly.

What about the young girl? I do like girls. She is young, so luscious.

Rachel's foot slipped, causing her to fall to a knee, slamming it onto a sharp rock. She swallowed a cry and scrambled back up. "Starr!" She was panicking, she knew that, but it didn't matter. She'd let them have one child; she was not about to let them have another. "Starr!"

She crested the ridge and looked down through the trees. There, at the bottom, where it flattened out near the bluff, stood the young teenager. This time she wore no clothes. She stood in the center of a makeshift pentagram that she'd built of rock and fallen wood. There, in the shadows, she swayed back and forth, her eyes closed, chanting loudly: "Come to me, Diane, I am yours. I abandon myself to your beauty and to your power."

And circling around her . . . Rachel sucked in her breath. She could see them clearly now. Circling around Starr were Rachel's deities, the dark, luminous forms that had battled one another on her bed.

"Starr!"

The girl did not hear. "Come to me, Diane—"

"Starr, don't!" Rachel started down the hill, slipping and sliding. "You don't know what you're—"

"I abandon myself to your beauty and to your power."

"No!"

The girl chanted louder, faster—enraptured in the moment. She began throwing her head from side to side. "I am yours—"

Rachel tripped again, tumbled, then staggered back to her feet. "Starr, don't!"

"I abandon myself to your beauty—"

"Starr!"

"—and to your power."

She reached the bottom of the slope, Starr twenty feet ahead. That's when the crying started. The screaming. The baby. The swirling entities rose above Starr, condensing into the shape of a giant bird just above her head. As it solidified it grew whiter, brighter.

Starr opened her eyes. "No!" She reached toward the bird. "Don't leave me! Come back!" It continued rising until it floated high overhead. Then it turned toward Rachel. With one mighty thrust of its wings it started for her—head lowering, wings pulled back . . . screeching.

"No!" Starr cried. "Come back to me! Come back!"

Rachel looked for an escape. There was none. No boulders, the nearest tree too far away. She ducked, turning. It did little good. The thing caught her right shoulder, spinning her around, throwing her hard into a fallen log. Her side burst with pain, a bruised rib, maybe broken. She lay a moment, catching her breath. Her side burned with every gasp as she looked up to see the bird glide through the trees, circling behind Starr. But it was no bird. She knew that. It was an angel. Baby Jessica come back as an angel.

Despite the pain she struggled to her feet. The edges of her vision grew white; she was passing out. No! She wouldn't! Not now. Not for Starr. Not for the baby. But how could it be her baby *and* her gods *and*—

The angel dropped down, coming in for another approach, this time behind Starr.

The girl had turned to face it. "Come to *me*! Come back to *me*!"

"Starr—"

She raised her hands for it. "I give myself—"

It pulled in its wings, picking up speed, resuming its shriek.

"—to your beauty, to your—"

But at the last second it tilted its wings, veered past her, and headed directly for Rachel. Good, good. Better her than the girl. Despite the pain, Rachel stood taller. She would take the full assault.

"That's right!" she shouted. "It's me. I'm the one who killed you. I'm the murderer!"

As she stared, it took on the face of a baby, her baby—but cracked and broken. Of course. They had to crush her skull during delivery. That's how it was with late-term abortions. Not only did they crush her skull but any other part of her necessary to—

The face wavered and changed into a frog's, like the gargoyles on her bed. It stretched out its hands, revealing claws, opened its mouth, showing fangs. Claws and fangs? The sight so alarmed her that against her will she ducked again. This time the creature's talons caught the top of her head, tearing into her scalp, ripping out hair. She screamed, dropping to her knees, but staggered back up, her vision growing whiter with every breath.

She caught a glimpse of Starr reentering the pentagram—arms outstretched, shouting. "Come to me, Diane! I abandon myself to your beauty and to your power."

"No . . ." Rachel staggered forward.

She heard the baby's scream coming from behind.

The girl stood a dozen feet ahead shouting, "Enter me!"

"Starr—"

"I am yours!"

Hearing the flap of wings, Rachel spun around, hoping to somehow block its path. It caught her dead center in the chest, the impact so strong she flew backwards. She hit a tree and crumpled to the ground. She may have lost consciousness, she wasn't sure. But forcing open her eyes, she saw Starr's blurry form just feet away.

"I yield myself to your power!"

The angel had dissolved back into the luminous shadows, swirling just above the girl.

Rachel tried moving, but her body refused. She watched helplessly as Starr, arms spread open, rose onto her tiptoes, her face lifted in eager anticipation.

"I yield myself to your beauty!"

"...no..."

The shadows condensed into a black, pencil-thin stream.

"I yield all that I—"

The stream shot into Starr's mouth with such force the girl's eyes bulged in surprise. She rose even higher onto her toes, and a helpless squeal escaped before she collapsed and fell to the ground.

"Rachel!"

David had passed Luke and Preacher Man on the ridge and was the first to spot the two women down at the bottom. Rachel, with a bleeding gash atop her head identical to what he'd seen in his dream, and Starr lying in her arms.

"Rachel! Starr!"

They did not respond. He ran, stumbling and sliding down the hill to join them. Rachel had draped her cardigan around the girl, but as best he could tell the child was not moving. "Rachel?" He arrived, kneeling at her side. "What happened?"

She glanced up at him, her face wet with tears and blood. She looked back down, brushing the hair from Starr's face, inadvertently smearing her own blood across the girl's cheek. "Starr ..." Her voice was a hoarse whisper. "Sweetheart ..."

She remained motionless.

"Starr ..."

No answer.

Rachel pulled her closer. Then, ever so gently, she began rocking.

Softly David spoke, "Rachel?"

She didn't seem to hear.

He tried again, reaching out and touching her arm. "Rachel?"

Still no response.

"David?" Preacher Man called.

He looked up the ridge and saw Luke and the old-timer making their way down. Albert followed farther behind.

"You be careful," Preacher Man warned.

David turned back to Rachel. She was stroking Starr's hair, tears streaming down her face, continuing to rock.

"Rachel ... can you hear me?"

He reached for Starr's mouth, feeling for breath.

The girl's eyes exploded open.

Rachel jerked in surprise. "Starr?" She pulled her closer. But the girl grew stiff as a board.

David moved into Starr's vision until her eyes registered him. Her mouth twitched once, then twice, before she spoke. "What have you to do with us?" It was Starr's voice but it wasn't. It was deeper. More guttural.

He threw a concerned look to Rachel.

"Starr?" she asked. "Sweetheart, are you okay?"

The girl said nothing, continuing to glare at David.

"Starr, are you there?"

"She's here," the voice growled. Then shifting her eyes to Rachel, it added, "And so are we."

It was Rachel's turn to stiffen.

"What's going on?" David asked.

A faint smile danced across Starr's lips. "Do you tell him, or should we?"

Without looking at him, Rachel replied, "I recognize that voice."

David glanced at her.

"It's one of mine."

Starr responded with a throaty chuckle.

"This . . . isn't right," Rachel stammered.

"Of course it's right," the voice answered. "It's her choice."

"But she didn't know. She didn't—"

"She knew. You taught her all she needed to know." The smile curled into a grin. "And for that we are grateful."

"David." Preacher Man was much closer. "Be careful. Both of you be careful."

"That's right, David," the voice sneered. "We wouldn't want to hurt you."

Once again David reached toward her face. "Starr—"

"Don't touch us!" The girl bolted from Rachel's arms, sitting straight up. She pulled the cardigan around herself, just out of his reach.

Still not understanding, he turned to Rachel.

"They're afraid of you," she explained. "They've always been." Without waiting for a response, she turned to the girl. "Starr, listen to me. I know you're there. You don't have to—"

"Silence!"

The cry stopped her, but only for a moment. "I know you can hear me. I know they've got you shoved down into some corner." She moved closer. "But you don't have to be afraid. You can still—"

Starr's right hand flew out. Her nails slashed deep into Rachel's cheek, immediately drawing blood. Rachel screamed and grabbed her face.

"Rachel!" David cried.

She held out her hand to him. "It's okay, I'm all right."

Starr rose to her feet. "This is not your concern, David Kauffman." She stood, glaring down at him. "If you continue tormenting us, you will pay the price."

"Price? What price?"

The smile again played on her lips. "Just ask your daughter."

He blinked, stunned, until his anger surfaced. "My daughter?" He rose to confront her.

Starr took a tentative step backward, and then another.

"What do you know about my daughter?"

"They know nothing, brother."

He glanced over his shoulder to see Preacher Man and Luke arriving.

"They're just tryin' to scare you." Preacher Man continued forward, past David and toward the girl. "But they're really the ones who are afraid ..." Turning to Starr, he finished, "... aren't you?"

Starr took another step back and sneered. "What does an old drunk know?"

Preacher Man dropped his head and shook it. "Not much."

"That's right," the voice taunted, "the drunk knows nothing."

"'Cept ..." Preacher Man looked back up, Luke still at his side. "I know Who I belong to."

"You are a failure."

He held her eyes. "That's right. But I'm *His* failure, ain't I." He took a step forward.

She stepped back. "Fool."

He nodded. "But a fool bought and paid for by the Blood of the Lamb."

"Silence!"

"By Jesus Christ Himself, Who died—"

"SILENCE!"

"—upon that cross and—"

"STOP IT! I DEMAND YOU—"

"—Who purchased me with—"

A loud *crack* sounded above their heads. David looked up to see a tree limb falling toward them. "Luke!" He started for his son but Rachel grabbed his arm. He shook her off and had only taken a few steps before the branch hit him, slamming him hard to the ground.

"Dad!"

He immediately struggled to his knees, fighting through the branches, searching for his son. He spotted him beside Preacher Man and Starr. The tree had just missed them.

"Dad?" Luke's voice broke in concern. "Are you all right?"

"Yeah . . . I'm okay."

"You sure?" Rachel asked. She was picking her way through the branches toward him.

He nodded, ignoring the pain in his shoulder.

She turned to Luke and Preacher Man. "You two be careful. You don't know their power."

Preacher Man nodded, then turned back toward the girl, deliberately taking another step forward.

Starr countered with a step back. "She is ours," the voice declared. "There is nothing you can do to change that."

"Maybe there is, maybe there isn't."

"Careful," Rachel repeated.

"Luke," David warned. "I don't want you—" That's when he felt the rumble, a fraction of a second before he heard it.

"Up there!" Rachel pointed behind them.

David turned. The forest was moving! A swath a dozen feet wide was slipping down the ridge directly for Luke and Preacher Man.

"Rock slide!" Rachel cried.

The earth had turned liquid. Dirt and vegetation swarmed around the larger trees, submerging or snapping off the smaller ones. Rocks and boulders bounced like toy balls.

David spun back to his son. Preacher Man was quickly directing him behind the upturned roots of a fallen tree.

"LUKE!"

But he barely heard himself as the rumble grew to a thundering roar ... as the earth shook ... as the ground continued sliding, roiling and boiling over itself, showing no trace of stopping.

You tellin' me it wasn't at your end?" Orbolitz shouted into a palm-sized walkie-talkie.

Helgeland replied, "We were holding rock steady at 61 percent when it occurred."

"Then what was it?"

"It's only a hypothesis, and I can't be entirely certain, but—"

"Cut to the chase, son."

"I'm guessing that song may have somehow increased their sensitivity to the Presence."

"A song?" Orbolitz demanded. "You saying all that light was their singing?"

"Or something associated with it."

"And the earthquake?"

"We're on a fault line; we always knew there was a possibility of unrelated seismic activity."

"But there's no connection between 'em. Strictly coincidence?"

"Heavy steam's been venting from Mount Baker's Sherman Crater for the past couple weeks now."

Orbolitz leaned back on one elbow against the steps. In his other hand he held the goggles. "And these things. I seen them smearing lights again, only it was like they were comin' right at me."

"Of that I'm not so certain. But if you'd put Jefferson on the line, I'd be happy to talk him through how to increase the filtering."

Orbolitz glanced to his bodyguard on the sofa, seriously doubting he had the extra synapses for the occasion.

"Shouldn't take more than ten minutes," Helgeland continued. "Either that or I could send up one of my boys from down here to—"

"No, I'll swing down there myself. Where's the group now?"

"Still at the bluff."

"As soon as they're clear, let me know."

"Will do."

"But why now?"

"Sir?"

Staring at the goggles he asked, "Why did they go on the blink now?"

Helgeland gave no answer.

Orbolitz rubbed his eyes and sighed heavily. "I don't like it, Dirk."

"How's that?"

"If they can control the Presence through simple singing, how else can they manipulate it?"

"I wouldn't be worrying much about that. It's all going to be over in twenty-four hours."

"No."

"Come again?"

"We don't have that luxury. Soon as we get these goggles up and runnin', I want to go to maximum power."

"Mr. Orbolitz . . . you saw what happened when we tried that in the lab."

"This ain't the lab, Dirk."

"But if we don't allow their systems time to adapt—"

"What are we at now?"

"We just hit 64 percent."

"So all we got left is 36 percent. An extra 36 percent ain't gonna hurt nobody." He waited for an answer, but there was none. "Talk to me, Dirk."

"It's just . . . in the lab, the last 20 percent, it always proved to be the most dangerous."

Once again Orbolitz sighed.

"Sir, all I'm saying to you is we don't have the assurance that—"

"We've got assurance of nothin', Dirk!" Both bodyguards glanced over and Orbolitz lowered his voice. "We're in uncharted territory here, son. No-man's-land."

"Could we at least stretch it out—say over the next seven to eight hours? That's still four times faster than the computer model suggested."

Orbolitz rubbed his forehead.

"Sir?"

"All right, seven hours. You have seven hours to bring us to full intensity." He glanced at his watch. "That puts it at 11:00. By 11:00 tonight, everyone here will be experiencing 100 percent of the Presence."

"Yes, sir." Another pause. Then a little softer, "And God help them all."

"No, Dirk."

"Sir?"

"God is the last person we want around at that time."

d ust was still rising as David picked his way across the rubble toward his son. "Luke!"

Rachel followed. Her ribs burned with every breath, but at least her head had stopped bleeding.

"Luke!"

"Over here," Preacher Man coughed. "We're . . . over here."

David turned, following the voice. "Are you all right?"

"Yeah," Luke answered, "we're okay."

The two appeared through the dust, crawling from the safety of the tree's upturned roots. Luke was bent over, holding his head.

David was immediately at his side. "What's wrong?"

Luke looked up. "Don't you—" He coughed. "Don't you hear that?"

"Hear what?"

"That hum, that buzzing? Don't you feel it?"

Rachel stopped breathing a moment to listen. She exchanged looks with the other men.

David shook his head. "We don't hear anything, son."

"You're kidding!"

"Is it what you explained to Albert?" Preacher Man asked.

Luke nodded, rubbing his temples. "Only worse. A hundred times worse."

Rachel strained to listen but still heard nothing . . . except a faint, distant groan. She turned toward the bluff, squinting through the dust. There it was again. "Starr?" She moved as quickly as possible around the mound of rubble, picking her away through outlying rocks and boulders. "Starr, are you okay?"

David and the others followed.

Another groan, louder. And then she caught movement. "Starr!" The girl was lying on the ground near the edge of the bluff. Rachel quickened her pace. "Starr?"

The child's head snapped around and she growled, "Stay back!"

Rachel slowed. The girl pulled herself closer to the edge, her left leg dragging behind, twisted in an impossible position.

"Starr, your leg, you're—"

"Stay where you are!"

Rachel stopped. David, Luke, and Preacher Man joined her.

"Sweetheart . . . your leg."

Another voice answered, "She's of no use to us this way."

"What . . . what do you mean?"

"We will not have a cripple."

An icy chill swept through Rachel. "But . . . the leg, it can be repaired, it can—"

"The leg will always be useless. She is useless."

Another thinner voice spoke, one Rachel instantly recognized. "Virile young men will not be attracted."

Her thoughts raced, grasping the implications. She eased closer. They were less than a dozen feet apart.

"Stay back!" Starr pulled herself closer to the edge.

Rachel froze.

"Stay back or we will destroy her!"

She hesitated, unsure what to do. Slowly she kneeled. "Starr, I know you can hear me." She tried to keep her voice calm and even, as if speaking to a child. "You can fight them. You can push them aside and come back to the surface." She waited, watching. "Starr . . ."

The girl's face twisted, then scowled—some sort of battle was obviously raging.

David quietly kneeled beside Rachel. "What's going on?"

She motioned for his silence as they both watched.

Starr's face continued to grimace, until her own voice finally broke through, a faint whimper. "Help me—" interrupted by, "SILENCE!"

Starr's voice returned again, "Rachel, please don't let them—"

"SILENCE!"

Rachel anxiously watched, waiting.

"What's happening?" David whispered.

She shook her head, not taking her eyes from the girl. Finally she asked, "So what do you want?"

The deeper voice replied, "We don't want her."

"Meaning . . ."

"We will find another."

Rachel swallowed, fighting to stay calm. "Really? And where is that?"

The voice gave no answer.

More firmly she asked, "Who will give you permission?"

Again, no response.

"You mean to tell me you're just going to wander this wilderness until you—"

"SILENCE!"

Rachel took a measured breath, working to hide her fear.

"We will leave the girl and we will return to you."

NO! Osiris shouted from inside Rachel's mind.

She agreed. The last thing she wanted was their return. She shook her head. "That is not possible."

"It is our right," the deeper voice insisted.

"Not anymore. You have left and I forbid you."

"We will leave the girl and we will return to—"

"No, I forbid—"

"We will return to you or we will destroy the girl!"

Rachel stopped. "What?"

They are bluffing! Osiris shouted from inside her head.

"We will destroy the girl."

She struggled to keep her panic in check.

Do not believe them!

Starr's lips curled into another smile.

They left! Osiris insisted. *They must suffer!*

Rachel needed little convincing. Once again, she shook her head. "You may not return."

The smile twisted into a mocking grin as Starr pulled herself so close to the edge a portion of dirt slipped away from under her right hand.

"Rachel . . ." It was David. He wanted to help but was obviously out of his league.

The voice repeated, "Allow our return or we will destroy the girl."

Rachel held Starr's eyes, though of course, they were not Starr's that she looked into.

Suddenly, the frightened girl resurfaced. Disoriented, she saw the drop-off immediately in front of her. "Rachel . . . help me . . ."

Rachel's mind raced, searching for a solution.

NO! Osiris commanded. *NO!*

Starr's hand, the one nearest the edge, started to rise.

"Fight them," Rachel urged. "You can fight them!"

Starr looked helplessly at her hand. She turned back to Rachel, her voice quivering. "Help me . . ."

NO! Osiris cramped Rachel's gut so hard she gasped.

Starr's hand slowly reached out over the precipice.

"Starr . . ."

The girl began shaking as her body shifted its weight toward the edge.

Try as she might, Rachel could think of no other solution. If she didn't let them return, they would destroy Starr.

NO! THEY MUST NOT! THEY MUST NOT RE—

". . . Rachel . . ."

NO!

Despite Osiris's rage, despite the intense pain and her own fear, there was no choice. It was the only way to save the girl.

More dirt slipped away, this time from under her knee.

"All right!" she yelled. "All right!"

NOOO! Osiris hit with full fury, cramping her so hard she dropped her head to the ground. But even as she collapsed, she forced open her mouth, gasping a "yes" as she breathed in, permitting the icy darkness to rush back inside and down her throat—with such force that it threw back her head.

"RACHEL!"

She opened her eyes. Starr reached out to her, her face filling with terror as the cliff under her began to dissolve.

"NO!" Rachel lunged forward but David caught her, holding her back.

The ground gave way. Starr's eyes locked onto Rachel's. They were filled with fear, confusion, and betrayal . . . as she started to fall.

Rachel broke free from David, scrambling to the edge, trying to grab the girl's outstretched hand. But she was too late. They barely missed as Starr slipped away, her face lifted toward Rachel's, crying out her name.

Rachel stared in disbelief as the girl fell, arms flailing, screaming ... until she hit a tree growing from the side of the cliff and was silenced ... her unconscious body tumbling head over heels like a rag doll, growing smaller and smaller, plummeting eight hundred feet toward the river below.

part three

ten

the group had returned to the lodge shaken to the core. Some had wept openly. Others sat in stunned silence. All were despondent, feeling the unbearable weight of the child's death, not to mention the hopelessness of their situation. Rachel had taken it the worst. David and Albert had all but carried her up to her room, where Reverend Wyatt remained behind to offer what words of comfort he could find.

That had been nearly an hour ago. Now the old man slowly descended the stairs. Albert spotted him first and quietly asked, "How is she?"

The Reverend sadly shook his head. Although his central white light and the surrounding orange-red glow had returned to what they were before the song, his darker shell had decreased substantially.

"Will this ever end?" Savannah muttered. She spoke from within her enormous violet shadow. Unlike the Reverend, her orange-red glow had actually decreased. David wasn't sure why, though he still suspected it had to do with the hollowness of her center core. The same could be said for Albert and Rachel—without the core light, they had nothing to combat their encroaching shells.

As he moved into the room, Reverend Wyatt asked, "What about Starr? Is it possible to retrieve her body?"

"From an eight-hundred-foot, sheer rock face?" Albert shook his head. "It'd be impossible for any of us to get down there. Not without the proper gear."

Savannah turned back to the Reverend. "Did you talk to Orbolitz; did he say anything?"

"He is not in his suite. One of the bodyguards said he left the premises but should return shortly."

"Left?" David asked. "How is he able to leave? How can he just come and go as he pleases?"

"He doesn't have these." Albert reached through his shadows of canine snouts and tapped his forehead, indicating the device that had been inserted.

"So now what do we do?" Luke asked.

David glanced over to his son. The boy appeared as dejected as the others. His eyesight was only a little better. But both his core and the orange-red glow had increased, making his blotches of violet even smaller.

Savannah sighed. "I don't know about the rest of you, but I'm so tired of dealing with this." She raised an arm encased in the grotesque, lumpy darkness. "The more I fight it, the bigger it gets."

Albert nodded. "Same here. Why bother. If this is how we're wired, maybe we should just sit tight for the next twenty-four hours and be done with it."

David scowled at his own bubbling layer. Like the Reverend and his son's, it too had decreased, but not disappeared. "You're saying we shouldn't resist this?"

Albert replied, "You saw what happened when we tried."

Savannah agreed. "It's only one more day."

"How can you say that?" David argued. "Remember what he said happened to the others, to those subjects in his lab?"

Reverend Wyatt quietly nodded. "They were killed. The Presence was too great for them and they were destroyed."

"But . . . he wouldn't do that to us," Savannah said.

No one responded.

"What type of person would just arbitrarily wipe out a dozen human lives?"

David turned to her. "*He* would. I've seen him in action. If he keeps increasing the Presence, there's no assurance that it won't also kill us."

"... or save us."

All heads turned to Preacher Man. He sat off to the side. Like David, his shadow had thinned slightly. And, just as Reverend Wyatt still had his sword, he still had the mysterious disk hanging from his side. His eyes were red from crying, or maybe from the booze, or maybe both.

He spoke with his head lowered, his voice thick and gravelly, consonants blurred. "Maybe ... we're goin' 'bout things all wrong."

"What do you mean?" Albert asked.

"I mean, 'stead of tryin' to escape all this dark ugliness"—he stole a tentative glance at the Reverend—"or hacking away at it ... maybe we should try usin' the Presence to destroy it."

Albert snorted, "The Presence is what brought all this on in the first place."

"No," Preacher Man shook his head. "It just made us see what we already were."

David glanced at the Reverend, who was listening, thinking it through.

Preacher Man continued. "If we're talkin' about the Presence of God Almighty—it shouldn't be a bad thing." He licked his dry lips. "You saw what happened when we sang, how the room got all bright and these darker shells faded." He turned to David. "How your own darkness stopped attacking and started behavin' itself."

David stared at the man. It was true. Though the Presence had made his problem clearly visible ... it had also, for a brief moment, overpowered it.

Nubee spoke up. Of all the group, his core whiteness burned the brightest, which made his orange-red glow the most brilliant. "So you are saying that we should look for ways to *increase* the Presence?"

Preacher Man stared down at his hands.

"Or at least," David thought out loud, "figure how to use it."

"Sure," Albert scoffed, "get ourselves killed early and avoid the rush."

"Maybe." Reverend Wyatt turned to him. "But we also become what we eat."

"What's that supposed to mean?"

"It means instead of fighting the outside with our own strength . . . maybe we should be feeding the inside with His. You saw what happened when we sang."

"I also saw what it did to Rachel . . . and what it did to Starr."

Silence stole over the room.

Preacher Man quietly agreed. "Bein' in the Presence of God can be a scary thing." He looked to David. "Ain't that right, brother?"

David nodded, remembering his own experience in heaven . . . The Man he'd seen carved in light, the Man with the holes in His hands.

Nubee quoted softly, "'When I saw him, I fell at his feet as though dead.'"

"From Revelation again," the Reverend observed, "when the Lord appeared to the apostle John, one of His best friends."

Nubee nodded.

"And if that was His friend's reaction, one can only imagine what ours would be should He appear to us."

"And yet," David countered, "as you said, the Presence did reduce our darker shells. Right here in this very room, when we sang, they all but disappeared."

"You really believe it can be used for good?" Albert asked.

Again Nubee quoted, "'He is a destroyer of evil, but a blesser of good.'"

"'. . . a sharp, double-edged sword,'" Preacher Man agreed.

"Still . . ." Savannah turned back to Preacher Man. "No offense, but it really hasn't helped you that much, has it?"

He looked back down at his hands. "All I know is . . ." He slowed to a stop.

"What?" Albert asked. "What do you know?"

He tried again, his voice growing husky. "The love I got in my heart for Him . . . it's greater than any darkness of my soul."

David watched the man as he felt his own emotions rise.

"So where do we go from here?" Albert asked. "If this Presence thing can be used for good, how are we supposed to do it?"

It was another excellent question. One nobody could answer.

"What about prayer?" Nubee finally asked.

"What about it?" Savannah said.

"We have seen what singing to God can accomplish. Perhaps we should try praying to Him as well."

The idea surprised David. Not the idea, more the fact that they'd not thought of it earlier. He glanced around the room. Others appeared equally as surprised, Reverend Wyatt almost embarrassed. But no one was opposed. Maybe unconvinced, but not opposed.

"Sure." Albert shrugged. "Why not?" He turned to Reverend Wyatt. "Go ahead, do your thing."

The Reverend hesitated.

"What's wrong?"

"I am not certain. That is to say . . ."

David looked on. It was the first time he'd seen the man at a loss for words.

The Reverend cleared his throat and tried again. "Perhaps I am not the best suited to lead us in this type of prayer."

"What?" Albert asked.

"Perhaps there are others." He turned to Preacher Man, waiting until he looked up.

"Me?" Preacher Man asked, incredulous.

Reverend Wyatt nodded. "You were the one who sensed we should sing. You were the one who realized there was goodness in the Presence."

David looked on, seeing the new respect between the two. By the looks of things the Presence was doing a much deeper work than simply increasing glows and reducing shells.

Though touched by the gesture, Preacher Man shook his head. "No, brother . . . You're the man God has called."

"But—"

"You go ahead. You take the lead . . . we'll follow."

David smiled. Yes, sir, a *much* deeper work.

The Reverend cleared his throat. "All right then, let us pray." He bowed his head. The others followed. "Dear Lord . . . there is much here we do not understand, and yet we know this to be true. Thou doth love us. Thou doth love us and . . ."

As the man prayed, David began to hear other voices. Whisperings. He opened his eyes but saw nothing. Nothing except the increased brightness of those with the lit cores. And with that brightness came the increase of their orange-red glows . . . their brilliance once again filling the room.

". . . Thou doth promise to protect and defend . . ."

He stole a look over to Albert, who watched with equal interest.

". . . And now, oh Lord, we seek Thy help, we seek Thy assistance . . ."

A faint mist began to appear within the room's glow. With it came a sweet smell. Like incense.

". . . as to how we might best submit to Thy perfect . . ."

The glow grew brighter, the mist thicker.

"Show us what Thou would have us do. How we may best yield ourselves—"

The scream echoed from upstairs. David instantly recognized it. Before the others responded, he was on his feet, racing toward the steps. He took them two at a time until he reached the landing, where he turned and sprinted down the hallway toward Rachel's room.

he knew the Presence had increased. Not only because of the light and mist downstairs, but because of what he saw when he threw open Rachel's door.

She sat crouched in the far corner, sobbing, "I'm sorry ... I didn't ... I'm so sorry ..."

Directly in front of her hovered a brilliant white bird, wings extended, four, maybe five feet across. Although its back was to him, David immediately recognized it from his dream. But of course it was no bird—not with the legs, arms, and head of a human. It was an angel. And it was crying, wailing in rage.

"I know ..." Rachel wept. "I'm so sorry ..."

"Rachel?"

She turned to him, eyes red and swollen. "David! David, it's Jessica ... it's my baby!"

The angel swiveled its head around to David. It had the face of a baby—but cracked, broken. And when their eyes met, he felt a strange coldness. Something wasn't right. Besides the shattered face, the eyes were wrong. He'd seen those who'd crossed over to the other side, in the Garden, those who walked and dwelled in the Light. Their eyes sparkled with the Light's joy, with Its love. But these ... instead of joy and love, these eyes were filled with fear ... and hate.

The creature turned back to Rachel, increasing its cries, its screams.

"I know ..." Rachel's voice caught. "I'm sorry ..."

David looked on, scowling. This was no angel. What had Gita told him, what had she been so adamant about when he tried to contact his daughter? *"The dead do not return."* Isn't that what she'd said? Isn't that what the Bible taught? And didn't it also teach that angels were separate creatures from human beings? Hadn't he said that very thing to Rachel earlier, down by the stream?

His chill grew deeper.

"Rachel . . ." He wanted to get closer but didn't know how to move around the creature. "Listen to me. Rachel, that is not your daughter."

"Yes," she whispered, staring at it. "Of course she is—"

"No."

"Yes, and I killed her. Jerry didn't want to but I . . ."

"Rach—"

"I killed my baby and now I must pay."

"No, that's not true."

"There must be justice. 'This is the lesson that thou must learn, thou receives only what thou dost—'"

"No." He inched closer. "Remember what I said? About forgiveness—"

The creature wailed louder, drawing her attention.

He kneeled. "Rachel."

Her eyes faltered, then glanced past the thing to him.

"You're right, there must be justice. Someone must pay. But it doesn't have to be you."

The creature continued screaming.

David leaned in as close as he dare get. "That was the whole purpose for Jesus coming, remember? That's why He died on that—"

The creature shrieked, spinning back around to confront him. The sheer hatred in its face forced David back. Seeing his fear, the thing drifted closer, a flickering smile playing upon its lips. For the briefest second the image rippled, and David saw the face of an amphibian—the same type that had guarded the wormhole passages to the Lake of Fire. He rose to his feet, fighting to hold his ground, but the fear was too great.

It continued to approach, its smile curling into a malicious grin.

David forced himself to breathe. Then, despite the fear, he declared, "I know what you are."

The grin grew bigger.

"You're no angel. You're an imposter."

"Mommy must pay." Though its lips did not move, a child's voice came from within.

"She's not—" David took a breath. "She's not your mother."

"Jessica ..." Rachel rose unsteadily to her feet. "Sweetheart ..."

It turned to her. "Mommy hurt me."

"I know, honey ..."

"And now Mommy must pay."

"No!" David argued. "She's not your mother! And somebody else has already paid." He turned to Rachel. "Remember I said how Jesus Christ—"

Again the thing cut him off, this time with a roaring wail. David paused. That was the second time it reacted violently to the name of Christ. Was there a pattern? He remembered the same thing happening on the bluff with Preacher Man. Was there something about the name they feared? And Albert? The air rippling every time he spoke it, his mouth catching fire every time he misused it.

David tried again, this time shouting over the scream, "Jesus Christ paid for her—"

"Stop!" the baby cried.

"When He died on that—"

"Stop it!"

"David!" Rachel shouted. "You're hurting her!"

But he didn't stop. He'd found the chink in the armor and went for it. "When His blood paid for our sins—"

"STOP HIM! MOMMY, MAKE HIM—"

"DAVID!"

"—on that cross and—"

The wailing shook the floor, filling the room with blinding light.

"JESSICA . . . !"

The roar faded, the light dimmed, and Jessica was gone. But she was replaced by somebody else. Staring into the remaining light, David saw the form of a person. A petite Asian woman. One he immediately recognized as—

"Gita!" he cried.

She broke into her sweet, gentle smile. "David."

Overjoyed, he started for her, until she held out her hand to stop him. He slowed, less than three feet away. "What? Why are you—"

"I have been sent to help."

"I don't under—" He started for her again and again she held out her hand.

"It is important that you leave, David." Pointing at Rachel, she continued. "You must stay as far away from this woman as possible. She is evil."

"But—"

"She is evil and she must pay."

David turned to Rachel. "That's—that's not true. Anybody can be forgiven. All they have—"

"She *cannot* be forgiven!"

He turned back to her. "But . . . what about Jesus Christ, what about—"

At the sound of the name, Gita's image rippled slightly, her voice taking an edge. "David, please. She is not worthy to even hear that name. She has killed her baby. She has tortured and murdered her only child!"

David's scowl deepened. It didn't add up. Was it possible that some people could *not* be forgiven? He tried again. "But Jesus Christ—"

"David!"

There it was again. The impatience. The fear. As on the bluff. As with the baby. He tried again. "Didn't Jesus Christ—"

"Stop it!" Gita demanded.

David's heart sank. As much as this looked like Gita, as much as he wanted it to be her, he knew it wasn't. He tried one last time. "Didn't Jesus Christ say—"

"Stop it! Stop it!"

He paused, deeply saddened. And, though he wanted her to stay, though he longed for her to remain present, he took a step forward and resumed. "Jesus Christ who—"

She covered her ears. "STOP IT!"

"—died on the cross, who—"

"*STOOPPPP* . . ." As she screamed, the pitch of her voice lowered, the word lengthening, drawing out . . . until the room again exploded in light. And smoke. Dark, ominous smoke.

Coughing, straining to see through the haze, David finally spotted Rachel. She held her hand to her mouth, staring in horror at a dozen smaller creatures surrounding her on the floor—two to three feet tall, with long sharp claws, exposed fangs, and gargoyle-like faces.

From the center of the group, the largest turned to him and snarled. "What have you to do with us, servant of the Most High?"

David tried swallowing, but his mouth had gone bone dry.

"You with the dark, murderous shadow." The voice was deep and guttural, similar but not identical to what he'd heard from Starr on the bluff. "Look at your darkness. Who do you think you are, speaking of forgiveness?"

In spite of himself, David glanced to his chest. His dark, bubbling light was still there. *Still there*. After all he'd been through, after all that he tried, and sang, and read, and prayed, it still remained. Forgiveness. What did he know of the subject? Who was he to speak of it? He of all people?

The creature broke into another grin. "You are a fool, David Kauffman. You are a failure."

David looked up, startled at the tone and words. Weren't they exactly what it had said to Preacher Man? And the response, what was the old man's response? "That's right . . ." His voice caught and he tried again, repeating what he remembered. "But I'm *His* failure, aren't I?"

Fear crossed the creature's face—the same fear it had shown toward Preacher Man. And that was all David needed.

Taking a breath for resolve, he finished the quote, "Bought and paid for by the Blood of the Lamb."

The creatures shuddered. More confirmation.

David took another step.

The leader growled a warning. "The thing is ours since its childhood. It will always be ours."

"No. She can be forgiven."

Struggling to hold his position, the leader hissed, "*Ours*. It will always be *ours*."

"Only if she wants to be." David took another step. The group cowered, huddling together, as frightened of him as he was of them. But not him. He'd already guessed the source of their fear. "Jesus Christ died on the cross for anyone, no matter what they've—"

"FAILURE!" The leader puffed its gills, blustering.

"Yes, I am." He looked over to Rachel. "And He still loves me. He loves me just as much as He loves—"

"Don't listen to him! He is a failure! He knows nothing!"

Almost smiling, David turned and repeated another one of Preacher Man's responses. "I know Who I belong to. I know what He's done for me." He turned to Rachel, softer. "And He can do the same for you. Your past doesn't matter. All you see here, all you're listening to is guilt. And He's already paid for—"

"SILENCE!"

"He's already paid for it, Rachel. Justice has already been served." David saw tears welling up in her eyes, knew he was getting through. "Jesus Christ has paid—"

"DON'T LISTEN TO HIM! HE IS A FAILURE!"

"All you have to do is ask. He will forgive anybody of anything."

She wiped her face, a trace of hope glimmering in her eyes.

"Just ask . . ."

She opened her mouth.

David smiled. "That's right. He'll do the rest. He already has."

At last she parted her lips, starting to speak ... when the room suddenly roared with wind. The creatures moved together, condensing into something larger. A man. Lying on his back. Filthy. Naked. Covered in blood. Nailed to a cross. Suddenly Rachel's hands were covered in that blood, holding a hammer and spike. She recoiled, screaming. The image fluttered and changed. Now it was her baby, little Jessica nailed to the cross, crying, writhing, Rachel covered in blood from the wounds of her little hands and her little feet.

The image was more than Rachel could bear. She screamed again, then again, unable to stop. She dropped the hammer and spike. They clanged to the floor, as the baby joined her screams.

"Rachel ..." David kneeled beside her. "Rachel!"

She could not hear; she could only stare at the baby, at her little wounds—

"Rachel ..."

—at her own bloody hands.

Laughter filled the room.

Overwhelmed, she wrapped her hands around her knees, pulling herself into a little ball, burying her face. As she did, the image of the baby collapsed, tumbling back into the group of gargoyles.

"She is ours," the leader taunted from the center.

Rachel began to sob.

"She is ours, and we are hers."

The sobs wracked her body.

"There is no forgiveness. Not for someone who tortures and murders their only child. You are ours, and we are yours. Isn't that right, dear? Forever and ever. Isn't that right? *Isn't that right?*"

David watched as, amidst the sobs, Rachel began to nod.

The laughter increased as the creatures dissolved into a thick black cloud that rose from the floor and wrapped around her—the same swirling darkness that had encompassed her for so many hours ... for so many years.

uke had continued in silent prayer after Reverend Wyatt had finished, after the group had broken up. And, to his surprise, as he sat in the quiet of the room asking for direction, he actually got something. It wasn't anything big or flashy, no singing angelgrams in the sky, no burning rose bushes. Just a type of . . . inner nudge. One that he was now asking Nubee about.

"Like a still, small voice?" Nubee questioned as Luke wheeled him down the hall toward Albert's room.

"Yeah, sort of. I mean it really wasn't a voice, more like . . . a knowing."

"You were still, and you knew."

"Yeah, like when I was in the woods. I was still and I knew."

"Cuul . . ."

Luke had to laugh in spite of himself. With all the changes, the guy really was funny . . . and smart. But there was something else. Nubee's orange-red glow had begun taking a distinct shape. It was no longer some vague light sitting upright within his body. In the past hour its edges had become sharper, forming something. Something Luke didn't recognize, not yet, but he figured he would, sooner than later.

"And that impression, it is telling you to go to Albert?"

"I think by working together, like you said, I think me and him can track down that hum. Remember, he said it was different from the electronic leash? And when we were down at the bluff it was like a thousand times louder. I know something's down there and I know the two of us can . . ."

As they arrived outside Albert's room, Luke slowed to a stop. Beyond the blur of the open door, he saw the ominous dark glows. Even with his bad eyes, he recognized Albert's snapping jaws, could see them tearing into another, even darker glow—ripping and gulping. A darker glow that, by its enormous bulk, could only belong to Savannah. But, strangely enough, the more he tore into her, the larger she grew . . . and the smaller he became.

"Albert, what are you doing?"

He looked up, his shadows snarling. Without a word he rose, crossed toward them—

"Albert—"

—and closed the door in Luke's face.

The boy stood a moment, more sad than angry. He knew what had happened. Albert had quit the fight. Like he'd said down at the meeting, he'd finally given in to his darkness. And Savannah? With her greed for money and possessions, he doubted the man was feeding upon her for free. In fact, by the way her shadow had grown since he'd last seen her, and the way Albert's had shrunk, Luke knew his tearing and devouring carried a heavy cost . . . for both of them.

"Well," Nubee said, "so much for that still, small voice."

But a second choice had already surfaced in Luke's mind. A choice he'd tried to ignore earlier, but would not go away. With a heavy sigh he answered, "Not necessarily."

"Really?" Nubee asked in feigned ignorance. "Who else is there to help you? Not Preacher Man; he is too intoxicated. Not Reverend Wyatt; he is too old. I wonder who . . ."

Luke turned the chair around and headed the opposite direction. "Spare me your sarcasm."

"Oh, yes, of course. Your father! Now why didn't I think of that?"

Not bothering to look at him, Luke replied, "You already did."

Nubee glanced up and grinned. "So did you, my friend. So did you."

Preacher Man stood, staring at the bottles and cut glass decanters on his dresser. Once again, Orbolitz's men had filled them to the top with their rich browns, their glowing ambers, their sparkling clearness. He closed his eyes. It was just a matter of time. He could resist an hour, maybe two, but eventually he'd step into their powerful whirlpool and be sucked back into the never-ending spiral. He glanced down to the faint image of the disc by his side. The shield of faith—he'd known what it was the moment he'd seen it. Others had asked, but he'd remained silent, hoping in his pride that when the time was right, he'd step forward and use it, show them how a real man of God operated.

But now it was barely visible. Useless.

He noticed movement in the mirror and looked up to see Reverend Wyatt standing in his doorway. More of his hood had dissolved into the orange-red glow. A glow that was taking on the definition of a much younger man.

Nodding to the bottles, Reverend Wyatt asked, "They're still here?"

"Yes . . . and they'll always be."

"I'm sorry."

Preacher Man looked to him, speaking before he could stop himself. "Got another Word from the Lord, brother?"

The Reverend's wince immediately made him sorry.

"I have just left Albert's room. Savannah is there." He hesitated, then continued. "They . . . have given up." He sighed in defeat. "Nothing I have said was of any help to them. As I have with you, I've succeeded only in inflicting more guilt . . . and more pain."

Preacher Man saw the remorse, believed it was real. "What about Rachel?"

The Reverend slowly shook his head.

"And David?"

"His struggle also continues. Everyone's struggle continues. Odd, isn't it? Here I am with all the answers, and yet I have been of help to no one." He looked down at his sword, then reached for it. It gave a resounding ring as he pulled it from its scabbard. He raised it before him, examining the glow, which now appeared to be words and letters.

Its very presence made Preacher Man cautious and uneasy.

Examining it, Reverend Wyatt quietly quoted: "'Nevertheless I have somewhat against thee . . . thou hast left thy first love. Remember therefore from whence thou art fallen, and repent, and do the first works . . .'" He paused a moment. Then, more softly, continued. "I used to love like you . . . reckless . . . passionate. I'd have done anything for Him."

Preacher Man looked on surprised, but remained silent.

"Then, somehow, the doing . . . somehow it replaced the loving." He blinked back the growing sheen in his eyes. "'I have somewhat against thee . . . thou hast left thy first love.'" He swallowed. At last his gaze shifted to Preacher Man. He spoke only two words, quietly, earnestly, "Help me."

Preacher Man turned from the mirror to face him. "Me, help you? With all of my sins, with all that I'm doing?"

"It's not just—" Reverend Wyatt cleared his throat and quietly repeated Preacher Man's earlier words. "It's not just the doing, my friend . . . it's the abiding." More gently, he added, "The doing is what follows." He looked again at the sword. Slowly, he lowered it to the ground. "With enough pride, with enough willpower, anyone can *do*."

Preacher Man waited until the man raised his eyes to meet his. Softly, he answered, "With enough weakness anyone can *abide*."

"How?" The Reverend's voice grew to a raspy whisper. "I have forgotten. Please . . . show me . . . how."

eleven

"**a**re you hearing anything now?"

"No, Dad."

David nodded as they continued down the hill toward the small flat area and the bluff beyond. "It gets pretty steep here, lots of moss, so be careful not to—"

"I can see that, Dad. It's not like I'm totally blind." He threw in another sigh just to make sure his father got the point.

David let it pass. He knew it had been hard for Luke to suggest the two of them work together. And now, having to hang on to his father's arm, being led around the forest like a child, well, few things could be tougher ... unless, of course, it was being the father to the son it was being so tough on.

Still, David was grateful for the opportunity. Once they'd gotten Rachel to bed and she'd fallen into a fitful sleep, Nubee had assured him he could look after her. Now the two of them were outside with the hopes of finding some way of escape ... and if they were lucky, not killing each other in the process.

"How 'bout now?"

"No, Dad."

"Are you sure. 'Cause we're—"

"I don't hear a thing."

"But we're reaching the bottom of the hill. The cliff is only a few dozen—"

"Wait a minute, you're right. I do hear something."

"Yeah? What? What does it sound like? What does—"

"It sounds like someone who can't keep quiet long enough to let me listen."

David closed his mouth. Fine. He wouldn't say another word. He'd answer only when spoken to. And if Luke chose not to speak (and those chances were pretty high), then so be it. Of course, it hadn't always been like that. In his younger days, Luke was an incessant chatterbox—ADHD on caffeine. It came in handy when they had to hold their own against Emily and her mother—two women who always left them in the dust with their verbal skills, not to mention their loopy female logic. But gradually, as they ran out of women, Luke ran out of words.

He stole another glance at his son. In the past hour, Luke's blotches of darkness had all but disappeared. His center core had continued to brighten, and his surrounding orange-red glow had begun to solidify. It was still taking shape and definition, but from what David could see, the glow of the gangly man/boy was being replaced by a full-grown man. His chest had become wide and muscular, his glowing legs thick and solid. It was hard to see for certain, but he appeared to be wearing some sort of jersey and running shorts. And on his head, he wore a hat or crown. No, not a crown, a wreath.

"There," Luke half whispered.

"What?"

"Shhh . . ." He turned to the right, toward the bluff.

David searched the ground, looking for any markings, any clues. He could stand for a lot more information, but this was Luke's show, he was in charge. The thought made him uneasy, particularly in matters so serious, but there was nothing he could do. He hated the lack of control, the feeling of dependence. Yet, somewhere in the back of his mind, he knew it was just the beginning of reversing roles. Someday this would be the norm. He hated that thought even more.

"Hold it." They slowed to a stop amidst the outlying debris of the rock slide.

David glanced around. "Which way—left, right? Maybe we should keep—"

"Shhh . . ."

David nodded, silently rebuking himself.

"It's everywhere now."

"What?"

Luke started forward. David followed, this time more successful in remaining quiet. They picked their way around the rocks and boulders until they came to a stop directly before the slide. Luke turned, scowling. He took a tentative step to the left, then to the right. "Don't you hear that?" he asked. "I can't believe you don't hear that."

David strained but heard nothing. "Too much Led Zeppelin in my younger days."

Luke's scowl deepened as he slowly zeroed in, this way then that, until he was facing the slide again. "Here."

"It's under the rock slide?"

"It's the strongest here."

"Are you sure, because—"

"It's the strongest here."

David nodded, squinting into the setting sun. At its highest, the slide rose ten, twelve feet above their heads—mostly dirt and boulders along with fallen trees, uprooted ferns, and underbrush. Everything smelled of dust and damp earth. Off to their left, thirty or forty feet, it melded into the hillside. To their right it continued several more yards before fanning out and coming to an end a dozen feet from the bluff's edge.

"Do you see anything?" Luke asked.

David shook his head. "Everything is just like we left it. Nothing of any—" A glint of metal caught his eyes. It came from within the slide, at the base of two large boulders.

"What?"

"Hang on." He started up the pile of rock and debris. The first couple steps were loose and he slid as much as climbed.

"Dad . . ." There was that exasperation again.

"I think I saw something." He finally got his footing and scampered up to a large rock.

But the reflection was gone, lost in shadow. He continued forward, keeping his eye locked on where he'd last seen it. All around him stones clattered and dirt sifted, but he made certain each step was safe before taking it . . . until the dirt wedged between two fallen trees gave way. He cried out as he fell between them, managing to catch himself by his armpits with a painful grunt.

"Dad!"

He hung there, feet kicking, until he found a foothold.

"Are you all right? Dad!"

"Yeah," he gasped. "I'm okay." With effort, he dragged himself up until he was straddling one of the logs.

"Be careful!"

"I'm all right."

"You've got to be more careful!"

He was surprised at the emotion in his son's voice.

"Maybe we should go back. Maybe we should get someone else to—"

"Luke, I'm okay." He turned but couldn't see his son through the branches.

"Just be careful."

"Right." He rose to his feet, took a step or two, then jumped to the first boulder safely . . . until it started to shift.

"Dad!"

He fought to keep his balance as it continued to move. He did not see the smaller tree swing around behind him until it caught him in the knees, knocking his legs out from under him. He fell hard, grasping at the slippery rock, as he slid down between the boulders.

"DAD!"

He hit the ground, trying to break the fall with his arms. A good idea except for the pain that shot through his left wrist. But he had little time to worry about it as his head flew back, slamming hard into the boulder directly behind him.

Preacher Man mused sadly as they sat together in his room—one broken-down black evangelist, one old, stuffed-shirt white guy. Two servants of God from opposite worlds, both lost in defeat.

"There were times He seemed so real," Reverend Wyatt was saying, "when I accomplished so much. Like becoming district supervisor, or teaching at the seminary. I even managed to author a book or two that—" He caught himself, then sadly shook his head. "I'm merely proving my point, aren't I?"

Preacher Man smiled. "Nothin' wrong with bein' smart."

"I'm not so sure."

Preacher Man gave him a look.

"While you Peter types are throwing your legs over the side of the boat and walking on water, we Thomases are in the back searching the Scriptures for less risky forms of ecumenical transportation."

Preacher Man smiled sadly. "We Peters may be the first to walk on water"—he glanced over to the bottles on the dresser—"but we're also the first to do the sinking."

Barely hearing, Reverend Wyatt quietly quoted, "'Love the Lord thy God with all thy heart and with all thy soul and with all thy mind.'" He took a breath, then quietly added, "Sometimes I'm afraid I've only given Him my mind. As if I'm educated beyond my faith, beyond what He can use."

"Hogwash."

The Reverend looked up.

"I'd give anything to have your brains and education. And as far as what He can use ... Know who my favorite role model is in the Bible?"

"Peter?"

"Nope."

"David?"

"Wrong again. Balaam's jackass."

Reverend Wyatt smiled.

"I'm serious. If God can use a jackass to accomplish His purposes, I know I qualify. And, no offense, brother, so do you."

The Reverend chuckled politely. "I'm not so sure of that."

"Course you do. Go ahead, name me another."

"Another?"

"You talked 'bout teachin' kids and overseein' stuff. Name me another time He used you."

"I really don't think now is the—"

"Bible says we're saved by the blood of the Lamb *and* the testimony of our lips."

"Well, yes, but—"

"So go ahead, testify. Give me some testimony."

Reverend Wyatt eyed him a moment as if checking his sincerity.

Preacher Man nodded. "Go ahead now. Testify."

"Well, let's see . . . last year, despite the worst year of giving for our diocese, we somehow managed to keep the inner-city lunch program going."

"That's good. Feeding the hungry. What else you got?"

"What else?"

"Go ahead now."

"I suppose . . . there was that unwed mother's home we started, despite some rather impossible zoning restrictions—"

"'Whatever you do for the least of these you do for me.' That's what I'm talkin' about. And God was right there, wasn't He? Workin' alongside you . . . doin' most of the heavy liftin', I imagine."

The Reverend slowly nodded, beginning to see the picture. He looked back at Preacher Man. "What about you?"

"Me?"

"How has He used you?"

"Nothing big like you're talkin' bout. Most of mine's just on the streets, preachin' to folks who don't listen and don't care."

"But you've met with some success."

"Sure. Some strung-out druggie, some kid dying of AIDS, but—"

"'What you do for the least . . .'"

It was Preacher Man's turn to smile. "You got me there. Your turn. How else you seen God use you . . . in spite of you."

"In spite of me? Well, now, that should be easy. Let's see . . ."

And so it continued . . . two old warriors remembering their battles, some nearly forgotten, recounting the victories God had given.

"It's like them altars that folks built in the Old Testament," Preacher Man said. "How they reminded them of God's faithfulness."

"I am afraid I don't understand."

"We're just buildin' ourselves some verbal altars, that's all."

And it was true. The more they recalled God's faithfulness, the more real it became—the more real *He* became. So real that Preacher Man actually found himself thinking less and less about drink. So real that during one of their lulls, he had started humming again. Softly at first, but eventually breaking into words:

"*Holy, holy, holy. Lord God Almighty.*
Early in the morning our song shall rise to Thee."

Reverend Wyatt looked at him a moment, then quietly joined in—a bit hesitant, a bit self-conscious. His voice was thin and reedy, his sense of pitch no better than Preacher Man's. But it didn't seem to matter . . .

"Holy, holy, holy. Merciful and mighty.
God in three Persons, blessed Trinity."

As they sang, Preacher Man noticed both of their center cores growing brighter until they flooded into their orange-red glows—which also grew, bursting through the remains of their violet shells and slowly stretching toward one another.

"Holy, holy, holy! all the saints adore Thee,
Casting down their golden crowns around the glassy
    sea;
Cherubim and seraphim falling down before Thee,
Which were and art and evermore shalt be."

Soon, their glows merged, filling the entire room with brightness until Preacher Man could no longer see where his ended and the Reverend's began.

"Holy, holy, holy! Lord God Almighty!
All Thy works shall praise Thy name in earth and
    sky and sea;
Holy, holy, holy! Merciful and mighty!
God in three Persons, blessed Trinity!"

At last the song came to an end. But neither man moved. Instead, they sat quietly in the silence, basking in the light . . . abiding in the Presence. It wasn't until Preacher Man opened his eyes that he saw the Reverend's violet shell had completely vanished. So had his. Their orange-red glows had also changed. They had come together forming an even brighter light—an image—the single and distinct form of a man—a giant, blazing with brilliance. He stood between them, nine maybe ten feet tall, looking much like a Greek or Roman warrior, with helmet, sword, and shield. The sword that had once been the Reverend's, and the shield that had once belonged to Preacher Man.

dad ..." Luke's voice floated into his consciousness—
along with the throbbing pain of his left arm and one
doozy of a headache.

"Dad ... can you hear me?"

He sounded concerned, maybe in trouble—enough to
force David to open his eyes. It was darker now and he was
covered in dirt. The two boulders loomed above him. On
top of one, he saw the silhouette of his son, lying on his
stomach, calling down to him.

"Dad ..."

"I'm—" He coughed the dust from his throat and tried
again. "I'm okay." It was a lie, but necessary, considering
the anxiety in Luke's voice. Then he heard something else.
Behind him. A hissing sound. He sat up, put too much
weight on his hand, and swallowed back a yell. The hissing
continued. He turned to his left and saw the source. Dirt
was sifting away, slipping into a hole two to three feet in
diameter, its edges outlined by ... metal. Jagged, galvanized
metal. Not far away, he spotted the remains of what looked
like the top of an air vent, sheered off and crushed.

"Dad ..."

He motioned for silence. As quietly as possible, he
pulled himself from the dirt and crawled toward the hole.
A blue-greenness glowed from within it.

"What is it?" Luke whispered.

He arrived but still had no answer. Careful of the torn
metal, he eased his head into the opening. Directly beside
his face, along what looked like a ceiling, ran several pipes
and cables. They continued through a long shaft. He looked
down to the floor, guessed it to be about seven feet below,
though it was hard to tell from the growing mound of dirt
and debris filling it. He removed his head and swiveled his
feet around to the opening, this time taking more care with
his arm.

"You're not going in there!" Luke whispered.

He looked up. "Yeah."

"You don't know what's there!"

"That's the whole point." He carefully placed his feet into the opening, down until it touched the mound of dirt.

"Dad!" The desperation in his son's voice stopped him. "You can't go in there. You could get hurt."

"It's a tunnel. I'll be okay, I'll—"

"No! You're all that's left. You can't leave!"

David slowed to a stop.

"Don't . . ." The boy's voice clogged with emotion.

David pulled his legs from the hole and with some difficulty lumbered to his feet. "Son . . . are you all right?"

The boy wiped his face but did not answer.

"Luke?"

He sniffed, wiping his face again.

It was the most emotion David had seen since Emily's death, and it made his own throat tighten. "Listen, you and I . . . we both know there's something down there, a passageway or something. It's what you heard and maybe it's the way out of here."

"Yeah, but—"

"If I go down there, we might be able to get out."

"It doesn't have to be you, it can"—Luke's voice cracked—"it can be somebody else."

"I'm already here, we don't have time to—"

"You're all I got!"

David stopped. Understanding suddenly flooded in . . . and his heart broke. How could he have been so stupid? He tried to answer but could not.

"You're all . . ." Tears swallowed the boy's voice.

David stood a moment looking up at his child. This was the old Luke, the Luke who had loved him so fiercely. That *still* loved him fiercely. It had never left. The silence, the walls, the sarcasm . . . they were merely defenses, just ways to protect that love. *You're all I got.* The distancing, the attitude—simply protection. David lowered his head, touching his own eyes. When he trusted his voice, he looked back up. "Luke ..."

The boy sniffed.

"Son ..."

"I know." He sniffed again. "I know, I know ..."

"Are you sure? Because I won't go, if—"

"No, you gotta go."

"Not if you don't want me to. If you don't want me to I'll—"

"I said go, didn't I?"

"But—"

"Go. Go. How many times do I have to say it. Hurry and go."

David watched another moment as the boy continued to struggle. Then, when he was certain Luke had control, he turned back toward the hole. He spotted a broken branch and grabbed it. It would serve nicely as a staff ... or club. "I won't be long, I promise."

"Whatever."

David stepped into the opening and onto the mound of dirt. "I'll be back."

"Go. Go."

He nodded. Slowly he slid down with the dirt. Then, just before his head disappeared inside, he heard, "Dad?"

He stopped himself. "Yeah?"

"Be careful, all right?"

"I will, son. You have my word."

The boy nodded.

David held his look, returned the nod, then lowered his head and dropped into the blue-green darkness.

Orbolitz's visit with Dirk Helgeland in the control center had taken less than ten minutes. In that time the head of operations had adjusted the goggles to a higher filtering factor, as Orbolitz watched Albert's image on the surveillance monitors. The computer whiz kid had finally managed to seduce the ex-model—or she him, it was hard to tell with those two. And though the gruntings and ruttings of animal lust always fascinated Orbolitz, he had been more concerned about getting back to the lodge. After all, this was the crucial time, when the Presence was approaching peak power, when the subjects would choose their final passions—the ones that would follow them into eternity. For some, like those he'd seen in the fiery lake, it would be an earthly passion that they would forever desire, forever embrace. For others, it would be their passion for the Almighty, forever desiring Him, forever embracing Him.

Of all the current manifestations, it was Rachel McPherson's that most intrigued him. Unfortunately, there was nothing he had been able to see on the monitors. Like the others, her images would simply not register. So, as soon as Dirk had adjusted his goggles, he headed back up to the lodge, making sure her room was the first he visited. He didn't bother to knock but simply donned the goggles and opened the door to see what he would see.

He was not disappointed.

She lay on the bed, feverishly tossing her head. And for good reason. Nearly a dozen creatures stood scattered on her chest, her arms, belly, and thighs. Each clawed and tore into her orange-red glow, ravenously feasting and gulping down what little of her light remained. He'd seen these things before, hundreds of times in the VR chamber and from past observations of other subjects. Subjects unable to live with their guilt and mistakes, subjects whose souls were literally eaten alive. Just as David Kauffman was being consumed by his churning shadow of hate and unforgiveness, so Rachel McPherson was being consumed by her own self-hatred and unforgiveness.

Beside her, in the wheelchair, sat the crippled kid. He glowed so brightly that it was impossible to see where the white inner core stopped and his orange-red glow began. To further confuse the issue, the orange-red glow had taken on a distinct definition, sitting tall and erect, so strong and muscular that the wheelchair appeared unnecessary. As Orbolitz entered the room, the kid was speaking to her with confidence and authority.

"David is right. God does wish to forgive you. Jesus Christ does wish to—"

The sound of the name sent Rachel's creatures howling, gnashing, and tearing into her more desperately. She jerked her head from side to side, gasping, crying out through gritted teeth, "You don't know what I've done. What awful things I've—"

"That is why it must be God's death. Only God's suffering is enough to pay for our sins."

"But I . . . I . . ."

"It is not about you, Rachel McPherson. It is about Him. It is about *His* love."

"I . . . can't—"

"That is correct. You cannot bear it. Only He can. And He has. Jesus Christ has—"

Rachel screamed, shrieking in pain.

Undaunted, Nubee spoke louder. "He has done it all, Rachel! All you need do is give Him permission!"

She panted, gasping.

"Allow Him. You cannot bear it. It must be *Him*. Allow *Him*."

She continued tossing her head but had quit arguing. Orbolitz took a step closer to watch.

Her lips began to move. Quickly. Silently.

Nubee cocked his head to the side, listening. He turned to Orbolitz. "Do you hear that?"

"What she's saying?"

"No . . ." He looked around the room. "That . . . singing."

Orbolitz strained to listen but heard nothing. The goggles were only good for sight, not sound. But, at the moment, sight was more than enough. For as he watched, he began to see a fog filling the room. Effervescent, swirling. At first he thought it was a trick of the goggles. But Nubee saw it too. As it thickened, it grew brighter, taking on a pink, rosy hue. And the brighter it grew, the more alarmed the creatures atop Rachel became. They tore into her more frantically, obviously trying to make her stop. She grimaced, she gasped, she writhed . . . but her lips continued to move.

Nubee smiled. He leaned toward her, speaking softly. "That is correct, Rachel McPherson. Ask. Simply ask and He will do the rest. Simply give Him permission."

Orbolitz continued watching, listening, having no idea what to expect . . .

twelve

david moved along the shaft, every sense alive. He strained to hear the buzz Luke had talked about but could hear nothing . . . except his breathing and the scrape of his feet against the rough concrete floor. He expected the air to be damp and stale like a cave. Instead it was surprisingly dry. A row of fluorescent tubes lined the ceiling, along with pipes, conduit, and cable. Ten feet ahead rose several steps. They led to a brown metal door. He arrived, glanced over his shoulder, and headed up them. Transferring the branch/staff to his bad hand, he reached out to a smooth lever-handle and pressed down. It gave a soft click and the door opened a crack. A breeze rushed through as he cautiously pushed it farther.

To his surprise he was standing outside again, surrounded by brush, several giant boulders, and a darkening sky. He was still on the flat section just before the bluff but appeared to be on the opposite side of the rock slide. He glanced at the door and saw the outside had been camouflaged in textured foam and painted to blend in. But why? Why build a tunnel to here? He turned and looked back into the shaft. Only then did he realize that he must be standing at its entrance. Of course. He'd simply gone the wrong direction, heading out of the shaft instead of in. He shook his head and stepped back inside, closing the door behind him.

Moving back down the steps, he retraced his route. He approached the mound of dirt that he'd originally slid down and pressed against the concrete wall, climbing up and over the smallest portion of debris.

"Dad, that you?"

Odd, he'd barely made a sound, and yet Luke had heard. He peered up toward the opening and whispered, "Yes."

"What'd you find?"

"Nothing yet."

"Be careful."

"Right."

He stepped off the mound and continued down the passageway. The best he figured he was heading into the hill now. Some twenty feet ahead lay another door, similar to the first but with no steps. Everything had grown strangely quiet, even his bubbling glow. In fact, the deeper he walked inside, the less of his light he saw or heard. And by the time he arrived at the door, the glow had completely disappeared.

He placed his good hand on the lever and pressed down. Another soft click. Then, taking a breath for courage, he pushed it open.

Before him stood a small room with a low ceiling, lit only by the blue, flickering aura of television screens. It reminded him of a TV control room with its rows and rows of monitors filling the wall. Directly in front of him, before the monitors, stretched a long black console with glowing white and red buttons. Not three feet away, an operator in short blonde hair sat with her back to him, watching the screens.

To her right, at the end of the console, stood four metal racks about six feet tall. Inside them were what looked like home computers stacked on top of each other. David knew from experience that these were how supercomputers were made—not giant colossus machines, with flashing lights and swirling gizmos, but simple, home-type computers wired to run parallel with each other. Beside the racks stood a large, pleasant-looking man with red hair and a bushy beard. Next to him sat a balding worker at a smaller console with fewer monitors.

"And a good evening to you, Mr. Kauffman." The man with the beard had turned to him. "I see you have discovered us."

"Who . . ." David cleared his throat. "Who are you?"

The man pressed an intercom switch on the wall beside him. "Martini, Tanner. We'll be needing you at the Control Room stat, please. We have ourselves a visitor." He returned to David. "I'm Dirk Helgeland, the head of this little operation. I spoke to you and the rest of the group yesterday when Mr. Orbolitz arrived."

David had forgotten the name, but remembered the Irish lilt.

"And how, might I ask, did you find us?"

"There was a . . . rock slide."

"Ah, the rock slide." Helgeland glanced to the wall of monitors. "The thing's knocked out some of our cameras."

David followed his gaze to the screens. As he looked closer he recognized locations in and around the lodge. The kitchen, the dining room, the hallway. Another monitor showed Albert's bedroom, with Albert and Savannah collapsed on the bed in exhausted sleep. Oddly enough, neither showed any signs of their dark glow. Another monitor displayed Preacher Man's room. Reverend Wyatt had joined him. The two were kneeling, heads bowed. Again, neither showed any light or glows. More monitors displayed more rooms, as well as the porch, and numerous outside locations—including, down in the far corner, the image of his son. He'd wandered from the rock slide and was closer to the bluff.

"So this is . . ." David cleared his throat again.

"The center of our little operation."

"How many of you are there?"

"The staff? We've got ourselves two shifts plus a couple support folk. The sleeping facilities are down a ways, just a short stroll from here—though I'm afraid that slide means we'll have to be taking the longer route through the generator shaft." He glanced back to study the smaller bank of monitors before him.

"Generator?" David asked.

"Um?"

"You said generator?"

He returned his attention to David. "That's right. We had to make ourselves a little hydroelectric plant. No choice, the way those towers suck up the power."

"Towers?"

"They're kinda like microwave towers. We've got them disguised all around the property. It's how we've been broadcasting the Presence into you people."

David frowned, not entirely understanding.

"That's what your son climbed. And that buzz he's been talking about, it's nothing but the cables running from our power source out to the towers."

"And the electronic fence or whatever it is—the one you buried in the ground to keep us here?"

"Same principle, different frequencies, though with a bit of a kick, if you know what I mean. Listen, I'd love to chat, but we're coming up to the final phase of this little get-together, so if you wouldn't mind to be taking a seat till my associates show up, I'd appreciate it."

David remained standing.

"There!" The balding technician near Helgeland pointed at the screen before him. "See the similarities?"

Helgeland stared a moment, then turned to the woman behind the longer console. "Jennie, would you be bringing up the McPherson room on your screen, please?"

She hit a switch and Rachel McPherson's room filled one of two larger screens at the center of the monitor wall. On it David could see Rachel still lying in bed. She was sweaty and worn but no longer had any light or shadows.

The same was true for Nubee, who sat beside her in his wheelchair, and Orbolitz, who stood near the door.

"What happened to their glows?" David asked.

"None of that registers on video. All we've been able to record and transmit are your reactions."

David turned back to the screen. All three of the people in Rachel's room were looking around, their faces filled with a type of wonder and awe. "What is it?" he asked. "What's going on?"

"If I'm not mistaken, it's the calm before the storm."

"Storm?"

Helgeland called to the woman technician, "Jennie, would you mind bringing up Mr. Ingram, please?"

She nodded, reached over, and pressed one of the lit buttons. An older patient in a white hospital gown appeared on the other large monitor beside Rachel's.

Helgeland explained, "That's Mr. Ingram, one of our volunteers back at the lab. I believe Mr. Orbolitz explained that in the beginning we made ourselves a few mistakes. Besides subjecting them to the unnatural laboratory environment, we exposed them far too quickly to the Presence."

"The same Presence we're experiencing?"

Helgeland nodded. "Back in the lab, at about the 90–95 percent mark, the subjects all had . . . well, they all had a nasty habit of blowing up on us."

"Blowing up?"

"So to speak." He motioned to a large digital display at the bottom of the monitor wall. "You see that readout there?"

The glowing blue numbers read:

87.55%

"That's the intensity you folks are experiencing now." Turning to the woman he said, "Would you mind giving me a close-up on the young man, Jennie?"

She reached for another control. The camera zoomed in on Nubee.

Helgeland continued. "Do you see the similarities of his expression and Mr. Ingram's?"

David stared at the two monitors. Both men's faces were filled with reverent awe.

"Now, fast forward to Mr. Ingram at 95 percent."

"He expired at 93," the technician replied.

"Then how about giving us a look at 91 percent."

The technician adjusted a control and Ingram's image flickered to a completely different expression. Now his eyes were wide in fear, his face filled with terror. There was no sound, but it was clear he was screaming as he fought against the leather restraints holding his arms.

"And 92 percent, please."

Another flicker. His eyes were bulging, his body convulsing.

"Is that . . ." David swallowed. "Are you saying that's going to happen to Nubee?"

"That's what we're here to be finding out."

"But you're saying there's a possibility it will happen to him?"

"Mr. Kauffman, there's a possibility it will be happening to all of you."

The matter-of-fact tone in the man's voice made David grow cold. He stared at the screen as the seizures grew more violent.

Suddenly the door behind Helgeland opened and two large men entered. Smaller than Orbolitz's bodyguards, they were still big enough to ensure they were used to getting their way.

The larger of the two asked, "There some trouble, Doctor?"

"Yes. I'm afraid you'll be needing to escort Mr. Kauffman here to our quarters."

"You're taking him out of the experiment?"

"He's taken himself out. He knows our location and he knows about the towers."

"What about the electronic parameter, how will he cross it?"

"Have you cleared that fallen tree in sector fourteen?"

"From the quake? No, sir. We were going to wait until they slept."

"Yes, well, plans have changed a bit. Take him across the tree. What is it, thirty feet above the gully and parameter?"

"A little less."

"But high enough to put him out of harm's way. Once you've crossed it, make sure you destroy the tree."

"It's big. They'll hear us cutting."

"Trust me, that'll be the least of what they hear."

"Yes, sir." He started toward David, who tensed, immediately drawing his staff closer.

Seeing his reaction, the man slowed.

Helgeland replied, "I'm sorry, Mr. Kauffman, we have no other choice."

"What about the others?" David demanded.

"In two hours it will all be over."

"How? Like that guy up there?" David motioned to the screen. "You're putting everyone through that?"

"As I said, there are no certainties."

The man started toward him again.

"No." David raised his branch as a weapon, wincing at the pain shooting through his wrist. "You're going to shut this thing down and you're going to release us. *All* of us. *Now*."

Helgeland laughed kindly. "I'm afraid we won't be able to accommodate your wishes, Mr. Kauffman." He gave a nod to the largest man, who resumed his approach.

Despite the pain and his instinct not to harm others, David leaned back, hesitated a fraction of a second, then swung hard. He hit the man in the shoulder, spinning him into the console. The woman technician screamed, leaping from her chair, but the smaller man was already coming at him. David swung again, catching him in the gut and dropping him to the floor.

"I'm not kidding!" David shouted, catching his breath, fighting the pain. "Shut this thing down!"

"Mr. Kauffman . . ." Helgeland approached, palms open in reason. "Please, it will all be over in—"

Unsure what to do, not wanting to hurt him, David spun around and smashed his club hard into the console. There were no sparks but plenty of flying pieces.

"What are you doing?" Helgeland raced for the console.

"Stay back!" David hit it again. Then again. Still no sparks, though the acrid smell of something burning filled the room.

The first man had risen and came at him from the side. David turned and tried jamming the tree limb into his gut. He missed and caught his hip, slowing the man but not stopping him. Helgeland continued to shout as David, clenching his teeth against the pain, leaned back preparing to hit the man again . . . until the smaller one, still on the floor, grabbed his legs, yanking him off balance. David started to fall, then twisted away and swung the club toward the smaller man's head. He missed but caught his other shoulder, just as the first grabbed him from behind and pinned his arms.

David kicked and squirmed but was outmatched by a good thirty pounds. The big man dragged him, none too kindly, past the console and computer racks toward the exit. David still clung to the club, but it served little purpose.

"How long . . . ," the man shouted to Helgeland. "How long do we keep him?"

But Helgeland was too busy bemoaning his damaged console to reply.

Realizing his hopelessness, David finally stopped his struggle . . . until his eyes landed on his son in the monitor. That's when he went crazy. With a burst of adrenalin, he kicked and squirmed with everything he had. He threw back his elbow, catching his captor in the stomach, knocking out his wind. He jabbed again and again in rapid succession, a wild man, not fighting for his own life, but for his boy's.

The man's grip loosened. That's all David needed. He tightened his hold on the branch, crying out in pain as he swung it around, catching the man along the side of the head, sending him stumbling backwards against the wall. The second man, who was already on his feet, raced at him. The first would soon return. David had only moments. He leaned back and swung his club hard into the closest computer rack. This time there were sparks. Plenty.

Helgeland shouted.

He swung again. More sparks. He was getting pretty good at this. He leaned back for a third but had the air knocked out of his lungs by a series of kidney punches from behind—so expertly delivered that the pain caused him to drop his branch. It hit the concrete only a second before he did. He fell to his knees, gasping, trying to catch his breath, trying to focus through the pain. He heard Helgeland yelling, braced himself for more blows. But none came—except for a brutal kick to his face from the first assailant. But even as he flew across the room seeing ceiling and stars, he realized that their attention had been redirected. They no longer cared about him; now it was their console and computers.

"Tower eleven is out! We've lost a tower!"

David struggled to move. Whatever he'd destroyed had taken the spotlight off himself and for that he was grateful. He rolled onto his hands and knees, shook his head. The shouting continued as he crawled for the door. He understood little of what they yelled as he pulled himself to his feet.

"It's gone!"

"What?"

"The rheostat; it's out!"

"It can't be; there's no way—"

"Look at the reading!"

David leaned on the door for support. He turned toward the room, squinting to clear his vision. The numbers on the digital readout changed so quickly they were nearly a blur:

88.64 . . . 89.00 . . . 89.14%

"Stop it! Can't you stop it!"

"It's out. We have no limiter. We can't control it!"

"What are you say—"

"We can't stop it!"

"What?"

"The Presence! We have no control!"

Rachel McPherson felt the fog's appearing as much as she saw it. A warmth caressing and embracing her. And the more she moved her lips in silent prayer, the stronger it grew.

"That is correct . . . ," Nubee whispered from beside her bed, "ask, simply ask."

And she did, fervently. Closing her eyes, she half whispered, half thought the words, *"I'm sorry . . . so sorry . . ."*

But they weren't the only words running through her mind.

Murderer! She knew it was Osiris perched on her chest, knew he was screaming. *There is no forgiveness for you!*

"He has done it all," Nubee continued.

No forgiveness!

"Simply ask; He will do the rest."

". . . I'm sorry . . ."

She felt the fog thicken.

Baby killer!

Other voices joined in, other gods screaming. There was no missing their desperation, their panic . . . and apparently their pain.

Stop her!
Make her stop!

She opened her eyes. The fog had grown darker, crimson-red. The smaller gods squealed and squirmed, trying in vain to slap it off their skin. For every place it touched, large welts raised. Ugly blisters. And the thicker it grew, the worse the blisters became, until they were actually bubbling, beginning to steam and smoke.

Make her stop!
Torturer!

"He has done it all for you."

Not you! Not for you! You are too evil!

Images suddenly filled her mind. Memories she'd long forgotten ...

Seven-year-old Rachel and her brother burning ants on the sidewalk with a magnifying glass. Watching with fascination as smoke rose from them.

Monster! Your whole life!

Now she was nine, shoplifting the pink vinyl diary she loved so much at Woolworth's ... now a teen screaming at her mother, words so ugly they made the woman cry ...

Rachel felt her own eyes beginning to burn. "Momma ..."

... now high school, whispering rumors behind Kimberly Johnson's back ... giggling at the girl's tears ... at the boyfriend's anger as he storms off.

Evil! Destroyer of all you touch!

"Don't stop praying," Nubee urged.

The memories came faster ... gropings in the back of Stan Moton's car ... the drinking binges in college ... the drug experimentation ... other boys whose names she barely knew ...

Whore!

"Just ask Him—"

... and Jerry. Dear, sweet, Jerry ...

Destroyer of all that is good—

... their fights over the baby ...

—of your husband, your family!

Tears spilled onto her cheeks. "Please, no more, please—"

... the clinic, the bright lights, faces smiling down, speaking empty words of assurance ...

Killer of all that is sacred!

... and Jerry, his own face on the pillow beside hers, tear-streaked.

Of all that is precious!

Again she held the spike and hammer in her blood-smeared hands, again the Man lay on the cross before her ...

Killer of all that is holy!

... such sorrow in His eyes, but not for Himself. For *her*. Concern for *her*. Love for *her*. Tears blurred her vision, but she could not look away from those eyes ...

"Ask Him, Rachel ... just ask ..."

... eyes so encouraging, eyes giving permission ...

"No ... ," she croaked.

That's right, the voices hissed, *you're not worthy. Others, but not you. NOT YOU!*

Still, the eyes would not release her, they would not stop loving her ... urging her.

She looked at the hammer and spike—

"He can bear it. Only God can bear it."

—then back to those powerful eyes. Their passion, their pleading for her to continue.

"It is okay, Rachel, it is what He wants, it is why He came."

Finally, with trembling hands, she set the spike against the open palm.

NOO!

Tears swelled in those eyes, tears of love and ... was it possible? Tears of joy? He gave a single nod. A single nod and she understood. With a ragged, uneven breath, she raised the hammer above her head—

NOOOO!

—and brought it down hard onto the spike. The metal clanged and the vision shattered.

She opened her eyes to see Osiris and the others leaping off, their bodies bubbling and cracking. But she did not hear their screams. Instead, she heard . . . singing. All around, coming from the fog, from the room. She didn't understand the words. But the melody, the intertwining harmonies were so beautiful she felt her throat tighten and ache. She turned to Nubee, whose eyes were also filled with moisture.

"Do you"—her voice choked—"hear that?"

"Yes."

"What is it?"

Quietly, he quoted, "'I tell you, there is rejoicing in the presence of the angels of God over one sinner who repents.'"

"Have I . . . did I do it?"

Nubee grinned. "You tell me."

Rachel listened, quietly marveling.

"Now let Him inside, Rachel."

She looked at him.

"Let Him enter."

She understood. Just as the gods had resided in and influenced her, it was time for Another, for the one true God, to take residence. But He would never be rude or mean or demanding. Not with those eyes. He would be there to gently encourage, to guide, to instruct. And most importantly He would be there to love her . . . and to be loved.

She took a deep breath, the deepest she'd taken in a long time. It was as if a great weight had been removed from her. Maybe it had. She looked down to her chest. Not a creature remained. There was nothing now but the singing and the fog and the—She caught her breath. Her darkness, her outer shadow, it was being drawn from her body into the fog. It was being pulled, absorbed into the mist, disappearing into its deep crimson cloud.

And as it disappeared, her orange-red glow grew more and more visible, glowing brighter and brighter. But the brightness did not come from the darkness leaving. It came from—

"Look," Nubee whispered. He motioned to the center of her chest—the small, empty core . . . that was no longer empty. The core that now burned with light. A dazzling brightness identical to Nubee's.

"Bless You, Lord. Thank You . . ." Over the singing she could hear him praying. "Thank You, Jesus, thank You . . ."

Without hesitation, she joined in. "Thank You . . ." She swallowed. "Thank You, God . . ."

Although her words were different from the singing, they felt the same. And with that assurance, she leaned back into her pillow, closed her eyes, and continued. "Thank You . . . Jesus. Thank You." She did not look back at her core; she did not need to. She could literally feel its intensity growing brighter and brighter and brighter.

uke!"

David slid as much as he climbed, painfully scrambling his way up the dirt mound toward the hole in the shaft's ceiling. He threw another look over his shoulder toward the door. No one pursued. At last he emerged through the opening, looking in all directions. It was night now. The sky above the boulders pulsed with lightning. Thunder clapped and roared.

"Luke!"

But the boy was nowhere in sight. He tried scaling the rocks once, twice, but there were no footholds, nothing to grip. He turned back to the hole, not liking the idea, but having no choice. He stepped back in and slid down the mound until he hit the side wall. Staggering, but staying on his feet, he half ran, half hobbled to the exit he'd been to earlier. He raced up the steps and threw open the door.

The sky churned with black clouds illuminated only by lightning.

"Luke!" He could barely hear himself over the thunder. He stepped out and scanned the top of the slide, the hill behind him. There was no sign of Luke. He turned, limping toward the bluff. He made his way around the boulders and debris until—there he was, on the other side of the slide, his glow outlined by the strobing light. "Luke!" He started for him, stumbling over rocks. "Luke!"

The boy turned, and David blinked in unbelief. Because he was no longer a boy. Now he glowed as a towering athlete . . . strong, powerful.

"Dad? What's going on?"

"We've got to get the others!" He stumbled again. "We've got to get out of here!"

"What happened to you?"

"What?"

"Look!"

Arriving, he glanced at himself. Like Luke, his glow had also solidified, but not into an athlete. It was something entirely different. He was dressed in some sort of robe. But not of cloth or material. It was light. His orange-red glow had hardened into a robe of light. It did not shine as brightly as Luke's, and his darker shell was still very much present, still bubbling and eating into the glow—but the glow had definitely taken a shape.

He grabbed Luke's arm. "Come on, we've got to go!"

"Where? How—"

"There's a way out. A tree's fallen over that electronic fence!"

Suddenly Luke pointed past him. "What's that?"

David turned just in time to see an orb of light dive toward them from the sky. He ducked, pulling Luke with him as the thing swooped past, then veered up and away. They turned and watched it disappear into the trees. He looked back and saw another coming in from their right.

And another. Swooping, diving, not directly at them, but close enough, before darting up and into the trees.

"They're everywhere!" Luke shouted.

"You see now? You can see them?"

"Those I can see! And listen! Do you hear that?"

"What?"

"That music . . . the singing."

"All I hear is thunder."

"No, under it! Under the thunder!"

Another light swooped by, just feet above their heads. As it passed David did hear something. More than the thunder. Underneath it. Singing! Cautiously, he rose to his feet, looking around. *They* were singing. The lights were singing. More importantly they were singing a song he'd heard before. In the Virtual Reality tunnel. The music that had filled the Garden. Not words, but sustained chords mixing and weaving into each other.

Luke rose beside him. "Cool."

The lights continued to dart and fly, every second becoming more and more defined. Another swooped past, so close David felt the wind of its . . . *wings*. The thing had wings! He ducked, but it did not strike. Like the others, it came close, but never struck.

"Come on!" They started up the hill. The lightning flashed continually now, the thunder a constant roar that David not only heard, but felt through his body—just as he heard and felt the music.

"Look out!" Luke pointed at a giant cedar directly beside them.

David turned but saw nothing. "What?"

"Get away!"

"What are you talking about?"

He pulled David so hard that they both lost their footing and tumbled half a dozen yards back down the hill. When they stopped, David scrambled to his feet. "What are you doing?"

"The tree!"

"What about it?" He turned to the cedar. "There's nothing wrong with—"

Suddenly, the tree exploded with lightning. Wood and splinters flew in all directions. David ducked, shielding his face as pieces rained around them. When it had stopped he turned to his son in amazement. "How did—"

"Come on!" Luke pulled him by the arm. "Let's get out of here!"

thirteen

At first Preacher Man thought the rattling were windows from the thunderstorm. But they continued until he realized another quake had begun, an aftershock. Opening his eyes, he saw the warrior of light still standing between Reverend Wyatt and himself. It was no angel, he knew that. No separate entity. It was both of them together—either how the Presence viewed them or how they actually were, it made little difference. Reverend Wyatt had put it best when he'd quoted, "'So we, being many, are one body in Christ.'"

Truth was, Preacher Man never liked that verse, or others similar to it. He was never comfortable being part of some group. He didn't like being responsible for other folks' success or failures, and he didn't like being accountable to them for his. The idea almost seemed un-American, like losing his independence. But this soldier, this warrior, was different. It was like his marriage to Dorothy. Somehow it made him bigger ... more complete.

The aftershock continued, growing stronger. The floor started to roll.

He rose to his feet, helping Reverend Wyatt do the same. As seasoned West Coasters they knew the safest place was hunkered down beside a heavy object—not under it where they would be crushed, but beside it so it would take the impact.

"The bed!" Reverend Wyatt shouted.

They started toward it when the mirror over the dresser exploded. Preacher Man spun to see shards of glass falling in and around the bottles of booze. Instinctively, he started for them.

"No!" Reverend Wyatt grabbed his arm, but he shook him off. "Billy Ray!"

He staggered toward the bar and reached for the vodka. Violet blue light shot from the bottle into his hand. He froze, watching in astonishment as it streamed up his arm, reforming some of his old shell, pumping it with its darkness.

"Billy Ray!"

He looked into the last hanging piece of mirror. Except for the flashes of lightning outside the window, the room was dark. The warrior had disappeared. Now there was only the Reverend, taking hold of the sword that had returned to his side. Preacher Man glanced down and saw his shield had also returned. He looked back to the bottles then reached for the rum ... until another dark light streamed from it into his hand. The floor pitched—so hard he grabbed the dresser to steady himself. He reached for a third bottle, the Scotch, which also shot its darkness into him.

"'If one member suffer, all the members suffer with it!'"

The Reverend's sword flashed in front of Preacher Man, crashing into the dresser, severing all three streams of darkness. Preacher Man turned to him, speechless. But the streams were no sooner severed before they again shot from the bottles, racing back toward his hands.

The Reverend raised the sword. "'Whoever abideth in him sinneth not'!" Again he brought it down with a crash, and again the darkness was severed. Momentarily.

Looking for some way to help, to protect himself from their return, Preacher Man remembered his shield. In a moment of inspiration, he reached down and grabbed it, raising it just in time to block the first stream of darkness, the vodka, as it raced back at him. It hit the surface with a loud hiss. Next came the rum's darkness. Again he was able to block it. Then the Scotch. He could feel each of their impacts against his shield, their vibrations as they shoved and pushed, but with effort he was able to hold it in place.

Suddenly the floor pitched so violently that it threw them both to the ground. A ceiling beam twisted and groaned. The window across the room exploded.

"We can't stay here!" Reverend Wyatt shouted as they struggled to their feet. "Everything is coming down!"

Preacher Man nodded and turned toward the door. To his surprise, the warrior reappeared, as brilliant as ever. Once again, he was armed with the Reverend's sword and Preacher Man's shield.

"Come on!"

Taking one another's arms, they headed for the door— the warrior between them . . . his light engulfing them.

the hallway floor bucked and tossed. Rachel clung to the wheelchair, fighting for balance as she rolled Nubee toward the stairs. In the past, Luke or Albert had always carried him up and down. He wasn't that heavy. But they weren't there and she had to get him outside.

"Move! Get out of the way!" One of Orbolitz's body-guards staggered past, nearly knocking her down.

"Jefferson!" Orbolitz shouted from down the hall. "Get back here. Get back!"

But the man didn't listen. He reached the stairs then half ran, half fell, until he hit the bottom and charged for the door.

Rachel arrived at the landing and quickly locked Nubee's wheels.

"What are you doing?" he asked.

"We have to get you out of here!"

Before Nubee could answer, Orbolitz barged past, throwing Rachel against the wall.

"Mr. Orbolitz!" she called. "We need your help!"

He did not answer as he stumbled down the steps, holding his goggles in place with one hand, clinging to the banister with the other.

"Mr. Orbolitz!"

"You go!" Nubee shouted. "I'll be okay!"

"No!" She slid her hands under his legs and tried to lift him.

"Rachel—"

"No!"

The ceiling planks above their heads popped, one after another. Pieces of wood fell along with chunks of plaster and streams of dust.

"Hang on!" She coughed. She pulled him from the chair, his weight so great that they nearly tumbled. She took the first step, leaned against the wall for support, until the railing in front of them suddenly groaned and fell away, the outside edge of the stairs dropping a good 30 degrees. The slope was so steep Rachel half dropped, half threw Nubee back to the landing as she fell, lunging for the wall. She slid toward the edge, clutching at loose carpeting which didn't hold. Her feet and legs slipped over. Then her hips. She screamed, reaching for anything, until her hand caught a remaining piece of banister. She grabbed hold, clinging for all she was worth, swaying as she dangled some twenty feet above the floor.

She looked up to Nubee. He lay on the landing beside his chair, struggling to sit up.

More wood and plaster fell. She tried pulling herself up, but only loosened the banister more, causing it to creak then slip another foot and a half before jolting to a stop. Desperately, she searched for something to grasp, anything. She noticed Nubee had managed to sit up and was struggling to stand!

"Back up!" she cried. "Get away from the edge!"

But he did not answer, his face filled with concentration.

"Nubee!"

Her hands started to cramp.

Nubee continued to struggle, dust sticking to the sweat on his face.

Another stream of plaster began to fall, some of it catching her in the face, her eye. She coughed, trying to blink it away but with little success. The banister slipped again, then gave way altogether. She screamed, falling, but dropped less than a foot before Nubee grabbed her wrist. She looked up, blinking, trying to clear her vision. It was true: both of his hands were holding her hand. Both of his *glowing* hands. She looked past them to his glowing body, bent over, clinging to her. But that was impossible. Not only was he defying his own physical limitations, he was defying gravity. She looked to his glowing knees. They rested at an unbelievable angle on the tilting step. Stranger still was his physical body, the part inside. It floated a good six inches higher. Somehow his physical body was being supported by his glowing one!

With great effort, he pulled her up and over the edge of the step to join him. They leaned a moment against the wall. Then, holding her tightly, he rose—his glowing feet on the stairs, his solid form hovering inside. Rachel watched, speechless, as he held her and took a careful step down, and then another. What she saw was beyond any law of physics. And, judging from Nubee's expression, he fully agreed.

They continued, one step after another, until they reached the bottom landing and he set her down. The earthquake had not stopped and the floor continued heaving as dust and debris fell faster. They turned and staggered toward the entry hall. Once they arrived, Nubee threw open the door. But he hesitated a moment, looking back up the stairs to his wheelchair.

"Looks like you won't be needing it!" Rachel shouted.

He turned to her, still amazed. "Apparently not."

A support beam slipped, then gave way. They ducked out the door and it crashed behind them, belching smoke and dust after them as they stumbled down the porch steps and onto the lawn.

Orbolitz was there, shouting into his walkie-talkie. "Helgeland? Helgeland, answer me!"

Rachel leaned over, catching her breath, but only until she noticed the singing that surrounded them on every side . . . and the strobing night sky. She rose and looked at the electrical storm, fiercer than any she had ever seen. It was terrifying. So were the balls of light that swooped and dove through the trees.

"Rachel!"

She spun around to see a violet shadow waddling toward her. Deep inside, almost hidden, Savannah and Albert were holding hands.

"Thank God you got out!" Savannah yelled.

"Look at you!" Albert shouted. "You're gorgeous!"

Before Rachel could respond, another voice called from behind. "Momma, Momma!" She turned and saw two children, a girl and boy, she guessed around five and seven years old. They raced to her and threw their arms around her legs, clinging for all they were worth. "What is happening? Where are we?"

Stunned, she could only stare at them.

"Please, tell us." The boy looked up to her, his eyes wide with fear. He had an accent, Eastern Europe. "What is happening?"

She wanted to give an answer but had none.

Orbolitz saved her the trouble. "It's overloading!" he yelled. "We're shortin' out!"

She turned to him, not understanding.

"This God of yours lives out o' time! Now you do too!"

"Momma!" The little girl pulled so hard and was so frightened that Rachel instinctively kneeled to her. The poor thing was crying, trembling. Rachel reached up to her smudged cheeks, pushed the hair from her eyes. "Who are you?" she asked. "I–I don't know—"

"They're yours!" Orbolitz angrily shouted. "From the future!"

She turned back to the child, at a loss for words.

"We've got to leave!" It was another voice. David's.

She looked toward the woods and saw the father and son racing toward her. "We've got to get out of here!" At least she thought it was father and son. The best she could tell, David's glow had hardened into some sort of robe, regal like a king's, only made of light. It wasn't extremely bright since the bubbling shadow still very much surrounded it, but its shape and form were clearly visible. Luke, on the other hand, literally blazed with light. He was no longer the gangly boy covered in pieces of shadow. Now he appeared as some great athlete, dressed in track-and-field garb, complete with an Olympic laurel wreath atop his head.

"We've got to go!" David repeated.

Still kneeling, Rachel glanced back to the little girl and boy. But they were gone. She looked about, to every side. They were nowhere to be seen. Confused, concerned, she rose to her feet. Only then did she notice the quake was finally coming to a stop.

But not the thunder.

Or the music.

"Now!" David shouted. "We have to go now!"

"You'll never get out!" Orbolitz yelled.

They arrived and between breaths David explained, "I was at the control center. There's a tree." Turning to Albert and Savannah's shadow, he continued. "Over the electronic leash or whatever it is. High enough to cross without—"

"You were—" Orbolitz could not hide his incredulity. "You were at the—"

"I saw Helgeland. Your setup. And your little super-computer, God rest its soul."

"He smashed the snot out of it!" Luke beamed.

Orbolitz sputtered. "You . . . you are the one responsible for—"

"Not bad, for an old guy," Luke bragged.

"Rachel . . . ," David exclaimed.

She turned to him.

He stared, practically speechless. "Did you—I mean . . . you prayed?"

She stepped toward him, not sure how he knew. "Yes."

"You asked Him?"

She nodded. "And you were right!" She reached out and took his hands. "You were so right."

He continued staring, searching for words. "Look . . . at you . . ."

She glanced down, expecting to see her blazing white center core. She did not expect to see that the glow surrounding it had also solidified. But instead of being royalty like David, or an athlete like Luke, she was dressed . . . she was dressed in a wedding gown! Dazzling white, so bright she could barely look at it. She turned to the others, not understanding.

Quietly, Nubee quoted, " 'For the wedding of the Lamb has come, and his bride has made herself ready.' "

She looked at him. "I . . . I don't . . ."

Again, he quoted. " 'Without stain or wrinkle or any other blemish, but holy and blameless.' "

"Blameless?" She practically laughed. "I'm not blameless."

"You are now," David quietly replied.

She looked to him, then Nubee, then back to David again. "After . . . all that I've done?"

Nubee again quoted, " 'If anyone is in Christ, he is a new creation; the old has gone, the new has come.' "

Suddenly her eyes burned. Was it possible? Was she really new? The words were too good to be true. Yet she'd seen what had happened in the room—the light, Osiris's exit, the crimson mist that bathed her, that removed her darkness. Before she could stop herself, she threw her arms around David. "Thank you." She pressed her wet face into his chest. "Thank you, thank you . . ."

He held her—how long, she did not know. But when they separated and he looked at her, she saw his own eyes brimming with moisture, staring at her in silent awe.

"Dad?"

Pulling himself from her, he nodded and turned to the group.

"We have to get out of here now!" He spoke to Albert and Savannah's bulging shadow. "That parameter we mapped out. There's a tree fallen across it. If we climb over it, Helgeland says it's high enough to avoid any effects. Is that true?"

"It's possible, sure."

"Fools," Orbolitz scorned. "All of you."

They turned to him. Only then did Rachel realize his bodyguards were nowhere to be found. Apparently David had noticed it as well, because his violet shell had begun bubbling harder.

"What about Reverend Wyatt?" Savannah shouted. "The Preacher?"

"Present!" Preacher Man called.

They turned to see the two men round the corner of the lodge. Each was surrounded in light, but a light that blurred into each other, forming a much greater light . . . like Albert and Savannah's dark light, but different. For theirs formed a third person between them, a warrior, several feet taller and very much stronger.

"Impressive," Luke called.

"We think so." Reverend Wyatt grinned.

David turned back to his son. "Luke, I want you to take the others back into the woods. Start at the gully behind the lodge and work your way around, following the parameter we mapped. Look for any fallen tree that might—"

"What about you?"

"I'll be with you soon."

"I'm not going without you."

"I'll be there—"

"Dad, I'm not—"

A searing sound filled the air, like frying meat, ripping fabric. Suddenly the night glowed red, but not from lightning. It glowed from the fiery ocean they were now standing upon.

"What is it?" Rachel shouted. "What's going on?"

Orbolitz yelled, his voice racked with pain. "I think it should be ... clear."

She turned to him and caught her breath. He was below them, standing chest-deep in the burning liquid—his body immersed in flame.

He gasped. "We've seen ... your future." Striving for control, he continued. "This is ... mine."

Around him stood other bodies, as far as the eye could see. Thousands of them in the fire, chest-deep in flames, molten pieces of their flesh dropping into the burning liquid. There was no singing now. Only pitiful shrieks and wails. Rachel looked down at her own feet. Like the others in the group, she did not sink, but stood on top of the burning liquid. But it wasn't *her* standing. It was her glow. Just as Nubee had been able to stand on the sloping stairs and float above them without falling, so she was able to stand over the flaming ocean. Her glow, the glow of each of the group, even Albert and Savannah's feeble light, was keeping them from sinking.

"It's the Lake of Fire!" David cried. "How did it get here?"

"It's always been ... here," Orbolitz gasped.

"What are you talking about?"

The ripping sound returned. The fiery lake flickered, then was gone. Suddenly everyone was standing back in front of the lodge. Orbolitz leaned over, trying to catch his breath.

"What do you mean, it's always been here?" Albert demanded.

"We're slipping into higher dimensions." Orbolitz rose, struggling for composure. "Dave's little temper tantrum with the computer shorted the system—tore apart our reality so we're catching glimpses through rips and tears into higher ones."

Again, the air flickered. The lodge and forest rippled, starting to change. The group cried out, but it was a false alarm. Everything shifted back to normal.

"And that's only the beginning, folks." Orbolitz gave a mocking chuckle. "Things should really start heatin' up now."

Without taking his eyes from Orbolitz, David ordered, "Take them, Luke. Get out of here and find that tree."

"But—"

"Take them."

Rachel threw a concerned look to him. She'd never heard him sound so cold, so seething. Even as he spoke, his boiling darkness thickened.

Luke must have seen it too. "Dad—"

"Now!"

Realizing his father meant business, Luke turned to the group. "Okay, everybody, you heard the man. Let's get going." With Nubee moving in to support his bad leg, Luke started forward. The others followed.

"You won't be long?" Reverend Wyatt called back to David.

"No, this won't take long," David replied. He stepped in front of Orbolitz to block his path. "This shouldn't take long at all."

as the group scrambled off in search of the tree, David stood alone with the unprotected Orbolitz, his hate rising to an all-time high. Images flitted through his mind. Glimpses of his Emily's raven hair as Preacher Man lifted her body from the muddy grave. "*Her eyes!*" the man had shouted. "*Someone's stolen her eyes!*"

Only it wasn't *some*one. It was *this* one. This man standing before him. This man who had murdered his daughter.

"Be careful, Dave." Orbolitz tried to sound casual, but even behind his goggles the fear was evident. "Your shadow is gettin' a lot thicker, son."

But David had no concern for shadows. Or their thickness. So many emotions churned and roiled inside of him. So many thoughts. But when he spoke, only one word emerged—a shaking, trembling, "WHY?"

Orbolitz cocked his head. "Why what? Why this? Well, I think I made that pretty—"

"*Why Emily?*"

"Now, Dave, we've been through all that. She's history, yesterday's news. I think a better question—"

David's hands shot to the man's throat. *"My daughter is not history!"* Despite the pain from his injured arm, he squeezed hard. Orbolitz choked, clawed at David's fingers, his face darkening.

Looking to David's chest, he forced out the words, gagged, constricted, "Now . . . you've . . . done it."

David glanced down and saw his robe of light was gone. The bubbling shadow had completely consumed it, and it had grown so dense he could no longer see his center core. But he didn't care. The one who killed his child was in his hands. He tightened his grip, the adrenalin helping him lift the man off the ground, writhing, kicking.

The ripping sound again filled the air. The burning lake returned. Only this time David did not hover above it. Now he stood in it. With no glow to support him, he stood chest deep in the fire. Flames ignited his legs, his gut, his chest, the pain unbearable. When he breathed, the fiery air singed his throat and lungs.

But Orbolitz was still in his hands. He tightened his grip. "Make it stop!"

"There's . . . ," Orbolitz gagged, ". . . nothing I can do. This is what *you* want!" He screamed. "This is *your* passion!"

The words were as much a shock as the flames. David turned to see the surrounding corpses, all burning, all trapped in their passions ... just as he was. This is what he'd seen earlier, last year when they'd been to hell. People locked in and forever living out their life's greatest passion. Sex, power, wealth, love.

Was it possible? Had his hatred, his hunger for revenge become so great?

Fine! Then so be it! He squeezed harder. If this was his eternal passion, then he would live it to the full. He would revel in it. Because, more than anything, at that moment, this is all he wanted.

"David? David!"

He looked up and saw Rachel above the fiery water shouting down to him: "What are you doing?"

Through clenched teeth he cried out, "He killed my daughter!"

"You have to forgive him!"

He did not reply. Could not.

"You said so yourself!"

"I ... can't!"

"'Forgive us our debts as we forgive our debtors,' that's what you said!"

"I can't!"

"He can help us do anything, remember?"

"I ... can't! I'm not ... that good—"

"'A new creation in Christ'! Isn't that what we are? The new has come and the old has gone away."

David heard the words, but that's all they were, words. What he gripped in his hands was far more real. And satisfying. The way the man kicked and writhed. The way he gasped and squirmed gave more satisfaction than anything he could imagine.

"David!"

"No," he seethed. "It does no good. It doesn't work."

"Of course it does. Look at me. *Look at me!*"

But he did not look. He knew what he would see. The glowing form, the core's blazing brightness—everything he had sacrificed ... for this.

"David!"

Ignoring her, he shouted at Orbolitz, "Take off the goggles!"

"What?"

"If I'm going to hell, I'm going to enjoy it. Take off the goggles so I can see you suffer."

"I—"

David squeezed harder.

The man nodded, choking, gagging.

He released his hold just enough for Orbolitz to reach up and rip off the goggles. And there, six inches away, face to face, David saw his daughter's eyes. The ones Orbolitz's team had transplanted. Those deep, incredible violet-blue eyes. The wave of emotion was so intense that he could hardly breathe. These were his child's eyes. His baby's. The eyes sparkling in excitement over the gifts he'd bought, the praise he'd given. The eyes so confused and imploring as they took her away to the hospital that final time . . . and the eyes that were filled with a love deeper than he thought possible when she and David were together in the Garden.

But it was more than his daughter's love in those eyes. There was another love present in them. The love that illuminated the Garden. The love in the eyes of the Man with the holes in His hands. Piercing, penetrating, unrelenting. Yes, they were Orbolitz's eyes, full of fear and humanity, and yes, they were his daughter's eyes, full of her love. But there was something deeper, something eternal in them that belonged to the Man. And David could not destroy that part, that eternal part. No matter how faint it was.

Orbolitz sensed his hesitation. "Go ahead," he taunted. "What are you waiting for?"

"David . . ."

So much of him wanted to continue, to revel in the suffering, to savor it, to make it his passion. But the eyes would not let him. Not their love, no matter how dim the flicker.

Angrily, he released Orbolitz, throwing him to the side and into the lake ... which suddenly turned into the lawn outside the lodge. It took only a moment to get his bearings, before he turned to Rachel. She reached out her hand and he took it.

"Let's go," was all she said.

They turned and started for the ravine.

Scrambling on the ground for his goggles, Orbolitz shouted, "You think it's over? You think you've won?"

David did not answer.

"Look at you! Look at your shadow. You're no better than me!"

David began to slow, but Rachel pulled him forward until they rounded the lodge and headed after the others into the woods.

"Our fates are the same, David Kauffman! You hear me? You and me, we're the—"

But his voice was drowned out by the rolling thunder ... and singing that had suddenly grown much louder.

fourteen

by the time David and Rachel joined them, the group was already scouting the parameter of trees they'd marked earlier along the gulley.

"Here!" Preacher Man shouted over the thunder. "Got another one here."

"And here!" the Reverend called.

Though they were fifteen feet apart, the warrior of light rose between them, connecting them both with its glow. It had no separate identity of its own but seemed a blending of theirs. The only time it moved was when they moved, always staying equal distance between them.

"See any fallen trees?" David shouted.

"We've got as many fallen as standing," Albert yelled. "The earthquake did quite a number!"

"We'll never find the right one!" Savannah complained as their shadow lumbered through the undergrowth. Like Preacher Man and the Reverend, Savannah and Albert were a team. But unlike the men's light, their darkness seemed to confine and hamper them.

"She's right!" Luke shouted. "It could be any one of hundreds of—"

Lightning sizzled through the air, exploding a tree immediately to David's left. Rachel screamed and he pulled her to the ground, instinctively covering her. Another tree exploded to their right, another in front. They huddled together as splinters and hot embers fell all around. He could feel the heat of the flames against his back, flinched at the hissing and popping that surrounded them. Cautiously, he raised his head. All three trees blazed with fury—their flames rising into one another, forming a single, swirling spire.

As he watched, the spire ignited a group of treetops to his right. And then another group, and another, moving quickly along their upper branches. Fascinated, he rose and helped Rachel to her feet. Only then did he realize there was no wind. Never had been. Here he was in the biggest electrical storm of his life and there was no wind. And yet the flame continued moving forward, not spreading out, not moving down the trunks, but traveling above their heads in a single, glowing column.

"It wants us to follow!" Luke yelled.

David could barely hear. "What?"

Nubee, who still remained at Luke's side, shouted back, "'The pillar of cloud did not cease to guide them on their path, nor the pillar of fire by night'!"

David exchanged puzzled looks with Rachel. She appeared equally as lost.

"It wants us to follow!" Luke repeated. "Come on!"

David hesitated before reaching out to help Rachel over a fallen tree and starting forward.

"Where is it going?" Albert shouted.

"We'll know when we get there," Preacher Man yelled.

The spire continued and the group followed, remaining twenty or so feet behind. They passed under trees whose tops, moments before, had fueled the fire. Trees that no longer burned but still steamed and smoldered.

"I'm not liking this," Savannah shouted.

No one disagreed.

"Listen," Luke yelled. "Do you hear that?"

"What now?" Albert sighed.

"In the thunder."

"You mean the singing," Rachel asked.

He shook his head. "*With* the singing."

David strained to listen. He did hear something. The thunder had begun booming and rolling in patterns. Patterns that interspersed themselves throughout the singing, separating the long continual chords, dividing the stream of harmonies into rhythms, shaping them into specific sounds and . . . syllables.

"I hear it!" Savannah cried.

Albert scoffed, "What are you talking—"

"Shh!"

David continued listening as the pattern grew tighter, as the same sounds and syllables repeated themselves over and over again:

Ho . . . l . . . y . . . ho . . . ly . . . holy . . .

It was a word! And he recognized it! Not only did he recognize it, but he marveled how it contained both the beauty of the voices *and* the power of the thunder.

Holy . . . Holy . . . Holy . . .

More words came, each one clearer, more beautiful and powerful than the last:

Is . . . the Lord . . . God . . . Almighty . . .

Then, just as the thunder had separated the chords into words, now the words began separating their reality into . . . well, at first, David wasn't sure what he saw.

The mountain began to shimmer, pulsating with the same light that filled so many of their center cores. The light he'd seen in the Virtual Reality tunnel, the Garden. It came in waves, the words, the light—washing through everything he saw. Each word pulsating with light that passed through the air, the ground, the trees—so powerful he could feel it strike and pass through his own body. The pulses came faster, more intense, until everything had grown so bright that he had to look down and shield his eyes. Only then did he notice his feet were on ice. Everyone was standing on ice, a giant sea of ice . . . but not ice. Glass. They were standing on a plane of glass stretching as far as the eye could see.

. . . Who Was, and Is, and Is to Come!

The light-words struck faster, harder—blows so powerful it became difficult for David to keep his balance. He was terrified, yes. But, at the same time, he was drawn to the source. Slowly, cautiously, he turned directly into the pulsing brightness. It blew his hair, pummeled his face, but he had to see. Mustering all of his courage, he forced his eyes to rise. And there, far away, he saw what looked like a throne rising from the plane. Around it sat other, smaller thrones. And encircling it were the same vibrant bands of color he had seen while traveling in the VR chamber— blue, green, red, yellow. And, though it was miles away, he saw Someone, actually sensed more than saw, a Person who sat on the throne.

But it wasn't a person. It was an animal!

He squinted into the pounding light. The animal had been slaughtered, covered in blood. A sheep . . . no, lamb. But it wasn't dead. It was clearly slaughtered, clearly covered in blood, yet standing alive. Alive and bathed in the blinding whiteness. Actually blazing as the source of that whiteness.

Holy! Holy! Holy!
Is the Lord God Al—

And then, as quickly as it had appeared, the light vanished. The sea of glass wavered, then was gone. The thunder fell back into its random booming; the words disappeared into the lovely chords that wove in and out of each other. Everything had returned to what it had been.

Well, not quite everything . . .

For a portion of the light remained. The blazing lamb. It stood at the opposite end of a giant cedar tree that had fallen across the ravine. High above it, the spiral of fire burned. Before David could respond, the ground started to shake again. Harder than the last. So hard it threw him down. He scrambled back to his feet, but the lamb was gone. So was the light. Only the column of fire remained.

"LOOK!" Savannah screamed.

David turned to see a distinct line of sifting rock and dirt at the bottom of the ravine. It snaked its way toward them, then passed under the cedar log, and continued beyond.

"It's splitting!" Albert yelled. "It's opening up!"

"Here!" Luke shouted. David turned back to see his son climbing onto the fallen cedar, motioning them to follow. "This is it! This is the way! Hurry!"

Struggling to keep their balance, the group started forward. But when David turned to check on Rachel, he saw her path had been blocked. The winged creature with the infant's face hovered before her—reaching out its hands, crying to her, pleading.

David called out, "Rachel!"

But she did not hear over the thunder, the singing, and the roar of the quake.

He looked back to the ravine. Rock and dirt slipped away; the chasm was widening. Without hesitation, he turned and ran toward her. The ground shifted like the floor of a fun house gone berserk ... with the added danger of trees cracking and falling. He staggered past Savannah and Albert as their shadow waddled toward the cedar bridge.

"Where are you going?"

He gave no answer.

Up ahead, Rachel, overcome with emotion, slowly sank to her knees. Her tear-streaked face glistened in the lightning.

"Rachel!"

She still did not hear. But the creature did. It turned within itself, facing David, hovering between them. It opened its mouth, but instead of the cry of a baby, it shrieked with a scream so frightening, David came to a stop.

When it had finished, he caught his breath and shouted, "Rachel! Rachel, we have to go! Now!"

Still staring at the baby, she cried, "She needs me!"

"That is not your child!"

"She's frightened, she needs me to stay with her!"

"She's not real! You know that! She's a counterfeit!"

The creature shrieked again—exploding into a flash of light and dividing. Like a cell under a microscope, it divided into two. The baby remained but now there was another. One with every appearance of—

"Starr!" Rachel cried. "Starr, you've come back!"

The second creature turned to her.

New tears sprang to Rachel's eyes. "I didn't—" Her voice choked with emotion. "I'm . . . I didn't . . . know."

It opened its mouth and spoke with a voice identical to Starr's. "I trusted you." The baby beside her cried louder and she repeated, "We trusted you!"

"I'm sorry . . . I didn't—"

"Rachel!" David moved around the creatures until there was another shriek, another flash of light. Now there were three. The baby, Starr, and . . . David gasped. For there it was again, in all of its loveliness, the counterfeit of Gita. Although its light was much brighter, it was the same face, the same engaging accent he'd heard earlier in Rachel's room.

"David . . . I was wrong."

But he would not be fooled again.

"David, the dead can return—"

"You are a liar!"

Sadly she shook her head. "Your friend is responsible for her baby's death . . . and for Starr's."

He turned to Rachel, shouting, "Don't listen to it! It's a lie! A counterfeit!"

The apparition continued, undaunted, gently reasoning. "She is responsible for their deaths . . . just as you are responsible for mine."

He spun back to it with a start. "What . . ."

"I am sorry. But it is truth, and you know how important truth is to me."

His voice thickened. "That's . . . not true. You are a—"

"And not only my death. There is another for which you are responsible."

He shook his head, suddenly fearing the worst. "No!"

"I am sorry, David—"

"No! *No!*"

"—but you've always known it to be true."

He shook his head harder . . . against the thought he had struggled with every day for the last year. A guilt that never lifted. He knew others were to blame—Orbolitz, the Life After Life program—but the ultimate responsibility, the final failure was his. No matter what others said, no matter how they rationalized, he was the one responsible. Another flash filled the forest, another split, and his daughter joined the group. She floated before him, so vivid, so real. Exactly as he'd left her in the Garden—brimming with youth and innocence, and like Gita, glowing with brilliance.

"Daddy . . ."

The word ripped his heart. Melted all reason.

"Emily," he croaked. Then, fighting for control, he shook his head. "No! *No!*"

"Daddy . . ."

Tears spilled onto his cheeks. He closed his eyes. He would not look at her. "*No . . .*"

"It's true, Daddy. You've known. You've always known."

His throat constricted until he could barely breathe.

"You're the one who made me take the medicine—"

He shook his head harder, beginning to sway like a wounded animal. "*NO!*"

"—who let them take me away."

He gagged on the pain. "Please . . ."

"And now you must pay."

"Please . . ."

"Daddy . . . Daddy . . ."

The words pried open his eyes. Wavering through his tears was that beautiful face, that raven-black hair. "No . . . ," he choked, "this isn't . . ." He gulped, "I . . . can't . . . I didn't know. I—"

But he did know. He had always known. *He* was responsible. And no matter how many times he read of Christ's love, claimed he understood God's forgiveness, there was always the doubt, the lingering fear in the back of his head that he was only fooling himself, that there were no free rides, that the scales of justice had to be balanced.

"Stay with me, Daddy." She floated toward him. "You left me once. Please, not again. Don't leave me alone again."

He could see them now. Those incredible violet-blue eyes. So full of compassion, so innocent, so imploring. She raised her hands to him, reaching out. He fought to breathe as hot tears streamed down his face.

"Please, Daddy . . ."

Then, ever so slightly, he began to nod. Yes. He would stay.

She moved closer.

Yes, he'd pay the price.

He felt her arms envelop him.

Yes, he would do whatever was necessary to make things—

"'Through his blood, the forgiveness of sins—'" A flashing sword swung down, missing his face by inches as the Reverend finished his quote, "'—according to the riches of God's grace'!"

The weapon sliced through Emily's arms, severing both of them. She screamed in agony. David spun around to see Reverend Wyatt and Preacher Man standing to his right. Towering between them, sword poised for another strike, stood the warrior of light.

"David!" Gita cried. "What have you done?"

"'Everyone who believes in him receives forgiveness of sins through his name'!" The sword flashed again, this time slashing into Gita's neck, cleanly decapitating her. But before her head even hit the ground, Starr, the baby, Emily, and what remained of Gita pulled together into a single creature—a towering gargoyle—amphibian face, protruding fangs, long sharp claws . . . nearly twice the size of the warrior.

"Uh-oh," Reverend Wyatt said.

Preacher Man nodded. "This could get interesting."

The gargoyle hissed as it stepped toward the warrior of light. It raised its arm and swung, razor talons glinting in the lightning. The warrior spun his shield around just in time to block it, though the impact knocked him backwards. Before he could recover, the gargoyle came at him and hit him again, and again, the third blow knocking him off his feet and crashing to the ground.

The creature roared in triumph and approached.

David spotted Rachel still kneeling, watching in horror. With the path now clear, he raced to join her.

"David—"

He turned to see Preacher Man shouting. He and Reverend Wyatt had moved as close to the fallen warrior as they dared, while the gargoyle stood, leering over its fallen victim.

"—start praying!"

He thought he'd misheard. "What?"

"Pray!"

He frowned. Pray what? Pray how?

"Now!" Preacher Man shouted.

He looked at Reverend Wyatt. The old man's lips were already moving.

The gargoyle thrust its long claws into both sides of the warrior, skewering him just below the ribs. The warrior jerked, struggling to get free, but could not move as the creature began lifting him into the air.

"NOW!"

Unsure where to start or what to say, David blindly jumped in. "God . . . we, uh, we ask for your help." His mind raced, searching for words. "Whatever that thing is, don't let it hurt that, uh, other thing—"

Not exactly articulate, but it seemed to work. At least the size of the warrior seemed to increase. Not a lot, but enough to force the gargoyle to stagger under the extra weight. It shrieked in protest, but continued hoisting the warrior until he was high over its head.

David bore down harder. "Give him power—give him the strength to fight back." The warrior continued growing. But not on his own. Instead, light began streaming into him from both Reverend Wyatt's and Preacher Man's glows. And, to David's surprise, from his own glow as well. Somehow even his light, as meager as it was, began feeding and strengthening him.

The gargoyle screamed again, stumbling under the warrior's added weight, until they both tumbled to the forest floor.

"That's it!" Preacher Man shouted. "Everyone keep praying. You, Rachel, everyone keep praying!"

David looked at Rachel, who appeared equally as shocked. But not wishing to mess with success, she took his hand and bowed her head. Still bewildered, but left with no other choice, he resumed his ramblings, watching in amazement as the warrior continued growing in size and strength . . . until he rolled onto his knees, then rose to his feet. So did the gargoyle, hissing, screeching. They were identical in size now as the warrior gripped his sword and began to approach. The creature stepped back defensively. It swiped at the warrior with its talons, once, twice, but the warrior continued forward.

David prayed harder. Rachel gripped his hand tighter.

The warrior raised his sword, preparing to strike when there was another flash. Once again the gargoyle had transformed itself into Rachel's baby. And once again it turned to her, this time with a helpless whimper, "Mommy ..."

Rachel lifted her head to see.

"Help me ..."

She started to release David's hand.

"Rachel, no!"

She looked to him, hesitating.

"You saw what it was."

"Mommy ... help me ..."

She turned back to the baby.

"It's not your child. It's a counterfeit. It's playing on your guilt!"

She turned to him, searched his eyes.

"You're forgiven! It has nothing over you or me. 'A new creation' ... We're *new creations*!"

Slowly, sadly, she looked to the ground ... and then she nodded. She was crying again, but she managed to whisper, "... yes." A moment and she looked up to him. "Yes."

The baby roared. They spun around just in time to see the warrior bring down his sword, striking it in the forehead, slicing through the skull and neck, splitting the thing in two. As the pieces fell to the ground they became smaller creatures. He raised his sword and struck the largest, breaking it into even smaller ones. And the largest again, creating smaller, and smaller, until nearly a dozen of the things, less than two feet high, were squealing, turning, scampering off through the undergrowth.

But there was little time to celebrate. The earth pitched wildly.

"Let's get out of here!" Preacher Man shouted, moving to David's side.

David agreed and, still holding Rachel's hand, they made their way toward the log bridge.

"Well now," Reverend Wyatt quipped as he joined them, "that turned out rather nicely."

"And we didn't even need their help." Preacher Man nodded toward the sky.

Only then did David see the winged creatures circling high overhead. Immediately, he stiffened.

"Relax," Preacher Man chuckled. "Them's the good boys."

"Angels?" David asked, still looking.

"You tell me."

"Why didn't they help their comrade down here?" He motioned to the warrior striding beside them.

"Son, that big boy ain't no angel."

"He's not?" David frowned, even more confused. "Then, what, who—"

The ground lurched violently.

"Hurry!" Luke waved from the fallen cedar. "It's splitting apart! It's all coming down!"

fifteen

et's go! Let's go!" Luke stood with Nubee on the far end on the fallen cedar. Together, they urged Albert and Savannah to step onto it and cross over.

"You must hurry!" Nubee shouted.

Luke glanced down at the gulley as it continued to separate. The rift had grown nearly a foot and showed no signs of stopping.

"We can't walk on that!" Albert pointed at the log.

"It's too narrow!" Savannah shouted from within their bulging shadow. "We can't make it!"

"It is the only way!" Nubee yelled.

The couple stared at the widening chasm.

Luke glanced past them to see David and Rachel approaching from behind with Reverend Wyatt, Preacher Man, and the soldier of light or whatever it was.

"You must try!" Nubee shouted. "There is little hope for your survival if you remain!"

The couple continued to hesitate until another tree cracked and fell with a *whoosh-thud* not ten feet away. That's all they needed. Taking hold of Savannah's hand, Albert went first. He placed a tentative foot on the log. Then another. The violet shadow undulated around him while stretching back to Savannah. It was so large and unwieldy it nearly pulled him off balance. But he continued forward.

"That is good!" Nubee shouted. "You are doing well!"

After several steps, Savannah followed. But she'd barely stepped onto the log before the additional bulk of her shadow spilled over the right side, pulling Albert with it. He compensated, leaning to the left, until his foot slipped and he started to fall. Spotting it, Savannah leaped off the log, pulling their shadow along with Albert back to safe ground.

"Try again!" Luke shouted. "Hurry!"

"No way," Albert yelled. "We can't make it!"

"You must!" Nubee insisted.

Savannah shook her head. "It's too narrow!"

Directly behind them Reverend Wyatt shouted, "'Enter through the narrow gate'!"

Albert turned just in time to see the warrior of light raising his sword. "No!" he cried. "Don't!"

"'For wide is the gate and broad is the road that leads to—'"

"Wait!" Preacher Man shouted.

The Reverend stopped. So did the warrior, his sword poised midair.

"It's gotta be their choice!"

"But . . . they must be separated," the Reverend argued. "They will not succeed together."

"*They* gotta decide," Preacher Man insisted. "It's gotta be *their* choice, not ours!"

"He's right!" Albert shouted. "Whatever he said, listen to him!"

"But . . ." Reverend Wyatt turned to him. "We can free you. We can separate you so you may cross."

"We don't want to be separated!" Savannah cried.

"I don't understand."

"There's got to be another way," Albert yelled. "I'm sure of it!" He and Savannah backed up, keeping a healthy eye on the sword.

"There is no other way!" the Reverend shouted.

"We'll find it!" Albert insisted. "We'll find another tree and cross over it!"

"But—"

The ground pitched fiercely. The log moved.

"It's slipping!" Luke cried. "Hurry!"

"Go ahead!" Savannah yelled to Reverend Wyatt as she and Albert continued backing away. "We'll meet you on the other side!"

"But—"

They turned and stumbled along the edge of the gulley, Albert shouting over his shoulder. "Don't worry about us. We'll be okay."

"Savannah!" the Reverend yelled.

"We'll find a way!" she shouted. "We'll be okay!"

The log shifted again, more dramatically.

"Let's go!" Luke shouted to Rachel and David. "You guys are next. Let's go! Let's go!"

David reached out and helped Rachel onto the log. Carefully, she began to cross, working hard to keep her balance.

"That's it!" Luke yelled. "You're doing fine!"

She was about halfway when the log suddenly rolled a good quarter turn. She fell and screamed but landed on it, hugging it with all fours.

"Rachel!"

She remained frozen, clinging to the log.

"We've got to hurry!" Luke shouted.

She looked up to him.

"You're doing fine," he yelled. "But you can't stop. You got to keep coming!"

She nodded, took a breath, and rose onto her hands and knees. She did not climb to her feet, but continued forward, crawling all the way. Once she arrived she gratefully allowed Nubee to help her off.

"Okay, Dad!" Luke shouted.

"You guys go ahead," David yelled to the older men. "I'll follow."

The Reverend nodded and was the first to begin. But instead of walking, he took his cue from Rachel. He dropped

to his hands and knees and crawled. "A bit unsophisti-
cated," he shouted over his shoulder, "but entirely accept-
able given the circumstances."

David nodded. "Whatever works!"

He reached the halfway point when Preacher Man, continuing the tradition, also followed on his hands and knees.
"When the man's right, he's—"

The earth lunged violently, causing the log to slip two
to three feet. Both men yelled, hanging on for dear life.
Once it stopped moving, they took a moment to steady
themselves and continued.

Luke waited impatiently, keeping an eye on the crevice
as it continued to widen. It was the longest quake he'd ever
experienced. At last Reverend Wyatt arrived and he helped
him off the log. Next came Preacher Man. Now there was
only his father.

"Okay, Dad!" he shouted. "You're up. But hurry! *Hurry!*"

david stepped onto the log and started across. But he'd
barely reached the quarter mark before he heard
shouting. He turned and saw Orbolitz, encased in his
shadow, hobbling down the slope toward him. "Help me!"
The man was injured and leaning heavily on a broken limb
for a crutch. "Don't leave me!"

As before, the sight of him made David go cold. But that
was all right. By the look of things, justice was about to be
served. Orbolitz had made his bed, and judging from the
way the mountain was crumbling, it appeared he'd soon be
dying in it. With grim satisfaction, David turned and continued across the log.

"Help me . . . please . . ."

The voice slowed him. Not the words, the voice. Because,
just as David had seen a faint glimmer of the Eternal in
Orbolitz's eyes, he now heard a hint of it in his voice. Some

part of the Man with the pierced hands remained connected to him; some part was still present.

And it was that Presence that brought David to a stop.

"Help me . . ."

He turned, hesitating.

". . . please . . ."

Then, more in anger than obedience, David Kauffman turned back to rescue the man he hated, cursing himself even as he went.

"David!" Rachel shouted.

"Dad! What are you doing?"

But he would not listen. He leaped off the log and, struggling to stay on his feet, ran the thirty yards that separated them.

"My ankle!" Orbolitz shouted as David joined him. "It's broken!"

David fought his hatred. He was grateful Orbolitz still wore the goggles, that he didn't have to see his eyes. *Her* eyes. Finally, angrily, he picked up the frail old man, the pain from his arm so severe he nearly dropped him.

"Careful!" Orbolitz barked.

David winced, doing his best to keep the weight on his good arm, while turning and carrying him toward the bridge.

"Dad! Hurry!"

It wasn't easy, carrying Orbolitz, fighting the pain, trying not to fall . . . while wanting to throw the man down with every step he took. If this was forgiveness, he didn't like it one bit. Nothing about it felt rewarding. Instead, it made him feel like a traitor. A traitor to his daughter. A traitor to Gita. A traitor to everybody . . . except the Man whose voice he had heard underneath, whose eyes he had seen within.

"We're not going to make it!" Orbolitz shouted.

"Shut up!"

"Baker's erupting! We're on a fault line! We're all going to—"

"Shut up!" Just because he had to save him didn't mean he had to listen to him.

They were fifteen yards from the bridge when the ground lunged so violently David dropped to his knees.

"Careful!"

The others continued shouting. And for good reason. When he looked up he saw the log was shaking loose. It was about to fall.

"Run, David! RUN!"

He rose back to his feet and continued. But suddenly he was no longer carrying Orbolitz. Now he was carrying his ex-wife, Jacqueline—whose departure had triggered Emily's illness and eventual death.

He stumbled in shock. "Jacqueline!"

She did not answer. But as he continued carrying her, he realized something was happening. Inside him. Somehow, through this deed, by risking his life to save hers, he was forgiving her. For the first time since their divorce he was actually forgiving the woman who had caused so much pain!

The sky pulsed and Jacqueline disappeared.

"Hurry, you fool!"

But it wasn't Orbolitz's voice. Or his body. Now he was holding Dr. Richard Griffin—the man who first lured him into the Virtual Reality chamber, the one most responsible for Gita's death, the one who made the final arrangements for his daughter's murder. Again, David felt a strange compulsion flooding through him, a need to save him.

More lightning and suddenly David was carrying . . . *himself*! Forgiving . . . *himself*!

"Stop that light!" It was Orbolitz again, turning his head away from David, shielding his eyes.

"Too bright! Stop it!"

The man's entire body was bathed in light. Brilliant. But it was not his light. It was the reflection of David's. The violet shadow that had once surrounded David had broken apart. As he ran, chunks fell to the ground, until his glow blazed with the same intense whiteness as his inner core.

"Stop! It's blinding! Stop it!"

They reached the log. The far end had loosened, rock and dirt pouring in all around it.

"Can you walk from here?" David shouted.

"Of course I can't! My ankle's broken!"

David looked dubiously at the log. Then, taking a deep breath, he hoisted the man higher into his arms. He started forward and began to pray. When he glanced up he saw Luke and the others doing the same.

The log twisted and he nearly lost his balance. He prayed harder, but no amount of praying would hold it in place. He'd taken only a half dozen steps before it broke loose and started to fall. Yet it dropped only a foot or two before bobbing to a stop. David looked up, confused. And for good reason. The far end was no longer attached to the bank. Instead, it floated freely with nothing to support it.

Well, not quite "nothing." Because there, at the end, a pair of glowing hands had gripped it, supporting it from beneath. Hands that obviously belonged to the warrior.

The group above gasped but did not stop praying. Nevertheless, the fissure yawned open wider and wider. David heard a roar behind him and looked to see the entire mountain crumbling, slipping away. The log wrenched from the warrior's hands ... and both David and Orbolitz began to fall.

Looking down through the rain of rock, dirt, and vegetation, David caught glimpses of the chasm. It had no bottom and seemed to stretch forever. Soon, he'd die ... for the second time. And that was all right. Strangely enough, it was all right. Because he knew where he was going. And he knew he would be accepted ... forgiven. Completely. He spotted Orbolitz falling beside him and a new word surfaced in his mind. One he'd heard Nubee quote from Revelation, but one

he didn't fully understood. Until now. Not only was he forgiven, but he, David Kauffman, had finally ... *overcome.*

Earth and rock pummeled him from every side. But the
pain would last only a moment. What had Preacher Man
said at their first meeting? *"Dying was easy, like a hiccup."*
The pain would last but a moment, eternity forever.

But David never hit the bottom; he never entered the
chasm. Suddenly he was being held. Suspended. It was the
same pressure he'd felt when he'd been deflected from hitting the fireplace two nights earlier—gentle but firm—as
if caught by a hand. But not the warrior's hand. This was
much larger and far more powerful. Everything else was the
same—the roar, the falling rocks, the dirt, the dust. But he
was no longer falling. He closed his eyes just for a moment,
just to get his bearings.

He closed them, but they did not reopen.

h e's waking up." Rachel's voice called from far away.
"David?" Then, a little closer, "David, can you hear me?"

He struggled to pry open his eyes, but they would not
obey.

"David?"

Finally they cracked just a fraction. Above him kneeled
the blurry form of Rachel. He blinked her into focus.

"Welcome back." She smiled.

He tried to rise up on his bad arm. A stupid move that
dropped him back to the ground with a groan.

"Take it easy," she said. "Everything's okay."

She obviously didn't feel the burning of his arm or the
throbbing in his head.

"Nice of you to finally join us, son."

He turned to see Preacher Man looking down at him
from the other side. Standing in the moonlight and with a
thick coat of dust on his face, he looked incredibly pale. In

fact, everything around David was covered in dust and moonlight, looking incredibly pale.

"What . . ." His voice was leather dry. He swallowed and tried again. "What happened?"

"You got yourself a nasty bump on the head, that's what happened," Rachel said.

Preacher Man motioned behind them. "And we lost ourselves a sizeable piece of real estate."

David turned. Not only had the log disappeared, so had the gulley . . . and the entire mountain beyond! Now they sat amidst fallen trees, overlooking a chasm covered by a thick cloud of dust.

He could barely find the words. "Is that . . . did it . . ."

"Yup—it's all down in the valley below."

His mind raced. "What about Savannah . . . Albert?"

He saw them exchange looks. Preacher Man cleared his throat. "We haven't seen 'em yet. Course, it's only been an hour, so there's still, you know, there's still a good chance." He tried to hold David's gaze but could not.

David closed his eyes. Not only over Savannah and Albert, but over Orbolitz's people, those folks in the control center near the bluff. By the looks of things, it was all gone— the lodge, the control center, everything . . . and everyone.

He turned back to Preacher Man. "And Orbolitz?"

Breaking twigs and rustling undergrowth drew their attention to Luke as he emerged through the darkness. But it was not the Luke David had seen the last few hours—no self-confident athlete, no young man with the dazzling glow. This was the clumsy man-boy with the ruined voice. "There's a road"—he leaned over to catch his breath—"'bout a quarter of a mile from here. It's all grassy but it's definitely a road."

"Perhaps an old logging trail," Reverend Wyatt suggested.

David looked over to see the Reverend sitting against a tree beside Nubee. Like Luke, this was the other Reverend. No light, no shadows, no sword. He turned back to Rachel and Preacher Man. The same was true with them. Everyone was normal. Only then did he notice that the lightning had also stopped, and the flying lights, and the music. Everything appeared as it had been the first night they arrived. Everything but the mountain.

"Dad." Luke had spotted him and moved to his side. "You okay?"

"Yeah." He struggled to sit up. "I'm all right." He stole a quick glance down to his own body, relieved and somewhat saddened that it, too, had returned to normal.

With a quiet groan, Reverend Wyatt rose to join the others. "So what is your opinion, Billy Ray?"

"'Bout the loggin' road?" Preacher Man asked.

The Reverend nodded.

"Followin' a logging road's better than followin' no road."

Reverend Wyatt agreed. "It certainly must lead somewhere."

"What about Nubee?" Rachel asked.

David turned back to see Nubee still sitting against the tree. Like the others he no longer glowed in light or power. Now he was the disabled young man with the drooping head.

"I can carry him," Luke offered.

"I don't know about that," Preacher Man chuckled.

"I'm a lot stronger than I look."

"Yes," Reverend Wyatt agreed. "I imagine you are."

"I'll be like in charge of him," he said, his voice cracking.

The two men traded glances with David, who hesitated but did not disagree.

"Go ahead," Preacher Man finally said. "You and Nubee get started; we'll join you."

"Great!" Luke turned and started for the young man.

"And if you happen to get tired, you just let one of us know."

"Sure," Luke called over his shoulder, "but I won't get tired. Honest."

Preacher Man threw David a wink. "If you say so."

The group smiled silently.

"Well," Reverend Wyatt sighed, "I suppose we should all get started." Turning to David, he asked, "You feel strong enough to travel?"

David nodded and Rachel reached down to help him to his feet. He thanked her and turned for another look at the devastation below. Where there had once been mountain and forest there was only rock and dust and darkness.

"You sure you're okay?" she asked.

"Yeah," he answered softly.

Sensing his need to be alone, she excused herself. He nodded and turned back to the valley, trying to drink it all in. So much had happened. In just seventy-two hours, so much revelation—about himself, about others. And if just a fraction of what they'd experienced could be trusted . . .

Preacher Man slapped a meaty hand on his shoulder. "You ready then, brother?"

Coming to, he nodded. "He never made it out, did he?"

"Orbolitz?"

David nodded.

"Not likely. Not if he stayed back at the lodge."

"The lodge?"

"Last place I seen him."

David turned to him. "No, he was here, remember? He was with me on the log."

"Last I saw of Orbolitz, you and him was havin' a little discussion in front of the lodge."

"No. He followed us to the gulley. I went back to get him, don't you remember? I went back and carried him across the log until it . . ."

Preacher Man was shaking his head and David came to a stop.

"You didn't carry no one, son. You was on that log by yourself when it went down."

"But . . . Orbolitz. We were—"

"And only by sheer luck did you land on that outcropping of rock down there."

David glanced to a small ledge several feet below them. "But I was . . . I landed in like . . . God's hands or something."

"You was in His hands, all right," Preacher Man chuckled. "But you landed on them rocks. And me and your boy, we climbed down there to fetch you."

David searched the old man's eyes.

"Speakin' of which, I'm bettin' your son could stand a little help with Nubee over there."

"What?"

"Your son?"

David turned to see Luke still struggling to get Nubee onto his feet. "Oh, right. I'll, uh, I'll be right there."

Preacher Man nodded and started to leave, then turned back. "You should really be proud of him. Your boy. He definitely rose to the occasion. He's gonna be somethin' someday, mark my words."

David glanced to the man, who flashed his crooked-tooth smile before turning and lumbering off to join the others. He looked over to his son and mused a moment. It was true. Earlier, he had seen an entirely different side of Luke. Strong. Intelligent. Mature. Then again, maybe that Luke had always been there—just invisible and hidden to the others. Hidden to everyone . . . but the Presence of God.

He started off to join him. "Here, let me give you a hand."

"I can manage," Luke gasped.

"I know, I know." He arrived and moved to Nubee's other side. "I just need something to do, to feel useful—if you don't mind."

"Well . . . all right. If you have to."

"Thanks." He slipped his shoulder under Nubee's arm. The young man's head flopped over to his side, a small trickle of saliva running from his mouth. David felt his throat tighten at the sight. "How are we . . ." He cleared his voice. "How we doin' there, Nubee?"

Nubee broke into his lopsided grin. "We go home now?"

With Luke's help he lifted him to his feet. "Yes, we're going home now."

Nubee's grin broadened.

Though the change in appearance saddened David, he knew that's all it was ... appearance. Because, underneath, there was something very different. Out of sight, hidden away, there was something of great eternal value. And not just in Nubee. He'd seen it in everyone—even himself. He'd seen it, and he hoped never to forget it.

He stole another glance over to Nubee, who caught his eye. "You read me Bible then?"

It was an old ploy and David had to chuckle. "Yes, Nubee. I'll read you the Bible then." They started forward, half walking, half carrying him.

"Revelation?"

"Yes, I'll read you Revelation."

It would be dawn in a few hours. They would reach the road soon, and after that, hopefully civilization.

"I like the angels. I like the monsters."

"I know you do," David said as they continued forward. "I know you do."

epilogue

"all set?" Rachel asked.

David scooped up the airline tickets from the counter. "Good to go." He turned to see Luke debating with a young tattooed employee, complete with a riveted nose.

"And I'm saying it's cool," Luke said, reaching for Nubee's chair. "We got it covered."

"Sorry, all disabled passengers in wheelchairs are supposed to be—"

"Nubee's not disabled."

"Whatever, they're supposed to be accompanied to the gate."

"Then accompany us from back there"—Luke jerked his thumb over his shoulder—"'cause I'm—"

The employee reached past him for the chair. "All disabled passengers in wheelchairs are to be accompanied—"

"I heard you, and I said—"

"Gentlemen, gentlemen." Preacher Man stepped in. "What seems to be the problem?"

The employee sighed. "The boy here's got some communication problems. He don't understand company policy."

"And you don't understand that Nubee's not disabled."

"He's in a wheelchair, man, don't tell me he's not—"

"Easy, fellas, easy." Laying a hand on the employee's shoulder, Preacher Man drew him closer and produced a ten-dollar bill from his pocket. "This should be improvin' everybody's communication skills, wouldn't you agree?"

The employee gave him a look.

"Sorry, it's the best I can do."

He threw a sideways glance, then snatched the bill. "I'll meet you at the gate." Without waiting for a reply, he turned and sauntered off.

David approached, marveling. "Did you just bribe him?"

Preacher Man shrugged. "I bought us a little peace."

"But . . . you're a man of God."

"That's right." Taking Nubee's chair he started forward with Luke. "And 'blessed are the peacemakers, for they will be called sons of God.'"

David and Rachel exchanged amused looks, then turned and followed the trio toward security.

It had been nearly a week since they hiked the logging trail to a dirt road, which eventually led to Highway 20. From there they were picked up by a group of migrant workers who had been turned away at Ruby Creek because of Mount Baker's eruption. Apparently, much of the North Cascades was a disaster—earthquake, mudslides, raging rivers. The Ross Dam which provided a fair bit of Seattle's power was all but wiped out. The west side of the mountains got it the worst, with floods and mudflows down the Nooksack all the way to Lynden, while the Skagit River destroyed much of Sedro Woolley and Burlington. The east side faired better, but not by much.

Their first stop was the city of Winthrop, where amidst the chaos they tried to file a report with the police—which no one believed, or had time to pursue. Then they traveled down to Wenatchee, where they visited the local ER. Here they checked David's arm and looked for any other broken body parts. They also examined Luke's eyes. Although they'd become extremely sensitive to light, forcing him to wear sunglasses outdoors and in, there appeared to be no permanent damage—though a specialist would more closely examine him once he got home.

Removing the tiny receivers that Orbolitz's goons had inserted was a bit trickier. It took Rachel's celebrity clout, not to mention Preacher Man's persuasive skills (plus an X-ray or two) to convince the doctors that they were for real. Fortunately, the devices, which were about the size of a large cold capsule, had already started working their way down their sinus cavities and it was fairly easy to remove them. The hospital would have insisted upon admitting them, but the eruption had put rooms even this far away at a premium.

After two days at a local motel where they caught up on several nights' sleep, Reverend Wyatt shared heartfelt goodbyes and headed up to Spokane to help his denomination coordinate disaster relief efforts. He promised to get back in touch as soon as things settled down.

The rest of the group rented an SUV and followed Highway 2 back over the mountains to Seattle. From there Luke and David rested another day and night at Rachel's home overlooking Puget Sound before they booked a flight back to Los Angeles. Preacher Man had planned to spend an extra week up in Everett with his sister and her five, or was it six kids. But after twenty-four hours, he was more than ready to head back home.

It was in Rachel's house, seeing her relaxed and in her element, that David once again realized how much he was attracted to her—her kindness, her laughter, and her depth of character. Then, of course, there was her beauty. Outside and in. She was lighter now, the inner darkness gone. And it had a profound impact upon the rest of her. She was a remarkable woman, and he couldn't help wondering what it would be like if they spent more time together. He and Luke could take another week off up here before the school officials started complaining. They could find a nearby hotel, relax, unwind. Maybe give her a hand at starting to put her life back together. For that matter, they could rent a house. After all, he could write his novels anywhere, and Seattle would certainly be a refreshing change from LA.

Then maybe, over time, if the chemistry continued to be so right . . .

He pushed the thought from his mind . . . more than once. Because he knew, they both knew, the relationship could never continue in that direction. They could be friends—after all they'd been through, how could they not? But it could go no further. There were too many reasons—the greatest being that she was still married to the man that she still loved.

"Any idea where you'll find him?" David had asked that final evening as they sat on her porch, watching a distant ferry cut through the water in the fading purple light.

"Finding him won't be the problem. Getting him to forgive me, that'll be the trick."

"I thought he had."

She sighed. "He says he has."

"If he loves you, he's forgiven you."

She mused quietly. "Funny . . . that's what he said."

He looked down at his coffee mug as silence stole over their conversation.

"You'd like him, David. You two have so much in common."

He smiled. "I'm sure I would." He took another sip of coffee, barely tasting it.

After a moment, she continued. "Listen . . ." It was her turn to look at her mug. "If for some reason . . . I mean if things don't work out . . ."

Against his will, David felt his hopes rise.

"I mean, you and I, we'll stay in touch, right?"

He took a breath, then forced out the words. "It'll work out, Rachel. If he loves you, he's forgiven you."

She nodded. "And even if he hasn't . . ." She looked up. "Even if he hasn't, that doesn't change the fact."

He stole a glance at her.

"That I'm still forgiven."

David smiled. More silence followed. There was so much more that he wanted to say—that he wanted to hope. But he remained silent.

"Here we are." Rachel's voice brought him back to the terminal.

He looked up, surprised that they'd already reached security.

"You have my number, right? Cell and home?"

"Yes," he said. "And you have mine."

"Absolutely. I'm sure I'll need some pointers along the way. It's all so new to me."

"I'm not that much further along, but I'll be happy to do what I can."

She nodded. Again, silence grew between them.

He tried filling it. "Starting a new career will be tough."

"Not with my typing skills." She held up her hands. "These puppies are good for ten words a minute. On good days, even twelve."

They chuckled. Another moment of uneasiness followed before she spoke, this time her voice thicker. "Thank you, David Kauffman."

He looked to her.

She blinked back a sheen of moisture covering her eyes. "I owe you so much."

"I just pointed to the truth you were looking for."

She smiled. "'And the truth shall make you free.' I'm free, David. For the first time in my life . . . I'm free."

He nodded. "Me too." He felt his own voice thickening. "Me too."

"Let's go, folks." He looked up to see the security guard waiting. Luke, Nubee, and Preacher Man had already passed through the detector. Now the guard was motioning to him. "Move along, please."

He turned back to Rachel. The moisture had filled her eyes. "I'll never forget you," she said.

"You better not." He forced another grin. He wanted to say more but didn't trust his voice.

She saved him the trouble. Quickly, before he could say or do something stupid, she rose up on her toes and gave him a peck on the cheek. Then, without looking at him, she turned and walked away.

David tried to speak but no words would come.

"Goodbye, Rachel," Preacher Man called out to her.

"See you later," Luke added.

She raised her hand and gave a wave, but continued down the corridor without turning. David stood, waiting for her to look back. She never did. Just as well. She didn't need to see the moisture in his own eyes.

"Sir, please step through."

He turned and gave his face a quick wipe before stepping through the metal detector. The alarm immediately sounded.

"Step back through again."

He stepped out, immediately searching the hallway for any sign of Rachel. There was none.

"Keys, loose change, anything in your pockets?"

He shook his head, reaching into his coat pocket to prove the point. But to his surprise, he felt something. A piece of plastic attached to wires. He pulled it out and stared at the remains of Orbolitz's goggles—one of the lenses and part of the frame with a few stray wires hanging from it. How was that possible? He'd never picked it up, never felt it in his pocket, until that very moment.

He passed it over to the agent, who took it from him with a scowl and called, "Nicholas?"

Another agent appeared as David stepped through the detector.

"What's it from?" the second agent asked. "Surveillance goggles or something?"

Still confused, he answered, "Uh, yes, something like that. What's left of them."

The two agents carefully examined the piece, turning it over and over. When they were convinced that it posed no threat, they handed it back to David. "Have a nice flight, sir."

"Thanks," David mumbled. He joined the other three as they turned and headed for the train that would take them to their gate. While they walked, Luke took the piece of goggle.

"I didn't know you had this."

"Neither did I."

The boy slipped off his sunglasses and brought the cracked lens with its dangling wires to his eye. "Hey, check it out."

He passed it back to David, who reluctantly lifted it to his own eye. He saw nothing but the darkened image of the airport.

"Pretty cool, huh?"

"I don't see anything."

"You're kidding." His son took the lens and peered through it again. "You don't see all those streaks of light?"

He held it back out to David, who declined. "Sorry."

A moment later they arrived at the train platform.

"Maybe it's your eyes?" David suggested. "You know, from the microwave burn or whatever."

"No way is this my eyes."

"Well, whatever it is, you need to put those sunglasses back on."

"Yeah, in a minute." He continued looking. "So you didn't see anything?"

"Zero."

He turned his head, looking up the train tracks, then down. "Can I keep them?"

"You can put your sunglasses back on."

"All right, I hear you."

"Now."

"All right, all right." With vintage Luke attitude, the boy sighed and replaced the lens with his sunglasses. "So can I keep it?"

"Knock yourself out."

The train approached and Luke turned to Preacher Man, showing him his prize. "Check it out."

"Don't know if I want to be messin' with anything connected to that man."

"Go on." Luke pushed the lens toward him as the train pulled to a stop in front of them. The doors hissed open and David stepped inside. He turned and watched the rest of the group enter—Preacher Man pushing Nubee, who remained slumped in the wheelchair, and Luke beside them, still offering the lens. "Go ahead."

With some reluctance, Preacher Man took the lens and raised it to his eye. The doors shut and the car lurched forward.

"See anything?"

"Nope."

"Just keep looking. There's these streaks of light shooting all around. Like what we saw in the woods with those receiver thingies in us."

David looked on, remembering all too well what Orbolitz had claimed he'd seen with the glasses.

"Can't see nothin'."

But now they were destroyed—just broken plastic and wires that no longer worked.

"You're not looking hard enough."

But apparently something was working, at least for Luke. Was it coincidence that he saw lights like they'd seen in the woods? Was it some trick of his eyes, of the burnt retinas that were healing? David certainly hoped so. But how had the piece of goggle suddenly appeared in his pocket? He'd never put it there. He frowned down at the tile of the swaying train. There were too many questions. And to be honest, much of him hoped they would never be answered.

But as he looked back up and watched Luke and Preacher Man examining the lens, he sensed, he knew, that would not be the case. *"There is much for you to do."* Those were the final words of the Man with the holes in His hands. The final words spoken to David when he left heaven over a year ago and returned to earth. *"There is much for you to do, but I will always be with you."*

And, deep in his soul, deep inside that core of blazing light that was no longer visible, David Kauffman suspected the questions would be answered.

They would be answered, but in ways he never dreamed possible . . .

A sample chapter from Bill Myers'

soul Tracker

If you enjoyed *The Presence* be sure to read its prequel, *Soul Tracker*, Book 1 in The Soul Tracker Series. Here's the opening chapter of *Soul Tracker* to give you a tatste . . .

one

It had started again. The voice. Five hours earlier in Wal-Mart. He'd been doing his usual stalking up and down the aisles, this time for laundry detergent. Why was it every month they moved at least one item to a new location? Over the years, since Jacqueline left, he felt he'd become quite the veteran shopper—reading labels, clipping coupons, even watching as the cashier rang up each purchase on the register. But this moving of products, especially to the least likely places, always frustrated him. He was reaching the peak of just such a frustration when he heard the child crying one row over.

"Daddy! Daddy, where are you?"

The fear in her voice brought him to a stop. It was the same panic, the same desperation that had haunted him for weeks.

"Daddy, come get me!"

The tone was so similar to another's that David forgot the laundry detergent. He hesitated, then pushed his cart to the end of the aisle. He slowed as he rounded the corner and peered up the next row. A little blonde, about kindergarten age, sat alone in a cart. She was bundled in a bright red coat, pink tights, and shiny black shoes. Tears streamed down her face as she cried.

"Daddy, please don't leave me!"

He scowled, glancing around. There was no one near. What parent would leave a child like this? Had the father no sense of responsibility? He pushed his cart up the aisle toward her. "Sweetie, are you all right?"

She turned, eyeing him, then took a brave, trembling breath.

He continued to approach. "It'll be okay, darling. I'm sure your—"

Suddenly her face brightened as she looked past him. "Daddy!"

He turned to see a concerned young man in a green fleece jacket and worn jeans stride up the aisle toward them. In his hands he held a new push broom, grasped tightly enough to assure David he would not hesitate to use it if necessary. David forced a reassuring grin. The young man sized him up and said nothing as he brushed by and joined his daughter.

"Oh, Daddy." The little girl sobbed as she stretched out her arms.

"I was just around the corner." Laughing, he scooped her out of the cart. "Did you think I forgot you?" She nodded and he hugged her. Then, pushing aside her damp hair, he kissed her cheek. "You know I wouldn't do that." Again, she nodded, but continued to whimper—an obvious attempt to make him pay penance.

David thought of stopping and turning his cart around, but that would be clumsy and awkward, only adding fuel to the parent's suspicion. So he continued up the aisle. As he passed, he felt he should say something to the young father, something instructive, something to remind him what a precious responsibility he held in his arms. He said nothing.

But the voice remained. A whisper in the back of his mind. It remained through the wooden conversation between Grams, Luke, and himself over dinner. It remained through the forced laughter as Grams recounted some scene from one of her daytime soaps. It even remained as David rode his son about the poor progress report they'd received in the mail from school.

And now, several hours later, as David Kauffman stood alone in the dark, silent living room, the whisper grew louder, becoming a more familiar voice. The one that always filled his head and swelled his heart to breaking.

"Daddy, I'll be good! I promise ... please ... please!"

He approached the overstuffed chair from behind, reaching out to its back to steady himself. He had not bothered to turn on a light. Across the room on the mantel, he heard the clock ticking. Outside, a faint stirring of wind chimes. He caught the shadowy movement of the cat—her cat—scurrying past and up the stairs to safety. David hated this room. Tried his best to avoid it. The memories were too painful—as bad as the upstairs bathroom, its lock still broken from when he'd busted through it to find her opening her veins . . .

The first time.

"Daddy . . ."

David closed his eyes against the memories, but he could still hear feet scuffing carpet, attendants' muffled grunts as they grabbed her flailing arms, pinning them to her side. And, of course, her pleas.

"I'll do better, I promise! Please, don't make me go!"

Images flashed in his head. Flying hair, twisting body, kicking feet, the appearance of a pearl-white syringe . . . Emily's eyes widening in panic.

"Daddy, no!"

"To help you relax," the attendant had said.

"Don't let them take me . . ." She no longer sounded sixteen. She was four, five. So helpless. *"Daddy . . ."*

He leaned against the chair, his throat tightening.

"Daddy . . ."

That was the deepest cut. The word. *Daddy.* Protector. Defender. *Daddy.* The one who always made things right. That was the word that had gripped him in Wal-Mart. The word that sucked breath out of him every time he heard it, that drew tears to his eyes before he could stop them. Even in front of Luke.

He tried his best not to cry when he was with his son. The boy had been through so much already. What he needed now was stability, and David was the only one who could provide it. If his twelve-year-old saw tears it would spell weakness, and weakness meant things were still out of control. No. Now, more than ever, Luke needed to know things were returning to normal, that there was someone he could depend on.

But David was by himself now. Alone. Luke was upstairs sleeping (or more likely working on the Internet) while Grams snored quietly just down the hall.

Emily's voice returned, softer, thicker. The drug taking effect. *"Daddy . . ."*

"Just a few weeks, honey," he had promised. *"You'll get better and then you can come home."*

He remembered her eyes. Those startling, violet blue eyes. Eyes so vivid that people assumed she wore colored contacts. Eyes glassing over from the drug. Eyes once so full of anger and confusion and accusation and—this is what always did him in—eyes that, at that moment, had been so full of trust.

He had held her look. Then slowly, with the intimacy of a father to his daughter, he gave a little nod, his silent assurance.

And she believed him.

She still sobbed, tears still ran down her cheeks, but she no longer fought. In that single act, that quiet nod, her daddy told her everything would be all right. And she trusted him. She *trusted* him!

David leaned forward onto the back of the chair, tears falling. He remembered the front door opening—bright sunlight pouring in, flaunting its cheeriness.

"I'll be right behind you," he had promised. *"Grams and I will be in the car right behind you."*

She could no longer wipe her nose. She could only nod and mumble. *"Okay."*

The last word she ever spoke in the house. *Okay, I believe you. Okay, I'm depending on you. Okay . . . I trust you.*

David dropped his head against the chair. He was trembling again, trying to breathe. The house was asleep and he was alone. "Where are you, baby girl?" He whispered hoarsely. "Just tell me. Let me know so I can help."

The screen door groaned. He looked up and quickly wiped his face. This was no memory. The boy was here. He'd called half an hour ago, asking if he could come over. David straightened himself, listening. There was a tentative knock. He took a breath and ordered his legs to move. Somehow they obeyed. He reached out to the cold door. He took another breath, wiped his face, and pulled it open.

The boy wore a gray sweatshirt with the word *Panthers* and red paw prints across his chest. He was tall and lanky, around six feet, with curly brown, unkempt hair. Long, dark lashes highlighted even darker eyes. His chin was strong and his nose slightly large, almost classical. David blinked. In many ways he was looking at a younger version of himself, back when he was in high school.

He forced a smile. "Rory?"

"Cory," the boy corrected. His voice was clogged. He coughed slightly and plumes of uneven breath came from his mouth.

"Well"—David opened the door wider, as if to an old friend—"Come in."

The kid swallowed. "No thanks, I gotta"—he shifted—"I gotta be going."

David's heart both sank and eased. Though he wanted this confrontation more than anything, he also feared it. This was the famous Cory. Cory, the sensitive. Cory, the "You'll really like him, Dad, he's just like you." Cory, the boy Emily couldn't stop talking about the last few times he'd visited her at the hospital.

And now this same Cory had come to meet the parent. A bit ironic. Maybe even macabre. But better late than never.

With long, delicate fingers the boy produced a cloth-covered notebook. "This is what I was telling you about." He cleared his throat again. "I know she'd want you to have it."

David took it into his hands, but he barely looked down. Instead, he was drinking in every detail of the boy, every nuance—those dark eyes, the frail shoulders under the too-big sweatshirt, his nervous, painful energy. He'd just been released from the hospital the day before yesterday. And, if possible, this meeting seemed even harder on him than David.

"She left it in my room the night she, uh ..." He lowered his head, examining the porch.

David nodded, watching. He looked at the notebook. It was six inches long, four wide, and nearly an inch thick. The cover was pale pink with a white iris on the front. It felt like silk. He stared at it a long moment.

The boy shifted.

Coming to, more on autopilot than anything else, David repeated, "You sure you don't want to come in?"

"No"—the boy cleared his throat again—"no, thanks." He motioned over his shoulder to a van that was idling. "I've got people waiting."

"Oh ... right." Hiding his neediness, David forced a shrug. "Well, maybe we can have coffee together or something sometime ... if you want."

Cory glanced up to him. "I'd like that." His eyes faltered then dropped back down. Speaking softer now, and still to his shoes, he added, "She was pretty amazing. I mean, I never met anyone like her. Never." He took a breath, then looked up.

David saw the sheen in the boy's eyes, felt his own starting to burn. "Yeah."

Cory glanced away, studying the porch light above them. "So ... uh ..."

David came to his rescue. "I'll give you a call next week, how does that sound?"

Cory gave the slightest nod.

David watched, waiting.

As if he'd completed an impossible mission, the boy took a deep breath and blew it out. He nodded more broadly and turned to start down the walk. David watched, absorbing everything.

Halfway to the street, Cory paused and turned. "I just, uh . . ." He cleared his throat. "It just doesn't, you know, seem right."

David swallowed, then nodded.

"I mean, she was getting so strong . . . so healthy. She was really happy, Mr. Kauffman. The happiest I'd seen her."

David wanted to respond, but he no longer trusted his voice.

Cory shook his head. "It just doesn't . . . things just don't seem right." With that he turned and headed toward the van.

David remained at the door. Moisture blurred his vision as he watched Cory arrive at the vehicle, open the door, and climb into the passenger's side. A moment passed before the van slowly pulled away. The boy never looked up.

It wasn't until the vehicle disappeared around the corner that David glanced down to the journal in his hands. He was trembling again. The meeting had taken a lot out of him. And it was still taking. Because he knew exactly what he held.

Emily's journal. Her final thoughts and hopes and dreams . . . and nightmares.

He turned and reentered the house, easing the door shut behind him. But he could go no farther. He leaned against the closed door and lifted the notebook to his face with both hands. He inhaled deeply, hoping for some fragrance, some lingering trace of his daughter. There was nothing. Only the faint odor of smoke and antiseptic. He brought the cover to his lips and kissed it. This was all he had left. All that remained.

"Where are you, baby girl? Where are you?"

Y ou never get married?" Nubee cried.
   "It is possible."

"But, must be somebody . . ." He hesitated looking for the right word.

"Somebody what?" Gita asked.

"Somebody blind enough to think you look beautif—*ow!*"

Gita gave her little brother a playful smack upside the head. Well, most of it was playful. It made no difference that he was thirty-two, so physically disabled that he could not look after himself, and that she was pushing his wheelchair on the walk past other residents. There were some things she just wouldn't cut him slack on.

"Help me!" he cried to Rosa, a passing staff member. "Help me! Help me!"

"You picking on your sister again, Nubee?"

"She beating me! Cruelty to animals, cruelty to animals!"

Rosa smiled. "How's it going, Dr. Patekar?"

"Very well," Gita answered. "And you?"

"Still breathing."

Gita smiled. "That is a good sign."

"At least around this place." The plump Hispanic chuckled as she started up the ramp toward the building.

Gita and her brother continued along the walkway. She lifted her face and closed her eyes to feel the warmth of the winter sun flickering through the bare mulberry branches. In her faster-than-the-speed-of-light world, these few hours a week spent with her little brother always brought a certain peace. Many saw her visits as compassion for her only living relative, but the truth was she needed them more than he did.

Gita had flown Nubee over from their home in Nepal as soon as she'd settled in. That was part of her agreement with the Orbolitz Group. She would work for them and commit her sizable experience to their new Life After Life program, a series of studies designed to scientifically track the soul after death. All they had to do was offer reasonable pay and pull a string or two to bring her little brother to the States so she could look after him. To her surprise, not only did they agree, but they made certain Nubee was admitted to one of the finest nursing homes in Southern California, and picked up the tab for his room and board. It was a gracious offer, but typical of Norman E. Orbolitz. Granted, he was an

eccentric recluse, a billionaire who owned one of the world's
largest communication empires. It was also true that he was
a master at playing hardball with any and all competitors.
But he was known equally well for his generosity and philanthropic outreaches. That fact as much as any other convinced Gita to move halfway around the world and join his
organization.

As a thanatologist, someone who studies death and
dying, Gita had made a name for herself by exposing one of
Great Britain's most famous psychics as a fraud. It wasn't
intentional, just the outcome of her unwavering, dogged
research. But it had created a stir that caught the attention
of the Orbolitz people. In a matter of months they'd convinced her to leave her position at Tribhuvan University in
Nepal and join their Life After Life program in the States.

Unfortunately, her focus quickly became something
more along the lines of *Hoax* After Life. Apparently the
Orbolitz Group—more precisely Gita's department head, Dr.
Richard Griffin—wasn't as interested in her research as he
was in her ability to expose false psychics, particularly those
who exploited the grief-stricken with promises of contacting their deceased loved ones. It wasn't exactly the program
she'd signed up for, but she had always seen the importance
of truth, the need to separate fact from fiction. And, like it
or not, she was getting quite good at it. No surprise there.
Dr. Gita Patekar enjoyed success at everything she put her
mind to.

Well, almost everything . . .

"So, nobody in all world think you pretty?" Nubee was
doing his best to get another rise out of her.

"I am afraid you are correct." She sighed, playing along.
Unfortunately, the opposite was true, and she knew it. For
better or worse, she'd been attractive all of her life. And not
just to the Asian community. Her petite frame, high cheekbones, coal black eyes, and well-endowed figure made her
fresh meat in any male shark tank—even at the church singles' group. Then there was the problem of her intellect. It

was supposed to be one of her better features, but she found herself having to use it mostly as a weapon of self-defense.

Last night's fiasco with Geoffrey Boltten was the perfect example. Was there some unspoken law that said after the third date men were entitled to have sex with a woman? Was that the new definition of lifelong commitment? Because, just like clockwork, after a romantic dinner and enjoying Mozart's "Magic Flute" at the Civic Arts Plaza, Dr. Boltten, respected surgeon and churchgoer, felt he was entitled to make his move.

Gita had barely let him inside her townhouse, supposedly to use the bathroom, when he grabbed her shoulders. Always the understanding type, she stepped back and tried to defuse the awkward situation with an obvious scientific explanation.

"It is okay, I understand. It is simply your phenylethylamine. Do not worry. Some was bound to have been released during our time together this evening."

"Oh, Gita," he gasped, pulling her to him. "I can't stop thinking of you." It was an old line, an even older move.

She shrugged him off and tried pivoting away. "With the rise of your PEA levels, you knew this would happen. You also know that further touching will increase both of our dehydroepiansdrosterone levels, which will lead to a rise in oxytocin." She was being as kind and forthright as possible.

"Oh, baby . . ." He grabbed the back of her head, pulling it toward his, forcing his mouth over hers.

Coming up for air, she tried one last time. "And now we must contend with testosterone and vasopressin. Doctor, you know you are merely reacting to chemicals being released within your—"

"No more talking." He yanked her toward him. "No more talking." That was when Gita realized the time for talking had indeed come to an end. All it took was one quick knee raise followed by a sharp blow to his larynx and the good doctor was on the floor, writhing, unsure what part of his anatomy to be holding in pain.

She looked down at him and sighed wearily. No doubt here was yet another man who would never call her again.

Nubee continued his teasing, pulling her from the memory. "Not to worry. We find somebody. Somebody blind . . . maybe deaf too."

She smiled weakly, because it wasn't just the culture's sexual promiscuity that she struggled against. There was something else. Something deep inside of her. And the books she'd read, the counselor she'd been seeing, they all pointed to the same cause. They insisted it stemmed from the nightmare childhood that she and her brother had lived while on the streets of Katmandu.

"These things can take a long, long time to heal," her counselor had said. "Someone who has endured your level of abuse may take years, even decades, to fully recover."

Gita hated that thought. She fought against it with every fiber of who she was. But deep inside she knew it was true. Deep inside she knew that loving another, that sharing her heart and soul with a man would be difficult. No, *difficult* wasn't the word. For her, there was another. And it was one that frequently brought tears to her eyes when she slept alone at night. It crippled and hobbled her heart as much now as when she was that eleven-year-old girl sleeping with men for food, for rupees, for anything to keep her and her brother alive. Because, as much as she wanted to give herself to another, as much as she begged God to free and heal her, Dr. Gita Patekar feared that when it came to love, she would now and forever be . . . *unable.*

"You make me listen to Bible now?"

She barely heard her brother.

"Gitee?"

They had arrived at their favorite bench, the one between two eucalyptus trees. Coming to, she answered, "Yes, it is time to make you listen to Bible again. What part do you wish to hear today?"

"More Revelation."

"Again?" She reached down and locked the wheels of his chair. She pulled the wool blanket up around his chest. "Are we not always reading Revelation?"

"I like the angels. I like the monsters."

"Of course," she sighed, "then we shall read Revelation." She sat on the wooden bench across from him and produced a small New Testament from her pocket. And there, in the warmth and cold of the winter light, she opened the book and began to read.

I'm hearing something now," the boy said. "Kind of a low hum, like a machine."

"Yes," Dr. Richard Griffin agreed, "that's fairly normal. Just try to relax." He caught a reflection of himself in the stainless steel tray on the bedside table. Who could believe he was fifty? Early forties would be his best guess, as long as he held in his stomach and paid close attention to how he combed and sprayed his hair.

He glanced at the digital readout over the subject's bed. It cast a blue-green glow upon the white tiles of the cubicle. They were coming up to the seven-minute mark. Seven minutes since he'd injected the kid with three milligrams of dimethyltryptamine, a hallucinogenic better known as DMT.

"Do you see any movement?" He peered at the boy. "Any type of ... beings?"

"No."

"Be patient, they'll show up," Griffin assured him. "And when they do, stay calm, don't panic."

Seventeen-year-old Jason Campbell nodded. He licked his lips in nervous anticipation and no doubt a little fear.

Dr. Griffin had picked him up as a volunteer from their "off-campus" site near Hollywood Boulevard. Kids, mostly runaways and street ilk, came to the place in droves looking to sell themselves as volunteers for various medical experiments. Experiments that weren't always legal, but that were absolutely necessary if the human longevity division of the

Orbolitz Group was to stay on the cutting edge of its research. For the most part, the procedures were harmless and everyone benefited—the kids got their money for drugs, important data was secured without jumping through bureaucratic hoops, local authorities were provided enough financial incentive to look the other way—and on those rare occasions when Griffin needed to cross divisions and secure a subject for his Life After Life program, they were there for the taking. It was win/win for everyone involved.

"There, I see something."

"The creatures?" Dr. Griffin asked. "Do you see the creatures?"

Jason's acne-ravaged face twitched under the silk eye-shades.

"Jason?"

"Yeah . . ."

"Do you see them?"

"Yes . . ."

"How many?"

"Just one."

Earlier, the boy had assured Dr. Griffin that he was a frequent user of psychedelics—LSD, ketamine, MDMA, he said he'd tried them all. Griffin had his doubts, but it really didn't matter. Although DMT was classified as a hallucinogenic, its devotees more commonly referred to it as the *spirit molecule.* It was a rare chemical that they insisted opened them up to a strange, mystical world, often populated by gargoyles and troll-like creatures. Creatures identical to several of the near-death experiences Griffin had recorded. If that was the case, if the same creatures that appeared in near death experiences also appeared while using the drug, then it was important he add at least one of the drug experiences to his database.

"There's another," the boy said.

"That's two?" Dr. Griffin asked.

"No, three . . . four, five." Jason's voice grew shaky. "They're everywhere!"

Griffin tried to soothe him. "Just relax. That's not unusual. Let them approach. It'll be okay." He threw a look over to Wendell Nordstrom, a wiry technician with red hair and a stringy goatee. Nordstrom stood on the other side of a portable console, watching the boy's readouts—heart rate, blood pressure, EEG ... and one very peculiar video monitor off to his left.

Jason's face twitched again. He scowled, then lifted his eyebrows, raising a black wire and fabric skullcap. The cap contained paper-thin electrodes strategically placed throughout it. These picked up the electrical firings from a handful of neural synapses within his brain. Firings that were amplified, sorted, and eventually fed into PNEUMA, the project's giant, fifteen-teraflops supercomputer.

Initially the skullcap was a cumbersome helmet that recorded tens of thousands of impulses. But gradually, thanks to the research of scientists such as Francis Crick of double helix fame, a small set of neurons leading from the back of the cortex to the front were isolated. To some, these few neurons were the elusive location of human consciousness—a small group of cells connected in such a way that they made us different from animals by making us self-conscious.

To others, it wasn't the cells or even their connections that mattered. Instead, it was what resided *within* those cells. Something the more religious might call ... the soul.

In either case, this drug, this DMT, seemed to stimulate those same neurons, particularly in the frontal lobe where so many near-death experiences are registered. And if those very same neurons were being fired by the drug, then their experiences had to be entered into the system.

"I can't ..." Jason scowled. "They're trying to talk, but I can't, I can't hear what they're saying."

"Relax. Let them have their way."

Jason gave the slightest nod. A thin veneer of sweat appeared across his forehead and above his upper lip.

Griffin looked at the clock. They were almost at the eight-minute mark.

Wendell's voice came from behind the console. "We're getting images."

Dr. Griffin nodded. This was the pivotal point of the experiment. For nearly four years they'd been studying the brain functions of the dying. They recorded those last few moments as the subject approached death, followed by the six to twelve minutes as the brain slowly shut down from the outside in. Theirs was an extensive, nationwide program involving over eighty hospitals and nearly two hundred hospice organizations. Each case was handled with care and sensitivity, as the terminally ill and their relatives were seldom in the mood to participate in experiments. Yet in the name of science—and with the added incentive of $2,500 per subject (thanks to the very deep pockets of Norman E. Orbolitz)—nearly thirteen hundred patients had agreed to wear the small, unobtrusive skullcap to record the last electrical firings of their brains as they died.

"Jason, can you hear them yet? Can you tell me what they're saying?"

The kid rolled his head. "I can't . . ." His face twitched again. "I can't make it out. But they're everywhere."

Dr. Griffin glanced at the empty syringe in the stainless steel tray. They'd given the kid three milligrams. The experts claimed that was more than enough to "interact" with the creatures. But if this was all the further they could go, after investing all their time and energy, then the experiment was essentially a failure. Griffin did not have time for failures.

He glanced at the vial beside the syringe. It contained another six milligrams. "Are they coming any closer?"

Jason shook his head.

"You must be holding them back. Relax, there's nothing to fear. Give in to the drug. Let them have their way."

Jason scowled again. It was obvious he was trying but still failing.

Griffin looked back at the vial on the table. He knew the answer to their problem, but hesitated. Not for ethical reasons. As far as he was concerned, ethics were man-made restraints created by timid moralists. This was science. More important, this was *his* science. Besides, Jason was homeless—street flotsam and jetsam that would never be missed. No, it wasn't ethics or even the fear of being caught that gave Griffin pause. It was simply the bother of having to go back to the Boulevard and begin the screening process all over again.

But the kid gave him little choice.

Dr. Griffin reached for the vial and syringe. He drew out another three milligrams, hesitated, then continued until the entire six milligrams was in the syringe.

"Dr. Griffin?"

Griffin didn't know if his assistant was calling out a word of caution or if he'd seen something of interest on the monitor. It didn't matter. The decision was made. He inserted the needle into the boy's right arm and emptied the syringe.

"Okay, Jason, I've increased the dosage. Now I want you to—"

"Inside . . . ," the youth whispered. "They want . . . inside."

"Inside? Inside what?"

Jason gave no answer. His face twitched again, then again. He began to roll his head. Harder. Faster. He flinched, then began to squirm.

Griffin reached for the leather restraint on the bed rail and buckled down the boy's right arm. "Jason . . . Jason, can you hear me?" He crossed to the other side and repeated the process. Then to each of the ankles. "Jason? You said they wanted inside. Inside of what?"

Faint crescents of sweat appeared under the arms of the kid's hospital gown. The sheen on his face had beaded into drops.

"Jason?"

His head continued to roll. Faint whimperings escaped from his throat.

"Jason? Jason, can you hear me?"

He opened his mouth, panting in uneven gasps. The whimperings grew louder.

Wendell called from the console, "Dr. Griffin, you need to see this."

Suddenly the boy's body contracted. His arms and legs yanked at the restraints. His head flew back, then rolled faster and faster. His whimperings grew to choking cries.

"Dr. Griffin!"

The doctor hurried to join Wendell behind the console. Readouts showed the boy's pulse at 148, his blood pressure skyrocketing. But it was the TV monitor to the left that grabbed Griffin's attention. The images were crude, like an eighties' video game—the result of raw data being translated by a portable, in-lab computer. They would become much more refined when fed into PNEUMA and prepared for the virtual reality lab. But for now there was no missing Jason's form, or at least how he perceived his form. He was floating in a dazzling star field. Closing in on him from all sides were the gargoyle-like creatures—some with amphibian faces, others more reptilian—all with sharp, protruding teeth and long claws. Several had already leaped on top of the boy's chest. More followed.

No wonder he was writhing.

"Jason?" Griffin called. "Jason, can you hear me?"

But Jason did not answer. His chest heaved then went into a series of convulsions.

"Pulse 185!" There was no missing the fear in Wendell's voice.

The boy screamed—then swallowed it into gagging coughs and gasps.

"*Jason!*"

"Two hundred!"

Griffin spun back to the monitor and stared. Two of the creatures had pried open the boy's jaw with their claws. Even more astonishing were the creatures on his chest. One after another raced toward his head and leaped into the air. As they hovered over his face they dissolved into a black, vaporous cloud that rushed into the boy's mouth and shot down his throat. Creature after creature followed. Black cloud after black cloud. Leaping and entering with such frightening speed that they soon became a thick, continuous stream of blackness.

Jason tried to scream but could only choke and gag.

"Jason!"

An alarm sounded.

"He's in V-fib!"

"Get the medical team here!"

Wendell nodded and hit the intercom as Griffin raced to the bed. "Jason! Jason, close your mouth!"

But the boy's mouth was locked open as he continued gasping, choking.

Griffin ripped aside the kid's hospital gown, yanking off a handful of the sensors taped to his chest, ready to begin CPR if needed.

The alarm continued.

The boy gagged as Wendell called for the medical team again.

But even as his assistant's voice echoed through the complex, Dr. Griffin changed his mind. Slowly and quite deliberately, he stepped back from the bed. It was better to do nothing. He knew that. And if the kid was lucky, the medical team would arrive too late to help. Granted, there would be some inconvenience in disposing of the body, but it was best for the boy. Griffin had seen these creatures before in the virtual reality chambers. He had seen what they did to a select handful of dying. The mental agony those patients endured, the impossible anguish they suffered . . . it was a horror worse than any pain of physical death.

It was a horror that the kid should not have to take back with him into the land of the living.

~

Things are finally falling into place. Bryan actually came up to my locker and started talking, which seriously is such a great emotional high. I feel like I could just run around twirling and jumping in the bright shining sun. I want to embrace life and give back so much. I know he's working up the courage to ask me to the dance. Kind of a spastic thought, but this gives me a great outfit to plan. I was thinking about like an off-white or purple dress. I have always liked purple; it has such an amazing regal feel to it. Seriously, I think that the hot guy in my math class might get jealous of Bryan, and what if Mr. Hot asks me to dance! How incredibly stellar would that be!!! I just want to bask in this moment of pure happiness and imagine two great guys fighting over my company. "Oh, I am sorry, were you talking about dancing with me?" Here is where the band breaks out into a slow, romantic tune and we gaze lovingly into each other's feverish eyes. His enchanting mocha browns settle deep into my dazzling violet blues. He softly joins in, singing to me, and my entire heart just melts. Ha-ha. I am so psyched!! I want to glide and sway here forever.

David lifted his glasses onto his forehead and rubbed his eyes. He'd been at Starbucks since the place opened three hours ago, sitting at the window counter, reading her journal. Of course he'd read it earlier, had been up all night devouring its two-hundred-plus pages. But like a man too starved to taste food, he'd gobbled down sentence after sentence, entire paragraphs without fully comprehending. And he wanted to comprehend, he wanted to savor every moment of his daughter's last few months. So, here he was, a mile from the house at his favorite writing hangout near the corner of Topanga and Ventura Boulevard, nursing his third cappuccino, trying to stay focused.

He might have had more success if it wasn't for the street preacher. The black, barrel-chested old-timer sporting the latest fashion from the Salvation Army stood just outside the window, as he often did, giving no one within earshot a break.

"You, brother!" His voice reverberated against the glass as he dogged a passing shopper. "Yes, I'm talking to you! Have you found the Lord? Have your sins been washed in the blood of the Lamb? Repent! Repent, or burn in the fires of hell that have no end!"

David watched with quiet distaste. The two of them had been coming to this shop for months, each plying their trades—the preacher outside searching for lost sinners on the sidewalk, David inside, struggling with his next novel on his laptop. Normally, the old-timer's rantings didn't bother him much—just another layer of coffee shop and street noise. But today, with no sleep and spent emotions, the self-righteous railings grew more and more irritating.

David sighed, pulled down his glasses, and turned the page to the next entry.

> I feel nothing. I just want to lie here in my warm, safe bed. Living has so entirely drained my blood of substance to the point that my parched veins are screaming for any form of liquid to fill them. My blood has been sucked out venomously by that stupid leach that I so often refer to as Kaylee. What a hypocritical jerk if I ever saw one. Honestly, I consider Kaylee my best friend in the entire world. Why would she not consider me the same ... is Amanda such a great friend considering she ditched you, Kaylee? I seriously stuck through everything with you! Just because I didn't know you as long as Amanda doesn't mean we can't be better friends than you and her. It's stupid, I know. All I do is wallow in this mental slush, swimming in the sewage hour after hour, holding my breath, unable to come up for air.

Talk about emotional whiplash—one page exhilaration, the next, devastation. But apparently roller-coaster emotions came with the territory of female adolescence.

He remembered one of their very first counseling sessions, the ones they started not long after his wife left. Emily was burrowed into the corner of the sofa, feet drawn up, playing with her hair. "It's just that he's like always shouting all the time."

He recalled his jaw going slack. "What? Honey, I never shout."

"Yeah, right." She smirked. "Like yesterday when I didn't empty the cat box?"

David turned to the woman counselor, lifting his palms. "It had been nearly two weeks. I merely made it clear that—"

"By shouting," Emily interrupted.

"I don't shout."

"Yes, you do."

"No, I don't."

"You're doing it now."

"Disagreeing with someone is not the same as—"

"Told you."

"Told me what?"

"You're shouting."

"I am not."

"Yes, you are."

"Emily!"

She turned to the counselor and shrugged. "See?"

David smiled at the memory. At the tender age of fourteen his daughter was already playing him like a fiddle. He recalled another session where he'd asked the counselor, "Does *every*thing in the house have to be ruled by emotion? Surely, truth and logic must count for something."

Once again the therapist broke out laughing. Apparently, he had lots to learn.

But the laughter didn't last long. The frenetic, topsy-turvy world of emotions eventually led to bouts of depression, which only seemed to grow darker and deeper until finally—

"Repent! 'I am the way, the truth and the life. No man comes to the Father but by me!' Turn to Him! Turn to the Lord before it's too late! Turn or burn!"

David squinted at the journal, trying to stay focused. But the lunchtime crowd was filtering in, opening the door more and more frequently, allowing the preacher's rantings to intrude more and more loudly.

"Time is short. You don't know what tomorrow will bring! Turn to Him and flee the torments of hell, where the worm does not die nor the fire is quenched!"

David shifted on his stool, trying to concentrate on the words before him. Emily loved to write. Sometimes the rambling stream-of-consciousness that he saw before him now, sometimes short stories, sometimes poetry. She cherished words. No surprise there. As the child of an author, she was always surrounded by stacks of books and magazines. Her favorite reading haunt? The tub ... which occasionally made for some careful maneuverings in the bathroom.

"I just want to find the toilet in the middle of the night without breaking a toe," he complained once over breakfast.

She nodded with the obvious solution. "Maybe you should drink less liquids before bedtime."

Again David smiled. It was true, when it came to books and writing he gave her plenty of leeway. Particularly with her mother gone. For Emily, reading was a way of affirming her emotions, of discovering what other women thought and felt. And her writing, no matter how emotional or over-the-top, was her way of exploring her own thoughts and feelings. So often she'd enter his garage office unannounced and plop down on the worn sofa behind his desk to write. And write and write and write.

He treasured those times together—back when she was open and sunny, back before the shadows of the disease had begun hiding her from him. For years she read to him from that sofa, those incredible eyes looking up, so eager for praise. And he gave it, abundantly. He never criticized, sensing that any negative comment would crush her already oversensitive heart. Instead, he would find authors she loved and encourage her to copy their work in longhand. That was how writers in the old days learned. It forced them to slow down and study each phrase, sip each word, and, most important, begin to understand the workings of the craft.

She practiced this advice religiously. Snips and fragments of great literature filled her journals. She was particularly fond of the poets. Emily Dickinson, her namesake, was her favorite. He flipped through the pages of the journal until he spotted one of the famous writer's poems:

> Some, too fragile for winter winds,
> The thoughtful grave encloses,—
> Tenderly tucking them in from frost
> Before their feet are cold.

> Never the treasures in her nest
> The cautious grave exposes,
> Building where schoolboy dare not look
> And sportsman is not bold.

> This covert have all the children
> Early aged, and often cold,—
> Sparrows unnoticed by the Father;
> Lambs for whom time had not a fold.

He tried swallowing away the tightness in his throat. Tears were coming again. How could someone so young, so full of life, become so lonely and full of death? He was near the beginning of the diary, before her hospitalization. During those black, nightmare times when she would not get out of bed, when her grades plummeted, when the two of them continually fought, shouting oaths and threats that he'd give anything to take back now. Those awful times when he had to physically force her to take the medication. Those beggings, those pleadings, those—

"Excuse me, brother?"

David looked up with a start. Through the moisture in his eyes he saw the preacher.

"This seat taken?"

David glanced at the stool beside him, then around the shop for an alternate choice. There was none. The place was packed. Exhausted, emotional, and with an overdose of caffeine, he replied, "Go ahead." He cleared his throat. "Just spare me the hellfire."

Unfazed, the man gave a crooked-tooth grin. "Some folks would say it's a pretty important topic."

David fought to hold back his anger. What right did this person have to talk to him about hell? He had no idea what he'd been living through these past nine weeks. The sorrow, the hopelessness, the absolute . . . finality. But instead of making a scene, he exercised all of his self-control and quietly seethed. "And what makes you an expert?"

The preacher pulled out the stool and eased himself onto the seat with a quiet groan. "I guess 'cause I've been there."

"We all have. Some of us more than others."

"Maybe." The man brought a latte up to his thick lips and slurped the foam. "But I'm talkin' the real deal."

David glanced away, angry that he allowed himself to be pulled into the conversation. But the old-timer wasn't finished. Not quite.

"You know what I'm talkin' 'bout. The real hell." His eyes peered over the cup at David. "That place you're so afraid your daughter is."

about the author

Bill Myers (www.billmyers.com) is a bestselling author and an award-winning screenwriter and director. His numerous books include *Soul Tracker*, *The Wager*, *The Face of God*, *Eli*, *Blood of Heaven*, *Threshold*, *Fire of Heaven*, *The Bloodstone Chronicles*, and *When the Last Leaf Falls*. His books and videos have sold over six million copies.

Soul Tracker

Bill Myers

Death has stolen your daughter. What if
you could search heaven and hell—
without ever dying—to find her?

This is the question facing novelist
David Kauffman. As a single parent he
is devastated when his young daughter
meets an untimely death. Desperate to
contact her, he meets Gita Patekar, a beautiful and committed
Christian with a scarred and shame-ridden past. She works for
"Life After Life"—an organization dedicated to tracking and
recording the experiences of the soul once it leaves the body.

Despite Gita's warnings that God is opposed to contacting
the dead, David uses the organization's computer to try to find
his daughter. In the process they discover Gita's organization
has some very deep and dark secrets. A suspense-filled game of
cat and mouse begins—both on earth and beyond the grave—
as the couple work together, fall in love, and struggle to expose
the truth . . . until they come face to face with the ultimate Love
and Truth.

Softcover: 0-310-22756-9

Unabridged Audio Pages® CD: 0-310-26229-1

Pick up a copy today at your favorite bookstore!

GRAND RAPIDS, MICHIGAN 49530 USA

WWW.ZONDERVAN.COM

What if you could hear the voice of God?
What if you actually saw his face?

The Face of God

Bill Myers

That is the quest of two men with opposite faiths . . .

THE PASTOR

His wife of twenty-three years has been murdered. His faith in God is crumbling before his very eyes. Now, with his estranged son, he sets out to find the supernatural stones spoken of in the Bible. Stones that will enable the two of them to hear the audible voice of God. Stones that may rekindle their dying faith and love.

THE TERRORIST

He has also learned of the stones. He too must find them—but for much darker reasons. As the mastermind of a deadly plot that will soon kill millions, he has had a series of dreams that instruct him to first find the stones. Everything else is in place. The wrath of Allah is poised and ready to be unleashed. All that remains is for him to obtain the stones.

With the lives of millions hanging in the balance, the opposing faiths of these two men collide in an unforgettable showdown. The Face of God is another thrilling and thought-provoking novel by a master of the heart and suspense, Bill Myers.

Softcover: 0-310-22755-0
Adobe® Acrobat® eBook Reader: 0-310-25702-6
Microsoft® Reader: 0-310-25764-2
Palm™ Reader: 0-310-25705-0
Unabridged Audio Pages® CD: 0-310-24905-8
Unabridged Audio Pages® Cassette: 0-310-24904-X

Blood of Heaven

Bill Myers

Mass Market: 0-310-25110-9
Softcover: 0-310-20119-5

Threshold

Bill Myers

Mass Market: 0-310-25111-7
Softcover: 0-310-20120-9

Fire of Heaven

Bill Myers

Mass Market: 0-310-25113-3
Softcover: 0-310-21738-5
Abridged Audio Pages® Cassette: 0-310-23002-0

Eli

Bill Myers

Mass Market: 0-310-25114-1
Softcover: 0-310-21803-9
Abridged Audio Pages® Cassette: 0-310-23622-3
Palm Reader: 0-310-24754-3

The Bloodstone Chronicles

A Journey of Faith

Bill Myers

Through the mysterious Bloodstone, which symbolizes God's great love for mankind, three children are whisked into strange and wondrous worlds. Soon they are visiting places like the Sea of Mirrors, where they are nearly crushed by the weight of their sins; or the Menagerie, whose prisoners are doomed to live in pure selfishness, or Biiq, where one doubting child is allowed to experience the same deep and unfathomable love that Jesus Christ has for us.

With the help of intriguing characters like Aristophenix, the world's worst poet, Listro Q—a tall, purple dude with dyslectic speech—and Weaver—who weaves God's plans into each of our Life Tapestries, the children learn the powers and secrets of living as citizens in the kingdom of God.

Hardcover: 0-310-24684-9

God and satan have made a wager. Now
it's up to michael steel to determine a winner.

The Wager

Bill Myers

Michael T. Steel has been nominated for
an Academy Award®, but his most com-
pelling performance has just begun. He
has been cast unaware as the lead character in a supernatural drama between good
and evil, heaven and hell.

Claiming that the Sermon on the Mount
is an impossible standard, Satan has chosen Steel to prove his point
in a wager with God, who agrees to the choice, insisting that
Michael can live out the truths of Matthew 5, 6, and 7 in the ten
days before the award ceremony.

The Wager follows Steel as he copes with his career, his crumbling marriage, and his struggles with faith—not to mention a few
diabolical tricks and temptations by Satan and some guidance and
encouragement from heaven. All this as Steel probes the depth of
the Sermon on the Mount and how one man might follow it in
today's world.

Softcover: 0-310-24873-6

Pick up a copy today at your favorite bookstore!

ZONDERVAN™

GRAND RAPIDS, MICHIGAN 49530 USA

WWW.ZONDERVAN.COM

We want to hear from you. Please send your comments about this book to us in care of zreview@zondervan.com. Thank you.

GRAND RAPIDS, MICHIGAN 49530 USA

WWW.ZONDERVAN.COM

talk with bill myers personally

If you have a book club/reader's group that has read this or any of my other novels, I'd love to chat with you and the group by speakerphone. That way we can all talk about the book together, they can ask me any questions they like . . . and I've found a good excuse to take a 30 minute break from writing! All that is necessary is for the group to have eight or more people, that they've read the same book, and that they have access to a speakerphone. If that sounds interesting, drop me a line at www.Billmyers.com and we'll set up a time and date.

Hope to hear from you!